about the author

Chad Kultgen is a graduate of the USC School of Cinematic Arts. His novels include *The Average American Male*, *The Average American Marriage*, *The Lie*, and *Men, Women & Children*, the basis of a feature film by Jason Reitman. He lives in California.

strange animals

strange animals

chad kultgen

HARPER PERENNIAL

NEW YORK • LONDON • TORONTO • SYDNEY • NEW DELHI • AUCKLAND

HARPER PERENNIAL

STRANGE ANIMALS. Copyright © 2015 by Chad Kultgen. All rights reserved. Printed in the United States of America. No part of this book may be used or reproduced in any manner whatsoever without written permission except in the case of brief quotations embodied in critical articles and reviews. For information, address HarperCollins Publishers, 195 Broadway, New York, NY 10007.

HarperCollins books may be purchased for educational, business, or sales promotional use. For information, please e-mail the Special Markets Department at SPsales@harpercollins.com.

FIRST EDITION

Library of Congress Cataloging-in-Publication Data has been applied for.

ISBN: 978-0-06-211957-5

15 16 17 18 19 OV/RRD 10 9 8 7 6 5 4 3 2 1

strange animals

"You're an animal. You're here to eat and fuck. That's it. There's no God judging you, no heaven waiting for you, no karma, no greater meaning, no purpose to life. Nothing you do on this planet will ever matter. You're an animal. You're here to eat and fuck. That's it." This was the advice Karen Holloway gave her friend in a crowded bar.

God and religion were constructs of humanity that had long outlived their purpose of explaining the natural world to a primitive population that had no means of discovering the truth. The universe was likely infinite, and although most of its makeup was unknown, there was no evidence that anything supernatural had had any hand in its creation or continued development. Despite our advanced scientific understanding of a wide variety of things, we had not yet evolved beyond certain animal motivations. Chief among them was the need for sexual interaction. In the modern

era, this need could be met without the once-unavoidable con-
sequence of pregnancy. And even when pregnancy was the accidental outcome of that animal impulse, a woman had options.
Choosing to have a child meant choosing a life of servitude and
obligation to that child, over any ambitions a person might have
for themselves, but there was no need to make that choice. These
were things that Karen understood to be true.

"As we know, I have a slight difference of opinion on literally
everything you just said. And I think it's sad that I'll be in heaven
hanging out with all of my family and friends—except you, because you'll be in hell, burning in a sea of liquid fire." This was
the response Tanya Campos gave to Karen.

God was a very real, conscious entity, and the various religions that had existed throughout history and into the present
were merely different methods by which that God spoke to different cultures. Science could explain the natural world, but religion explained the spiritual world. Evidence of God's hand in
the universe was in everything from the miracle of childbirth to
the design of a snail's shell. Human beings were the only creatures that God imbued with souls and free will, which separated
them from the animal world and gave them dominion over it. As
for sex, it was ideally something to be shared with a spouse, but in
the modern era, as long as your partner was someone who at least
loved and respected you, then it was impractical to abstain until
marriage. With proper use of contraceptive methods, a woman
could choose when she was ready to start a family. And while the
pursuits of personal fulfillment outside of raising children were
certainly worthwhile, being a mother was the most important
thing a woman could do, and if that ultimately meant abandoning other individual goals, then so be it. These were things that
Tanya understood to be true.

Karen said, "Okay, let's address your retarded idea of heaven
first. Then we'll get to why you can't complain about not getting
laid when you're standing in a bar full of guys who would gladly

fuck you, and then when I give you advice about letting go of your hang-ups, you tell me that I'm going to burn in hell. That's a seriously shitty best friend."

Tanya laughed and said, "Here we go."

"Yep, here we go. So you think that when you get to heaven, it's going to be all of your family and friends, right?"

"Yeah, that's the idea traditionally held by literally billions of people all over the world."

"But no one ever thinks to mention that maybe old Uncle Jimmy who molested a couple of kids in the family might be in hell, do they? Nope, it's always all of your friends and family. No one missing."

"Maybe old Uncle Jimmy was genuinely sorry and he repented, so he gets to go to heaven, too. And maybe we all forgive old Uncle Jimmy, because once you're in heaven you're at peace in a way you've never experienced before, and you understand things much better than just a human brain is capable of."

"Fair enough, but what about old Grandpa Johnny who killed a few dozen people in whatever war was going on in his generation, and nationalism told him that as long as he was doing it for his country, it was perfectly fine, so he never repented? Old Grampy Johnny is always right there waiting for you in heaven. Everyone gets in, no matter what, it seems like."

"I just said *you'll* be roasting in hell, and I'll be sad about that."

"Okay, asshole, then what about the people who claim to have died on the operating table and come back to life? Their immediate family are the only people they ever see in the white light. Wouldn't your grandma also have her heavenly entourage, which would include her grandma, so on and so forth, until you have a giant group of dead people that includes every fucking person who has ever fucking lived on the entire fucking planet? You never hear that story, do you? You never hear some idiot saying, 'I went to heaven and I saw every person who ever lived, even cavemen, because we're all related if you go back far enough'?"

"I can't wait for you to die, so you'll get answers to these questions and you can stop being an asshole all the time."

"When I die and when you die and when anyone dies, we're not getting any answers. We're just going to fucking rot in the ground. So live it up while you can." Karen raised her glass and took a long swig of beer, then said, "Does this beer smell weird to you?"

Tanya sniffed her beer and said, "No."

Karen said, "Weird. It smells metallic or something."

Tanya said, "Maybe it's a bad tap. I don't smell it, though."

Karen said, "Whatever," and she took another sip.

Tanya laughed again. "Anyway, you were baptized. You still have a chance to avoid eternal damnation."

"Bitch, please. You know what really kills me about you religious assholes?"

"There's something else, besides everything you just mentioned? Your well is deep. Please enlighten me."

"You all think we live in a religious society. But we don't."

"You mean America?"

"Yeah."

"You know the stats better than I do, probably, so you have to know you're talking bullshit now."

"Obviously we live in a dipshit country. More people believe in angels than climate change. But I'm not talking about opinion polls. I'm talking about the nuts and bolts of our society—how things are actually run. If I went out tonight and I killed someone, and then in my trial I said, 'Well, I believe in God just like everybody else, and I think he's all powerful just like everybody else, and I know we all believe that he can talk to people if he wants to. And he *did* talk to me. He told me to kill that person, so I did it. I don't know why God wanted that person to die or why he wanted me to be the one to kill that person, but I don't ask questions. When God tells me to do something, I do it. I was just following God's plan.' If I said that shit, even if the entire jury was full of evangelical idiots who speak in tongues on Sundays and really think that God talks to them every day, I'm either going straight to jail for life or getting the death penalty. Period."

"Right, because you broke the law."

"But a jury of my religious peers, who all supposedly believe it's possible for God to tell me to kill someone, should forgive me for breaking man's fallible law in order to carry out God's divine will. They should believe that I was operating under orders from above, and who are they to judge me anyway? Isn't that one of the basic tenets? Judge not lest ye be judged?"

"Yeah, but that's not how God operates."

"Bullshit. If God knows everything that's going to happen, if he has some plan that we all have to follow, then he knows about every murder before it happens and he lets it happen, even though he has the power to stop it. In fact, he sets up every murder in the first place. I mean, fuck, if you boil it down, every second of human suffering and misery was designed and carried out by God."

"You're really fired up tonight. I thought this was supposed to be a night where I get to bitch about getting dumped, and you get to cheer me up."

"I know. Sorry. I'm really bitchy lately. I'm stuck on my dissertation, and it's driving me a little nuts."

"You still haven't turned in your proposal? Jesus."

"Oh! Lord's name in vain! See you in hell."

"I'll repent."

"See, you're not as religious as you think. No one is. That's all I was saying. Another round?"

"Okay, but then I need to get back. I have to finish that paper tonight or I'm screwed."

Karen didn't mention religion or God again during the rest of the conversation with her friend. Instead she found herself thinking how strange it was that although we are all animals with roughly the same mental capacity and roughly the same access to information, both general and specific, we can come to such radically different conclusions about the nature of reality. She wondered if it would always be like this, or if at some point in the future a general knowledge base would be accepted by the whole of humanity on which every individual would base their view of existence. She hoped this would be the case, but became sad as she reflected that she wouldn't live long enough to see that future.

"It's not even midnight. I thought you guys were going to turn it up now that Tanya's single again," was the greeting Paul Barkley gave Karen as she walked in the front door of their apartment.

God and religion were very likely constructs of humanity, but no one would ever be able to disprove or prove the existence of a God, and argument of first cause would never be solved. The universe was vast and mostly unknown. It was just as likely that it was created in the big bang as it was that the entirety of existence was the result of a computer simulation in which every human being was merely a subroutine or an algorithm producing and analyzing data for a purpose that would never be known to them and might not even exist. Sex could be a recreational activity, but it could also be something sacred shared between two people. Having children necessarily meant not being able to work as hard or as often as you'd like on personal endeavors, but the idea of being old without children, without a family, wasn't pleasant. Love was an electrochemical reaction in the brain, but it was very real and no less consuming than if it were the same intangible, magical enchantment that most people seemed to accept as an explanation. These were things that Paul understood to be true.

Karen replied, "I know. She had a paper to write or something. I think she's probably just afraid to try and find another guy because she has got to be terrible at giving head."

"How do you know that?"

"She's only had sex with three guys."

"That doesn't necessarily mean she's bad."

"Come on. Yeah, it does."

"Wait, so are you saying that the more people you've had sex with, the better you are at it?"

"Of course. How can that not be true of anything? The more you do something, the better you get."

"Then you must have been a serious fucking slut before I met you."

Karen laughed. "Fuck you."

"Hey, that was a compliment."

"You always know how to flatter a lady. How was your day?"

She sat next to him on the couch and kissed him. He said, "Long. Jobs suck. You should milk this PhD thing as long as you can. Stay in school forever."

"I'd love to. Unfortunately I don't think I can get another extension on my dissertation proposal."

"And how close are you to finishing it?"

"It's hard to say. I mean, I can tell you that I've written exactly zero percent of it, but since I don't know how long the final proposal will be, I can't really tell you how close I am to finishing."

"You're insane."

"And that's why you decided to move in with me." She kissed him on the cheek again. Paul reached up, turned her head so their lips met, and kissed her with obvious sexual intent. He said, "Actually, *that's* why I decided to move in with you."

"Ooh, such a sexy man." Karen took off her shirt and her bra and playfully shook her breasts at her boyfriend. She took him by the hands, stood up off the couch, led him toward their bedroom and said, "Now I want to show you why I moved in with you. We can sleep in. Tomorrow's Sunday."

chapter
two

"Amen," was the response James Dobbs gave to his pastor's recital of the prayer that began the Sunday service he attended habitually.

God was the creator of all things. He existed beyond space and time and knew every person's thoughts and actions. He had a plan for everyone, and although he could dispense ultimate punishment, God loved all his children. God's plan included every atom in existence, but the things that took place on Earth were the only ones worth concerning yourself with, because human beings were the only creatures in the entirety of God's glorious kingdom that were blessed with free will. Although some scientific endeavors proved beneficial to society, science as a whole was part of a ploy by Satan to convince humanity to accept lies as truth, to pervert the spiritual lives of human beings. Sex was an act to be shared only between a man and his wife for the purpose of procreation. Life began at conception and had to be protected at all costs. These were things that James understood to be true.

James sat alone and silent a few rows back from the pulpit in Woodstone Church. He had been raised in this town, and Woodstone was the only church he had ever attended. James grew up in the foster system and never truly knew any parent as well as he felt he knew God. Nor did he feel that any of his foster parents cared for him as much as God had throughout his life. He never had the opportunity to make any close friends, and he didn't mind this. As a child, he spent every night praying to God to bring meaning to his life, and that habit continued. As an adult, he took enough pleasure in his relationship with God, his frequent prayer, and his attendance at church services to have what he considered to be a rich and fulfilling social life. In his mind, God had given him everything he needed.

"If you'll turn to Jeremiah 29:11 and follow along with me: 'For I know the plans I have for you,' declares the Lord, 'plans to prosper you and not to harm you, plans to give you hope and a future,'" was how Pastor Gary Preston delivered the opening reading from the Bible.

Jesus Christ was the son of God and he died for all of humanity's sins. Spreading the word of God was every Christian's duty, and there was no more exalted a manner in which to spread it than ministry. Certain people who allowed Satan's temptation to overtake them, or who abused the free will they were given by God to engage in lives of sin, would suffer ultimate punishment in hell. But God still loved these people just as a father still loves his child, even though he must punish the child from time to time. Sex was generally something to be shared only between a husband and wife, but all people make mistakes and all people sin. As long as people truly repented, they could be washed clean of their sins in the eyes of God. The healthy amount of money his ministry brought in was simply God's blessing for the good work he was doing, and there was no need for modesty where material wealth was concerned because it was a gift from God himself, and all of God's gifts were to be openly celebrated. These were things that Gary understood to be true.

"'For I know the plans I have for you,' declares the Lord, 'plans to prosper you and not to harm you, plans to give you hope and a future.' Now what are we hearing here? *For I know the plans I have for you.* This is God telling us what? Is he telling us that *we* know the plans he has for us? No. He's telling us that *he* knows the plans he has for us. He knows. Not us. And this can be one of the hardest things to accept as a Christian. You may be sitting there thinking that you know that God's plan for you has to include a brand-new Mercedes-Benz, or it just has to include fifty-yard-line tickets to the next Super Bowl, because you want those things so bad, but guess what? What you want, no matter how bad you want it, might not be what God has in his plan for you. And it's not just cars and Super Bowl tickets we're talking about here. I know some of you out there right now are suffering, really suffering. Maybe you have family members who are in the hospital, and you pray so hard every day that they'll get better, and you know God hears every word you pray to him, but your brother, your sister, your mom, your dad . . . they don't get better. You know why? Because God has a plan for that person, too, and you don't know what it is, and they don't know what it is. But he does. And that's all that matters. Learning to accept that God has a plan for you, and no matter what you think you should be doing with your life, that's secondary to what God knows you should be doing—well, that's one of the hardest things about being a Christian.

"So let's say you get to that point. Let's say you're okay with giving up all your own personal desires in order to do whatever it is that's in God's plan for you. The next step might even be harder. I mean, how will you know what God's plan is? Is he just going to tell you? Well, yeah, he is just going to tell you. Isn't that funny how sometimes God can use the simplest thing to work his miracles? But he can only do his part. He can tell you his plan, but that doesn't mean anything if you don't hear it. I don't know how many times I tell my kids to take out the trash, but guess who ends up taking it out? Yours truly—because my kids, God bless 'em, might be on their Xbox or their phone, or listening to music, and they don't hear me because they have so many distractions. It's hard to do, but it's a two-way street. God's gonna talk to you, but you have to hear him.

"So how do you hear God? You listen. Sounds simple again, right? But it's not. How many of us in here today can honestly say we're listening for God every day, all day? None of us can. My kids have their Xbox and their music and their phone, and you might have your bills or your job or your boyfriend or girlfriend or husband or wife. We've all got distractions. But that's okay. God knows that. And God knows that the best time to talk to us is when we're really listening, when the distractions are gone and we're just open to hear whatever it is he has to say. So the best thing we can do as Christians is listen for God's voice as hard as we can, as often as we can.

"And once you hear God, then what? Well, then you have to do the hardest thing of all. You have to *act*. You have to actually do what God tells you to do. And I know that's hard. It's a lot easier just to say, 'Well, God, I know you told me to get a job or to help my family or my community, but there's some awfully good TV on tonight.' Well, that won't cut it. You ever hear that expression 'When I say jump, you say how high'? That's exactly how God wants you to react to his voice when he tells you to do something. I mean, what do you think happened when Jesus heard his dad say, 'Son, I have a big favor to ask of you. You might not want to do it, but it's all part of my plan, and you just have to trust me'? You think Jesus said, 'Dad, I'd love to help you out, but I have some TV to watch'? No, Jesus went to his disciples and he told them he was going to die for all of us, and not to worry, because even though that might sound bad, God told him it was what he was supposed to do. No matter what it is, you have to be willing and ready to act on whatever commands God gives you, to complete his plan for you. And that gets a big fat amen."

The rest of the congregation, James Dobbs included, echoed back, "Amen."

James spent the rest of his Sunday at home, listening for God to speak to him, just as Minister Preston had outlined in his sermon. Just like every day prior to that Sunday, God did not speak to him. James wondered what God's voice sounded like and wondered if he'd ever hear it. He assumed that God spoke to everyone at least once, and he vowed that he would be ready when the time came for him to carry out whatever command God delivered.

chapter three

Karen was late for an appointment with her PhD supervisor.
She woke up on time but was too nauseous to leave her apartment. She had recently been feeling like her hangovers were getting worse and worse, and sometimes after what she considered a
smaller than usual amount of alcohol. She tried to force herself
to drink a glass of water but felt repulsed by the idea of her teeth
possibly touching the glass, a fear that a hangover had never produced before. She hoped her supervisor would understand or not
even bring up her tardiness.

She had developed a certain amount of dread concerning this
appointment, due to the misgivings she seemed unable to escape
where her dissertation was concerned. She had started writing
two proposals over the past six months, but she had lost interest
in both. She didn't want her dissertation to be the same as every
other philosophy dissertation at UCLA: read by an approval

committee, published in an esoteric journal, then filed away in some obscure library, where it would never be seen again. She was thinking about this as she walked across campus to her supervisor's office, hoping that her desire to do something important, something noteworthy, would garner her some more time to settle in on a subject for her dissertation.

As she walked toward Dodd Hall, Karen was stopped by a student she identified as undergraduate by his age and dress. "If you have a second, I'd like to ask you if you've accepted Jesus Christ as your personal savior," was his greeting to Karen.

Based on all the strife and suffering in the world, it was clear the end times were close at hand. Although a college education was important to secure a good job and become a high-functioning member of society, being a disciple of Christ was much more important, and was clearly much more worthy of a person's time than studying the knowledge of man. In the final days of the world, there was no greater endeavor than attempting to save as many souls as possible. Sexual intercourse was to be engaged in only by a man and his wife, and if God saw fit to initiate Armageddon before he delivered every man a wife, then it shouldn't be questioned, because that would be part of his plan, and dying as a virgin would be acceptable. The fornication and experimentation with drugs and alcohol that almost all college students participated in were sins; and while they were redeemable sins, if the world ended while a person was engaging in sinful behavior, that person would be sent to hell without the opportunity to repent. And since no one had any foreknowledge about the exact moment of Armageddon, it was better to avoid such behaviors altogether. These were things that this young student understood to be true.

Karen never passed up the opportunity to engage with religious people. It gave her a certain satisfaction to express her contempt for them openly. Karen said, "Why would you want to ask me that?"

He said, "Because I care about your soul and about its salvation."

"You know the God that you pray to, that you claim loves everyone . . . He—" She paused. "You do think God's a man, right?"

"Well, the Bible did say God made man in his own image, so . . ."

"What do you think this male God does with his penis? Do you think he fucks with it? If so, what does he fuck? Does he pee? If so, what does he drink in order to produce urine?"

"I hadn't thought about that, but I'd guess he just doesn't use it."

"Not even to masturbate?"

"Masturbation is a sin."

"I'm fucking with you. I just wanted to make sure you thought God was a man so I could correctly identify you as the regular kind of misogynist piece of shit that usually stands out here and bothers people. So that same big-dicked God that you claim loves every person on the planet also kills every person on the planet. But before he kills most of them, he makes them suffer through some of the worst circumstances you can imagine—war, famine, disease, all kinds of bad shit. And even if you're lucky enough to be born in a place and into a class that allows you to escape the garden variety atrocities that most of the world deals with, you'll age, at least, and your body will experience pain as it slowly shuts down over the course of your life until you die alone in a hospital somewhere."

He said, "It's true, we all age and we all die, but here, in this country, we're blessed to be comfortable for most of our lives, so we have the ability to spread his word."

Karen said, "You assholes will never understand how arrogant it is to claim you're blessed, will you?"

He said, "It's not arrogant. It's actually the opposite. By admitting that everything good in your life is a blessing from God, you give him glory, and you understand that you can achieve nothing on your own, nothing without God's divine favor. It's actually a statement of ultimate humility."

Karen said, "I know you think it is, but you're wrong. Let me help you out. By saying that you're blessed in not having to worry about the problems most of the rest of the world deals with on a daily basis, you're actually saying that you truly believe God likes you more than everyone else he's making to suffer. God has blessed you with a cancer-free body. Does that mean that anyone with cancer is less blessed? God must not like them as much as he likes you, right? I mean, why would he give them cancer when they clearly don't want it and let you walk around completely healthy?"

The student stammered slightly, "It . . . it just means that I'm thankful for what I have, and I recognize I have it because God wants me to have it."

Karen said, "Exactly. Other people want what you have, too, but they don't have it, and you really honestly think that's because God wants you to have it more than he wants them to have it. You believe you're favored by a God you claim loves all his children equally. Which is fucking disgusting."

With that, Karen continued on her way to Dodd Hall as the young student called after her, "I'll pray for you."

I'm very much hoping that you have a proposal for me, Ms. Holloway," was the first thing Professor David Noone said to Karen as she sat down across from him in his office.

Although no scientific evidence supported the existence of a God, there were certain undeniable spiritual human experiences that made an outright stance of militant atheism impossible. The universe was vast and magnificent in a way that almost certainly attested to a design or some conscious influence in its creation and arrangement. However, it was very likely that none of the major world religions were correct in their assumptions. It was far more likely that God and the realm of the spirit were much too complex for human beings ever to understand, and that we created art and philosophy in an attempt to describe those elements of the human experience that hard science never could. Sex was an animal act, but it was also a spiritual act and one of the most beautiful acts a human being could ever perform. These were things that David understood to be true.

Karen said, "I don't."

David said, "Karen, I've given you more extensions than any student I've ever had in the program. You have to come up with something. What about your proposition from last year? I thought it was very good. I know you have a specific disdain for religion, and I really thought you were able to get past the base-level vitriol you usually rely on with any religious debate and objectively explore the sadomasochist mind-set of the true Christian. Why don't you continue where you left off with that?"

She said, "Everyone already knows that the basic Christian ideals are contradictory and psychologically harmful, and . . . I just I don't want to do something that no one cares about."

David said, "So are you saying that every other student in the program is doing something no one cares about?"

She said, "I didn't say that. You did. But, yeah, basically."

David sat back in his chair and said, "Karen, you're very bright, obviously. Everyone in this program is. But I think you're failing to understand exactly what a dissertation is supposed to be. It's not meant to change the world or revolutionize the way we think about anything. It's meant to be a document that I can read and the rest of the committee can read to show us that you have enough understanding to warrant a PhD. That's all. Once you have the PhD, once you leave here, or stay here and become a professor, that's when your real work will start. And I don't want to rain on your parade, but this is philosophy. There's not a lot of new ground to tread, even after you complete the program.

I know you're still young, and you still have that drive to blaze a trail, but eventually you'll come to understand that the trails have already been blazed, and it's rewarding just to walk down them."

She said, "Are you serious?"

David said, "Very."

She said, "So do you think *you're* just walking down the paths of other people? Because the work you did on the negative costs of altruism, why it's bad to be good—that's why I came to this school, and that was a path that, to my knowledge, didn't exist before you."

David thought for a moment, the compliment having its calculated effect. He said, "You might get one chance at something that becomes meaningful to the world of philosophy. But I did that work years after my PhD candidacy."

She said, "Well, think of it this way: I want to do something important now. If I fall a little short and it doesn't revolutionize the world of philosophy, then it will still be a pretty amazing dissertation, right? Remember how you felt when you started thinking about altruism? You got that little spark and you knew you were onto something. I'm just asking you to give me a little more time to try and find that spark, and if I can't, then I promise I'll throw myself into my old proposition with reckless abandon and deliver you the best unimportant dissertation you've ever seen in your life."

David couldn't help but like Karen. She didn't remind him of himself when he was young. She reminded him of the types of girls he fell in love with when he was young. He said, "Okay. But you can't stretch this out much more. A few more weeks at the most, okay?"

Karen said, "Okay."

chapter
four

James Dobbs finished eating dinner in the kitchen of his one-bedroom apartment and put on his work clothes. He had had the same job on an overnight cleaning crew at Dillard's in the West Ridge Mall since graduating high school seven years earlier. The work wasn't difficult, and James considered how he didn't have to deal with very many people to be a perk.

As he drove, James thought about a girl named Rebecca. She worked at Dillard's and sometimes stayed late enough that James would see her leaving as he was coming in to begin the night's cleaning. He had never spoken to her, but he knew her name because she sometimes forgot to take off her name tag when she was leaving for the night. James wondered if God had put Rebecca in his life to teach him something or if, perhaps, she was the girl God meant for him. James said a prayer asking God to give him a sign that night. If Rebecca was the girl that God intended for him to marry, James asked only that God give him some unmistakable signal that this was the case.

As he turned off Wanamaker Road and into the West Ridge Mall parking lot closest to Dillard's, he could see Rebecca emerging from the building. James spotted her red Toyota Camry, with its Kansas State Wildcat bumper sticker, and he parked next to it. He waited in his car for a few moments longer than necessary, then got out and made his way toward the building so that his path to the door would cross Rebecca's. He looked at her in anticipation of the sign he asked God to deliver, but Rebecca didn't return his gaze. She was talking on her phone and looking down into her purse, completely oblivious to James and everything else around her. He silently repented for his sin of pride, for asking God for something so foolish and petty.

And then Rebecca's phone, precariously perched between her ear and shoulder, fell onto the ground an inch from James's feet, cracking its screen. This, he was certain, was the sign from God that he'd prayed for. He bent down, picked up the phone, and handed it back to Rebecca. She said, "Thanks. This is the second phone I've ruined digging for my keys."

God was probably real, but it seemed that praying was a waste of time. Whichever God created Earth certainly didn't care about what happened to the planet or the people on it. The solar system was the same thing as the galaxy and the universe— they were all just different ways of describing space, which was essentially anything beyond Earth. Science was good when it made the complications of living a little easier to deal with, by creating things like the Internet and cell phones, but there was no real need to waste time and money on space exploration or smashing atoms. Sex was a natural and instinctual part of being human, and no matter what any person's sexual preference, as long as it wasn't illegal, there was no need to bring religion into it. Abortion was a viable option for any girl who wasn't ready to raise a child. It wasn't something to take lightly, just a medical procedure. These were things that Rebecca understood to be true.

With a confidence that came from knowing that God had ordained this event, James introduced himself and told Rebecca that he saw her from time to time when he was coming in to start his shift. He told her that he'd wanted to stop and say hello, but he was too embarrassed. James went on to ask Rebecca if she'd be interested in getting dinner or seeing a movie with him on a night when she wasn't busy. James was confident that Rebecca would agree to go out with him, given that God had just given him a sign to ask her out.

Rebecca said, "Oh my god, that's seriously really sweet of you to ask, but I have a boyfriend. Sorry."

James stood in front of her, too confused to reply. She said, "Well, have a good night," and got in her car. As he walked into Dillard's and took the floor polisher out of its storage closet, he silently asked God if he had done something wrong, if he had misinterpreted the sign. He listened closely for any sound of God's voice, for any answer. All he heard was the loud hum and bristling of the brushes polishing the tile floor in the housewares department as he pushed the machine back and forth.

On his break, James avoided his coworkers and ate a sandwich in his car. He looked out his window at the spot on the ground where Rebecca had dropped her phone. The sign God had given him was a phone breaking. He began to understand that this sign was a negative sign. It wasn't a dove flying overhead, a beam of golden light parting the clouds, an angel trumpeting from the heavens. A phone hit the ground, and its screen shattered. It became clear to him that Rebecca was a temptation from Satan, and the sign he had prayed for, the sign that was delivered by God, wasn't meant to motivate him to ask Rebecca on a date. It was meant to warn him. God had given James a sign to say away from her.

This is what Pastor Preston had been talking about. James

assumed that God's plan was to bring Rebecca into his life, but it had become clear to James that this was incorrect. James understood that his own human desires were clouding his ability to surrender to God's plan. James finished his sandwich and thanked God for looking after him. He promised God that he would try to be more observant of his signs and more understanding of them. He promised God that he would do his best to suppress his own desires and his own thoughts about what should happen in his life so that he could more easily be used in whatever manner God intended.

chapter
five

Karen's menstrual cycle was fairly regular. It had been this way since she got her first period in junior high school. She would occasionally skip a period. It wasn't common for her to do so, but it did happen. But only one of those occasions came after she became sexually active. She was a freshman in college, and she had engaged in unprotected sex a few times with a fellow student who became her first college boyfriend.

The month after these initial unprotected sexual encounters, Karen did not get her period. When she began to suspect she was pregnant, she went to the campus health center, only to find out that she wasn't. The doctors there told her that it's not uncommon for girls entering their freshman year of college to miss a period due to the stress of such an extreme change in their lives. The doctors also said that an increased intake of alcohol and drugs can be contributing factors. Although Karen didn't admit this to the doctors, she felt that this second explanation was far more plausible in her case.

Paul had already gotten out of bed, made himself breakfast, and left for work by the time Karen woke up. She could still smell the bacon he cooked. She knew she had missed her period the month before, which she attributed to mounting stress concerning her dissertation. But she was now aware that a week had passed since her period was due again, which meant that she had missed her second period in a row. This was something she had never experienced. After checking her phone's calendar to see that she had only one afternoon class to teach, she decided to spend the morning buying and taking a pregnancy test, just to be on the safe side.

Once inside her neighborhood CVS, she paused for a moment to really absorb the experience. It was the first time she had ever purchased a pregnancy test, and she viewed it as a strange kind of a rite of passage—something that was available to women only recently in the overall timeline of humanity. She tried to imagine what it must have been like before pregnancy tests, before women had options. Then she tried to imagine what it would be like for women in the future. She wondered if it would be better, if there would be some kind of male birth control, if there would be no social stigma associated with an abortion, or if it would be worse. She knew it was possible that the future could see a return to more restrictive laws and social norms where reproduction was concerned, where a woman's freedom was concerned. In Karen's mind it was completely plausible that the next superpower to govern the world after America could be any one of the currently existing misogynistic societies around the globe. Without any foreknowledge of what might be in store for future generations, she considered herself lucky to live in the time she did.

She made her way to the family planning aisle and realized she didn't know enough about the variety of pregnancy tests to make a quick selection. As she looked over the dozen or so possible choices and read the back of some of the boxes, Karen became aware of other CVS patrons watching her. She didn't know if this was an accurate assessment of the situation, but it felt accurate. She questioned her uneasiness in this moment, but she gave into it nonetheless, grabbing a First Response test without inspecting it and walking to the front.

Paul always made some derogatory comment about automation being the downfall of society when they encountered self-checkout machines in grocery stores, but Karen was glad that CVS had an entire bank of them as she purchased her pregnancy test. But as she walked back to her car, she mentally scolded herself for feeling any shame at all about her purchase.

At home, as she sat on the toilet urinating onto the plastic stick, she knew what she would do if she was, in fact, pregnant. She would have an abortion. Both she and Paul had discussed with certainty how neither of them ever wanted children. This made the possible positive result of the pregnancy test seem more like an injury or illness that Karen would have to seek medical care to treat. In her mind it was more of a significant and horribly unpleasant inconvenience than a life-changing decision.

She pulled her pants back up and stood in the bathroom for the three minutes the box indicated were necessary for the hormones from her urine to react with the chemicals on the stick. As the final seconds of those three minutes ticked by, Karen watched two pink lines materialize in the small oval window at the end of the stick. She said, "Fuck," and flipped open her laptop to Google the nearest Planned Parenthood.

She found that the Hollywood Health Center was the closest to her. As she called to make an appointment, she soothed herself by rationalizing that the Hollywood Planned Parenthood office had probably done more abortions than any Planned Parenthood in the country, so their skill level should be high at least. She made an appointment for the following day, and then called

Tanya and asked her to come over. She told Tanya that she had big news.

Karen knew that Tanya didn't share her views on abortion, and she also knew that the situation had more innate gravity than she was willing to acknowledge. "Guess what?" she said to her friend when she arrived.

Tanya said, "What?"

Karen said, "I'm preggers!"

"Wait, what?"

"I know. It sucks. I don't know what happened. There were a few days two months ago when I had the flu and I didn't take my pill, but Paul didn't come inside me for at least a week or so after that. Anyway, doesn't matter now. What's done is done."

"Holy shit. What did Paul say?"

"He doesn't really, uh, know at this point."

"Holy shit. You have to tell him."

"Stop holy shitting me and calm down. I don't have to tell him at all. I obviously have to do something, but telling him is not that something."

"That's not cool. That's his baby, too."

"It's not anybody's baby right now. It's not even a fucking baby at all. It's a little ball of snot stuck to the wall of my uterus. That's it."

"You can't be serious. You're really not going to tell him about it?"

"No, I'm not. And neither are you."

"Why wouldn't you tell him?"

Until that moment, Karen hadn't thought about why she didn't want to tell her boyfriend about the pregnancy. Practically, the situation would be resolved by the end of the following day. She didn't see the need to involve Paul. But beyond that, she realized that she was feeling a certain amount of shame, guilt, and embarrassment for having gotten pregnant in the first place. She thought about all the conversations she and Paul had about not having children, about all the times they had laughed at their friends when they replaced their Facebook profile pictures with sonograms, about how they each hated the idea of willingly replacing themselves. This one shared view was something they took pride in and had built at least some part of their relationship around.

She felt that the pregnancy was somehow her fault, an easily preventable mistake. She knew logically this wasn't the case, but she couldn't help how she felt. On top of that, she knew that there was at least some chance that if Paul should find out about the pregnancy and the abortion that would follow, it might alter their relationship. Even though Karen knew that Paul would agree with her decision and take her to the appointment and care for her after the procedure, she felt it was better to leave him out of it. This wasn't an experience she wanted him to have to share.

Karen said, "I just don't want him to know, okay?"

Tanya said, "Obviously, I'll do whatever you want me to, but I'm telling you, you should seriously think about telling him. I know you're probably trying to downplay this in your head, but it's is a bigger deal than you think."

"No, it's really not, and that's how it's going to stay."

"Okay, fine."

"And I need you to take me to Planned Parenthood tomorrow."

"What? I'm not helping you get an abortion."

"I went to church with you that one time your boyfriend dumped you on Easter."

"I can't believe you're making jokes about this."

"I'm sorry. I know this is seriously against everything you stand for and all of that shit. But I really need your help, Tanya. You're my best friend, and I called you because you're the only person I want to know about it. You're the only person I really trust. Will you help me, please?"

"Are you serious right now?"

"Yes."

Tanya took a moment, exhaled a long breath, gave Karen a hug, and then said, "You know the fucking irony here, right? As a Christian, I have to help you when you're in need and I can't pass judgment. So I'll take you. But I don't agree with this at all. At all."

"I know you don't, and that's why you're my best friend."

That night Karen ate dinner with Paul, watched television with Paul, and had sex with Paul without telling him that she was pregnant with his child. While they had sex he said, "I think your boobs are getting bigger." Karen denied it, even though she knew he was right. Her bras had been getting tighter. She knew that after the following day, her hormones would return to their normal levels and her breasts would return to their normal size. Karen knew that this would be the closest Paul would ever come to finding out she was pregnant.

As Paul slept, Karen remained awake, building dread by imagining the procedure she'd have to endure the following day. She rubbed a hand over her stomach in small circles and thought to herself that this would very likely be the only interaction she would have with a child of her own.

chapter
six

Proverbs 12:11: Whoever works his land will have plenty of bread, but he who follows worthless pursuits lacks sense.

This was the opening line of James Dobbs's profile on ChristianMingle.com. James had studied this specific line from the Bible since he was a child. It had always held special meaning for him. Throughout his childhood and early adulthood he had felt contempt for his peers because he felt that many of them followed worthless pursuits while he worked his metaphorical land. He felt that this proverb was the simplest and best way to describe himself, the life he led, and the future he hoped to share with a wife. The work ethic he created based on these words was something that he tried to apply to every aspect of his life.

Even though his year-long membership on ChristianMingle. com had yielded him only two dates, neither of which led to a second date, James logged in to his account every night before work and made a habit of sending at least five personal messages to women with whom the site had matched him. He felt that God would not simply place his wife in front of him. He had to show God that he was ready for her and that he was willing to work in order to get her. God had to know that he was deserving of such a blessing.

In the first six months James was active on the site, he sent a standard cut-and-paste message to every woman he felt was a good match for him. It read:

"Hello. My name is James Dobbs. I haven't been on this site for very long, but after reading your profile it seems like we're a pretty good match and I'd love to get to know you more. If you find my profile interesting, please message me back. —James"

The message took James several nights to craft. He was unsure of what a good first message on an Internet dating site should include. In the end, he decided that keeping it short was the best strategy. He never received any replies to this message, however, and after reading complaints on several prospective matches' profiles that they were tired of having their inboxes filled with meaningless cut-and-paste messages from guys who clearly hadn't taken the time to read their profiles, James abandoned his standard message strategy. He rationalized that if he was sincerely going to work the land of ChristianMingle.com, he should put in the time required to personalize each of his messages.

His first message of the night was sent to a woman with the username "ChicaDeJesus." She was five foot three, Caucasian, twenty-five years old, had a bachelor's degree, and worked as a nurse. She described herself as having a goofy sense of humor and loving animals, including her two cats. She claimed to be looking for a hard-working guy who would be a good provider for the family she wanted to start as soon as possible. Jim imagined himself married to ChicaDeJesus, sitting in the backyard of some house he didn't yet have, watching their children run around after church squirting each other with water guns.

He wrote:

"Hi. I saw your profile and it seems like we have a lot of things in common. I really like comedy movies and it seems like you do, too. I don't have cats but I really like them and have no allergies or anything like that. Where do you nurse at?"

James felt that ending the message with an innocuous question about something he could only have learned by reading her profile increased his chances of receiving a response. He sent two similar messages to two similar profiles before he saw the small Christian Mingle instant messenger window open up in the bottom right of his screen. James was receiving an instant message from a user named "Eyesofblue." He saw that she was five foot seven, Caucasian, twenty-eight, and had graduated from high school, though she listed no job. James had always initiated first contact with women on this site, and he began to wonder if this could be the sign from God that he had been waiting for.

Eyesofblue's message read, "What do you do for a job? You don't have it listed."

James explained that he worked at the mall in Topeka.

Eyesofblue replied, "Like in a store?"

James explained that he worked at the Dillard's department store.

Eyesofblue replied, "Do you sell stuff? Like suits or something?"

James explained that he worked nights as part of the cleaning crew for that store, mainly, but sometimes they also cleaned other stores in the mall or the mall itself if the regular mall cleaning crew was unavailable, which happened a few times a year.

Eyesofbue replied, "Are you trying to save up money to move to Kansas City or something?"

James explained that he was not.

Eyesofblue replied, "Are you going to school?"

James explained that he was not.

Eyesofblue replied, "Oh. You just want to clean Dillard's for-ever? Lol."

James explained that the job paid his bills, and if the Lord had different plans for him, then James was sure the Lord would let him know.

Eyesofblue replied, "True. So what do you do when you're not working?"

James explained that he spent his free time either in church or reading for the most part. He then asked Eyesofblue what she did in her free time.

Eyesofblue replied, "Watch TV, I guess. So are you busy this weekend?"

James explained that he was not.

Eyesofblue replied, "Maybe you should ask me out, then."

James had never encountered a girl so forward. He wondered if God had sent her his profile and then compelled her to mes-sage him. He wondered if Eyesofblue was his soul mate. He asked her if she would like to get dinner with him.

Eyesofblue replied, "OMG! You read my mind. Lol. I'd love to."

They exchanged phone numbers, made plans for their date, and then James logged off. As he polished the floor in Dillard's that night, he prayed to God to help him decide what he should wear on what would be his first date in almost a year.

chapter seven

Karen had instructed Tanya to pick her up at 10:00 A.M., an hour and a half after Paul left for work. Karen assumed this buffer time would ensure that Paul wouldn't find out about her clandestine plan, preventing Tanya from having to lie about why she was at their place, if the two ran into each other. Tanya arrived on time and tried to stop herself from initiating any kind of conversation about the events at hand. She told herself she was just going to be a good friend. She told herself that she would remain neutral. She told herself this wasn't about her or what she thought should be done. But she couldn't help herself.

The drive to Planned Parenthood was silent at first. Then, about ten minutes in, Tanya said, "I know you don't want to hear this, but I have to make sure you've really thought this through. It's only been a day since you even found out. You can take some more time before you decide anything."

Karen said, "I don't need to think about it anymore. I've thought about this my entire adult life. I made the decision before I ever even got pregnant."

"I know. I know. It's just that there's no harm in waiting another week, and who knows? You might change your mind. Some kind of motherly instinct might kick in or something."

"That's why I need to do it now. If there's even the slightest possibility that some flood of mom hormones might make me change my mind, I need to make sure I take care of this first."

"That's a really shitty thing to say."

"Why is that shitty? I think making an informed decision based on logic and reason is far better than basing it on hormonal fluctuation and emotion."

"Okay, robot. I'm obviously here for you and I'm obviously supportive of you, but, I mean, don't you think about the baby at all? That baby can't speak for itself. Don't you feel like as a human being you have even the slightest obligation to let it live?"

"Here we go. I still don't know how or why you champion that pro-life bullshit rhetoric. You know the people at the heart of the pro-life camp—not you and the regular people who just don't like abortion, but the ones who get laws passed and try to shut down Planned Parenthood—those fucking pieces of shit are the ones who started that whole line of reasoning. The baby can't defend itself, so we have an obligation to defend them. Those fucks don't give two shits about the unborn babies they're supposedly saving. All they care about is control. They have to control women, and having women with the freedom to choose what to do with their bodies is a scarier proposition to them than letting women vote. Because on some very primal level, men see it as women controlling life, controlling the future of the species, and they certainly can't have that. And somehow their bullshit has sunk into your head and stuck. I know this is just one of those things between us that will probably stay like this until we die, and I've learned to accept it, but please, for the love of your

God, the one who tells you not to judge people and to be accepting and loving of everyone, can we just check this conversation today? Just today. Just let me get through this, and then you can tell me how bad it is to take the choice away from a blob of cells all you want."

They drove in silence for a minute or so. Karen felt like she might have gone a little too far in her reprimand, but she felt she had no alternative. She just wanted to get through the day with as little stress as possible.

Tanya eventually said, "Sorry. It's just tough to be a good friend in a situation like this, I guess."

Karen said, "I'm sorry, too. I know how hard it is for you to even be driving me to get this done. I'm sorry I put you in the situation in the first place. But you're my best friend, and I wouldn't want anyone else with me, to tell you the truth." This confession eased the tension between the two friends for a moment.

Tanya said, "Okay, last thing, and then I'll shut up. There's a compromise here that you might not be thinking of."

"What?"

"You could have the baby and give it up for adoption."

"Are you fucking crazy? If I'm worried about hormones changing my mind if I wait a week to do this, what do you think would happen to me after nine months?"

"I don't know. I just had to make sure you were thinking about all of your options before we get to the place."

"You know what would actually be hilarious? If I had the kid and gave it to a gay couple. How do you think your pro-life pals would feel about that? That's exactly what I'm talking about, by the way. They don't give a shit about the kid—they just want to force their moral agendas on everyone else. God, if I did that and blogged about it . . . Or what if— Wait, hold a second. Pull over."

Tanya, sensing that Karen might be changing her mind, pulled over. "What is it?"

Karen said, "Turn around. You're right. I'm going to think about this for a few more days."

"Are you serious?"

"Yeah. But you're still the only person who knows, and I want to keep it that way. Paul can't know what's going on."

Tanya said, "Okay," then made a U-turn in the middle of the street and headed back to Karen and Paul's apartment, hoping that whatever Karen was thinking about would save the life of this child. Tanya couldn't help but feel that God had a hand in whatever was going on.

Eyesofblue's real name was Beth. James had learned this and a few other general details about her through a series of text messages, and he hoped that her profile pictures were accurate. He was waiting for her outside the RowHouse, a restaurant Beth suggested after James admitted that he didn't know many nice‑ places to eat. It was five minutes past eight o'clock. She was five minutes late. Punctuality was something James took very seriously. He checked his phone to see if Beth had sent him a text, but she had not. When he looked back up, he saw her walking toward him from the parking lot. She looked very similar to her profile pictures. The only difference was that she was slightly heavier in person. James felt it would be a sin to judge her for this, so he tried not to, and he immediately forgave her for her tardiness.

She walked up to him and said, "James?"

God was definitely real and he definitely created everything in existence. Jesus Christ was definitely his son and he definitely died for the sins of humanity. The universe and space and aliens were things that only scientists and moviemakers thought about. They had no real impact on anything that occurred on planet Earth. While on Earth, it was every good Christian's duty to lead a good and righteous life, but God wouldn't have made fun if he didn't want people to have it. Although drinking, doing drugs, and having premarital sex were sins, God wouldn't have created the ability for human beings to repent if he didn't already know that there would be a need for it. Birth control, too, was something the church might be against, but God wouldn't have created it if he didn't expect people to use it. Birth control was something that gave a woman more flexibility in finding the right person to marry and spend the rest of her life with. Using it after marriage was something to be discussed with a husband, but using it before marriage was something God clearly intended for any woman who saw the need. These were things that Beth understood to be true.

James introduced himself and held the door open for Beth as they entered the RowHouse. When James approached the front desk and asked for a table for two, he was informed by the hostess that without a reservation the wait might be an hour. Beth said, "Oh, I made a reservation just in case. Beth Garner."

James felt slightly embarrassed that he hadn't known to make a reservation. He didn't dine out often, and when he did, it was rarely at a place that required reservations. He explained this to Beth who said, "It's totally fine. I picked the place. The least I could do was call and make a reservation."

James and Beth were shown to their table, and they struck up the regular small talk that two people make on a first date. When the server came to take their drink orders, James learned that Beth had no problem with the casual consumption of alcohol, as she ordered a Manhattan. Beth learned that James didn't drink alcohol at all when he ordered an iced tea and explained to her that he had never had even a sip of anything alcoholic. He told her that he passed no judgment on anyone who chose to partake in alcoholic beverages, but he had decided a long time ago that he would never poison himself in such a manner. He believed it to be insulting to God, who created his body with purity in mind. Beth began to think that James was possibly a little too Christian for her, but he was extremely polite and she did find him attractive, so she chose to ignore his hard-line stance on sobriety.

By the end of dinner, Beth was feeling the effects of her third Manhattan, and she asked James if he'd like to continue the date at a nearby bar. James was surprised to find that Beth's insistence on drinking alcohol throughout dinner, and her suggestion to continue drinking alcohol at a bar, didn't bother him that much. He always tried to remain neutral in matters of judgment where legal vices were concerned. He knew the social norms regarding alcohol dictated that Beth was doing nothing out of the ordinary, and it had been several months since he'd been on a date with a girl he found as charming as Beth.

He knew that this was very likely a test from God, but he was confused as to what God might be testing. It seemed too obvious that God would test him to see if he could resist temptation. And because Beth never tried to get him to taste even a sip of her own drink, James thought a test of temptation was unlikely. It seemed more reasonable that God might be testing James to see just how accepting of others he could be, how willing he was to indulge in activities that were out of his comfort zone. After deciding that this second test was the one God had probably set before him, James agreed to accompany Beth to a nearby bar.

Once in the bar, and halfway through her fourth Manhattan, Beth said, "So James, you seem like a pretty straightforward guy. You're polite. You don't seem like you're too weird or anything. Why aren't you married yet?"

James explained that he had dated a few women who seemed

like likely candidates for marriage, but for one reason or another, things just ended up not working out.

Beth said, "Does that make you sad at all?"

James explained that it didn't make him sad. He was confident in God's plan for him, whatever that was, and he knew that when the time was right, God would bring him together with whoever he was supposed to marry. Beth said, "Who knows? Maybe that's what God's doing right now," then leaned close to James and kissed him on the mouth.

James was surprised at how forward she was, but it made sense, given how forward she'd been online. There was alcohol on her lips—the first time James had ever tasted it—and he began to wonder if his first inclination might have been correct. Maybe this was a test of temptation.

Beth had one more Manhattan before she and James decided to leave. James walked her to her car, and they had a brief conversation about what a good time they each had and how they'd like to see each other again. As Beth was getting her keys from her purse, she stumbled, fell, and spilled everything in her purse onto the ground. She was very clearly drunk. She said, "Crap. I think I might be too drunk to drive home."

James offered to call her a taxi.

Beth had a different suggestion. "You could just drive me home. I can leave my car here until morning." Even if it was a test in temptation, as a Christian man, James knew he couldn't leave a woman in need, so he agreed to drive her home.

James followed the GPS directions to Beth's apartment and tried to engage her in some small talk on the drive, but after a few blocks Beth passed out. James let her sleep until he pulled up to the address she'd programmed into his GPS. He put the car in park, turned off the engine, and gently nudged her until she woke up.

Beth said, "Oh my god, did I seriously just pass out? I'm really sorry."

James explained that there was no need to apologize. As he helped her out of the car and walked her to her front door, he was surprised to find that Beth seemed more attractive to him in some way as a result of her inebriation. There was something in her needing his help that made him feel like he was fulfilling his purpose as a man.

At her door, Beth kissed James again, and again he could taste the alcohol in her mouth. She said, "Do you, you know, want to come in for a second?"

James thought it would be the polite thing to do, if only to make sure she didn't pass out on her kitchen floor or something similar. He agreed to come in to help her get into bed safely.

Once inside, Beth excused herself to the bathroom and told James to make himself comfortable. James didn't plan on staying very long. He went into the kitchen and filled a glass of water from the tap, then sat on the couch. He heard the faucet in the bathroom turn on, then off, then the bathroom door opened. Beth said, "Come here."

James followed the sound of Beth's voice to her bedroom, where she was already sprawled out on top of her comforter. He extended the glass of water and explained that she should drink the whole glass through the course of the night. Beth said, "Thanks. Just put it on the nightstand." James did as he was instructed, and as he approached the nightstand Beth reached out and pulled him down on top of her, kissing him sloppily and aggressively.

James pulled back and asked her what she was doing.

Beth said, "I invited you in. Why else would a girl do that?"

James explained that he genuinely thought she might just need some help getting into bed. Beth laughed at him and said, "Wait a minute. Are you one of these guys who doesn't believe in premarital sex?"

James explained that this was indeed the case.

Beth laughed again and said, "And you've never been married. So . . . you're a virgin?"

James explained that he was a virgin and he saw nothing wrong with it. He claimed that he would remain a virgin until God saw fit to change that. Beth said, "Well, it's possible he's trying to change it right now," and leaned out toward him, reaching to grab him again.

James explained that, while the offer was extremely flattering, he was saving himself until marriage just as God had commanded all his servants to do. He told Beth that he didn't judge her for her decision to ignore this command from God, but he wouldn't be able to see her again knowing that she could so easily disobey what he saw as one of God's most immutable laws where men, women, and love were concerned. James left the apartment, wiping a stray bit of Beth's saliva from his mouth.

On his way back home he hoped God was pleased with him.

chapter nine

In the days that followed Karen's decision to postpone the abortion, she became increasingly aware of the unique position pregnancy afforded her. Her hatred for religion and the patriarchal culture it inspired in America was something she'd felt from a very early age. She'd never been able to understand why any woman would adhere to the constraints of Christianity, or any major religion for that matter. Most of them described an ethos of subjugation for women in their primary texts.

The event that stood out in her mind as the moment she became aware of her active hatred for religion was in junior high school. She was walking to algebra class, and she began to feel something making her underwear wet. It was her first period.

She looked up and down the halls for a female teacher, but the only adult she could find was the male physical education teacher, Mr. Forman. She explained what was happening and asked Mr. Forman for help. Mr. Forman explained to her that all women menstruate, and that this was their punishment for Eve eating the fruit from the tree of knowledge in the Garden of Eden. He further explained that she'd have to deal with this punishment every month of her life, forever, then turned and walked away down the hall, offering her no assistance. Embarrassed and ashamed, Karen tied a sweater around her waist and sat through her next class hoping no one would notice. At lunch she was able to get to the nurse's office, where her mother was called and she was allowed to go home. She never told anyone about her encounter with Mr. Forman, and for a few years she assumed this was the way all men thought of women: as the reason humanity was cast out of paradise, as inconsiderate children who must be punished regularly, as the objects of men's disappointment.

As she gained reason with age, she grew to understand that only the most devout Christians felt this way about women, and it was on this topic that she focused her academic mind. She was curious to find out why Christian men had such an innate disdain for women, beyond the simple explanation that it was written into the Bible, and she became anxious to end that mode of thinking if at all possible. She began to study every Christian and conservative sect and mode of thought she could find, believing they were all simply new ways to hate women. Pro-life activism, the drive to defund Planned Parenthood, to protect the supposed sanctity of heterosexual marriage, to enact stricter voter identification requirements, and several other movements were all simply ways for men to maintain control over women, in Karen's mind.

As she sat at her computer, considering ways she could use her pregnancy to draw attention to the double standard that existed in Christianity, she began to think that what she was doing was much bigger than just a dissertation. For the first time in her life, she began to feel that she could do something that changed the way people thought, something that could have impact beyond the insulated world of academia.

Her initial idea, as she'd told Tanya, was to have the child and publicly give it to a gay couple who was seeking to adopt. This would very clearly outrage the religious right, and she was more than happy to be the cause of that outrage, but she realized that the idea wouldn't uncover any new hypocrisy in the church. It was already widely known that Christians viewed homosexuality as an abomination, and although they sought to protect every unborn child, they condemned those same children if they grew into anything other than heterosexual Christians. Her first plan would shed no new light on this subject.

She searched the Internet for statistics about percentages of gay and straight couples who were actively trying to adopt a child as compared to percentages of couples who were granted the ability to adopt on a per capita basis. There was clearly a double standard, but again this felt like old news. Karen understood that one more log on that fire wouldn't make it burn bright enough to draw much new attention.

Searching for other statistics, she found that of the 314 million citizens of the United States, 51 percent described themselves as pro-life. The number was shocking to Karen, who assumed it would have been much lower, but it began to give her an idea. If there were 157 million Americans who would honestly claim that saving a child's life was a moral imperative for them, then there had to be some way she could force them to prove this claim or be revealed as hypocrites.

After teaching a class later that afternoon, an idea came to Karen as she was driving home. It might be the best idea she would ever have, the idea she would be known for academically for the rest of her life. If executed properly, she knew, it would garner attention far beyond her supervisor and the PhD board. It could make national news, maybe even global. After thinking through some possible outcomes of her plan, she realized that some of them frightened her. The outcome that frightened her most was the one she most hoped for. For that reason, she knew she had to carry it out—and that she would have to remain anonymous in her efforts.

So, without consulting Paul, the father of her unborn child, Karen turned her car around and drove back to campus. She entered one of the public computer labs there so that what she was about to do couldn't be traced back to her personal computer. She sat down and began to craft a rudimentary website. The website was a single page of text that read:

I am a twenty-six-year-old female. The direction in which this country is headed, in terms of its treatment of women, is deplorable, and I feel is due in large part to the influence of the religious right in the guise of the pro-life movement. In an effort to expose the hypocrisy in that movement, I would like to extend the following public challenge to the 157 million Americans who identify as supporters of the pro-life ideology.

I'm currently eight weeks pregnant. I live in a state that allows me up until the end of the second trimester of my pregnancy to decide whether or not I want to have this baby. At the bottom of this page you'll see a link for donations. If the donations reach 100 million dollars by the end of my second trimester, then I'll have the baby, give it up for adoption, and every cent of that 100 million dollars will be put in a trust fund to be released to the child when he or she turns twenty-one. I'll keep none of the money for myself, so if I am to be vilified in this process, it can't be for that. If the 100 million dollar goal is not met by the end of my second trimester, any and all donations that were received will be refunded, and I will have an abortion. Mathematically this means that every pro-life American only needs to donate about 64 cents to save this child's life.

What I aim to prove in doing this is that the conservative movement in America doesn't actually care about the life of a child. They care about controlling the lives and decisions of women.

As Karen typed the last period, she looked over her shoulder to see if anyone near her might have been paying attention to what she was typing. She realized her paranoia was unwarranted, but the possible ramifications of what she was doing seemed so enormous to her that she could already feel their weight. She read over what she had written, and without publishing the page live onto the Internet, she saved it to a USB storage device, which she unplugged and dropped in her purse. Then she purged the computer workstation of any evidence of her project and left the computer lab. As she walked back across campus to her car, all she could think about was the storage device in her purse. She felt almost as though she were smuggling drugs across a border or carrying a loaded weapon in public. She told herself that she'd think about this for a few days before making it live. Once she put this out in the world, she knew, there was no taking it back, and once again she was scared.

James entered one of the meeting rooms of Woodstone Church a few minutes before seven on a Thursday night. At the end of the prior Sunday's service, Pastor Preston mentioned to the entire congregation that he would be holding the inaugural meeting of a new proactive outreach group he had decided to name the Anointed. He explained that his goal for this outreach group was to be as involved in the community as possible, and to help spread the word of Christ to nonbelievers through action. He extended an open invitation to anyone who wanted to know more.

James took a seat along with a few other people, only one of whom he recognized from church, in a small grouping of chairs directly in front of Pastor Preston. Pastor Preston looked at his watch and said, "Okay, folks, thanks for coming out tonight. It does my heart good to see that there's real interest in helping spread the word. So many Christians think they can come to church on Sunday and that'll make them right with God, but real Christians know you have to praise his name every day, all day. And let's not forget that all of you are here tonight because it's part of God's plan. He wants you here just as much as you want to be here, or you wouldn't be here at all. Keep that in mind as we proceed tonight. So again, thanks for coming tonight. Now, before I get into the nitty-gritty of what this is all about, I thought we could go around and say a little about ourselves. Just because we all worship at the same church doesn't necessarily mean we know each other. To get the ball rolling, I'll start. I'm Pastor Gary Preston. I first heard my calling when I was just a little boy, and now I'm fulfilling it here at Woodstone. God has blessed me with four lovely children, twelve, eight, four, and seven months, and a beautiful wife. And all of them have their own deeply personal relationships with Jesus Christ. When I'm not here at the church, I like to golf and watch KU football. Go Jayhawks. Other than that, I'm just humbled every day by the beauty that my Lord and Savior, Jesus Christ, bestows upon me."

With that, Pastor Preston nodded to the man seated to his left, indicating that he should speak next. The man said, "Hello, everyone. I'm Phil Hagerman. I've been coming to Woodstone for about a year now, I guess. Me and my family—wife and six-year-old daughter—moved here for my job, and a few of our neighbors recommended this place. So far we like it a lot, and I just thought I'd get more involved, seeing as how we're trying to be better Christians and set a good example for our daughter now that she's getting a little older and dealing with other kids at school, who are, you know, not really Christian. It's just kind of scary, you know? There's a kid in one of her classes who's Hindu or something. I just want to make sure I'm doing everything I can to keep her safe."

The world was a scary place, filled with countless potential evil influences and life-threatening situations. The only way to avoid these things was to accept Jesus Christ as your personal savior and pray to him for protection and guidance. The price of gas, putting food on the table for your family, and when your wife would next allow you to have sex with her were the only things worth worrying about. Although contraception was a sin, the consideration of being able to properly financially support the endeavor of bringing a child into the world warranted using it. No one should have more children than they were financially capable of caring for. People who did were one of the chief reasons America was in such turmoil. He hoped God would help America, but he knew better than to question his motives for initiating the current state of affairs. These were things that Phil understood to be true.

Pastor Preston said, "Very good, Phil. Glad to have you out tonight." He nodded to the man sitting next to Paul. "What about you?"

The man said, "My name's Brad Fine. I have two children, both grown and out of the house. Uh, this next part is still kind of fresh and hard to talk about, but I feel I'm among friends here, so . . . I'm newly divorced, and I've recently come back to the church after a long time away. I kind of figured out that the reason my marriage was having so much trouble was that I was having so much trouble spiritually. I wish it didn't have to end the way it did, but I understand God has a plan, and I don't question it. If it took the end of one relationship to repair my relationship with God, then I'm thankful. Now I'm just looking to throw myself into Christ, and do everything I can to show him that I'll never turn my back on him again."

Although there was no positive, concrete evidence of his existence, God was very real. It was this absence of evidence that made faith such a difficult thing to adhere to, but it's also what made it so powerful and personal. Even though God never intervened in human affairs, he was constantly watching and judging, so that everything a person did, no matter how small, was noted and cataloged for the final day of judgment, when all souls would be granted access to heaven or condemned to spend eternity in hell. Science had its place, but only as a supplement to faith, only where technology could enhance our understanding of the spiritual world. Sexual intercourse was a gift that was given to us by God Himself to be shared between a loving man and wife. The perversion of this act, when engaged in without love, without commitment, or between two people of the same gender, led to spiritual ruin. Children were God's way of letting a small piece of our spirits live on after we are called back to heaven. These were things that Brad understood to be true.

Pastor Preston said, "Brad, it means a great deal that you're willing to be so open with us here and now—and not just to me, but to Christ." Pastor Preston got up from his chair and patted Brad on the shoulder, then said, "And how about you?" nodding to James.

James explained that he was single, with no children, and that he was still waiting for God to deliver into his life the soul mate he knew was out there somewhere, waiting for God to bring James into her life. He said that he wasn't in a hurry, because he knew God had a plan, and part of that was understanding patience. He went on to say that he had never heard the sound of God's voice, that God had never spoken to him, but he knew that meant he just needed to listen harder, and that's why he was there. He felt that every act he could do in God's name would bring him one step closer to hearing his voice.

Pastor Preston said, "Well, James, that certainly is a very thoughtful and, um, personal introduction. Thank you. Let's keep going."

The woman next to James said, "Hi, everybody. I'm Brenda Tammer. I've been spiritual all my life, and I've always felt like I had a really great relationship with Christ, but my family is a different story. My husband and my kids, I mean, all they do is watch TV and play video games. I just really want them to have what I have with Christ, you know? I mean, it's the greatest feeling in the world to be that loved and to know that he's there with you in everything. I just want them to have that. So when I saw the flyer for this group in the hallway last Sunday, I kind of felt like maybe instead of trying to force a stronger relationship with Christ on my family, I should strengthen my own and show them what they're missing."

Jesus Christ was the best man who had ever lived. He was perfect in every way, and unyielding faith in him was the only way to heaven. But while on Earth, a relationship with him was the most fruitful and fulfilling relationship a person could have, and it would strengthen all other relationships in a person's life if they allowed it. Christ had the power to do anything, but he left it up to people to make their own choices and come to him of their own free will. Scientific endeavors and matters of academia were things that the average person had no business thinking about. Sex was something that could have dire consequences if the participants weren't right with God before they engaged in the act. Ideally, sex should only happen within the context of marriage, but sex outside marriage was acceptable as long as the people involved intended to marry at some point in the near future. Having a child was a blessing from Christ himself. Children were magical and to be protected at all costs. The best way to protect them was to introduce them to Jesus Christ. These were things that Brenda understood to be true.

Pastor Preston said, "I think it's great that you're taking it upon yourself to help your family get closer to God. Really great. Thanks for coming tonight. And how about yourself?" Pastor Preston indicated the next person in the group, an older woman.

She said, "I'm Gail Lafleur. Honestly, I haven't been involved with this church or any other church for a while. I, um, got some bad news earlier this year, that my dad was diagnosed with cancer, and I've been taking care of him for the past few months, and I've started to feel much more in touch with spiritual things. I've been coming to Woodstone a few days a week to services, and that's been helping me a lot. So I thought I'd see if coming to something like this could help me even more. That's about it."

Life was so complex, and filled with so many conflicting emotions and thoughts, that there certainly had to be some kind of God who created it all. And each human soul was too precious to end in death. There had to be something more—a heaven, a hell, maybe reincarnation, just something more. Everyone deserved to see the people they loved in life again after death. While medical science had certainly advanced enough to prolong lives, it never really saved anyone. All people died, and science would never be able to stop that from happening, so before you died it was a very good idea to let God know that you put your faith in him. Sex was something that could be engaged in for a wide variety of reasons, and in a wide variety of circumstances, none of which would prohibit you from going to heaven. As long as you were a good person, you would get in. These were things that Gail understood to be true.

Pastor Preston said, "As we begin to see our loved ones near their time to journey back into God's glorious kingdom, sometimes it reminds us that we need to be a little more aware of God ourselves. I'm happy to have you here tonight." Pastor Preston nodded to a man sitting next to Gail and said, "And I know this next great guy here, but no one else does, so tell us about yourself, please."

The man seated next to Gail said, "I do indeed know the good Pastor here, because I'm a pastor myself over at Forrest View—Pastor Jacobs. You can call me Ron. I've been a pastor there for almost seven years. I have a wife and two sons, who I love like Christ loves me—unconditionally, unless they get out of line, and then I show them wrath just like God does me. Just kidding. Just a joke. Anyway, I know that Jesus wants me to be the best pastor I can be, and I really think that means being as involved as I can be in as many Christlike things as I can be. So I try to stay active in as many different church groups as I can, especially groups outside my own church. I think you can lose sight of being a good Christian if you get locked into your own little spot, and you forget that there are other Christians outside your church who might do things a little differently. Anyway, I just want to help as much as I can, and when Pastor Preston told me he was starting up this group, I told him he could count on me to be here. So here I am."

Every person on the planet who has ever lived or would ever live had a calling from Jesus Christ and his father, God Almighty. Following that calling to the best of your ability would lead to eternity in paradise. Ignoring that calling to engage in personal pursuits was a sin punishable by eternal damnation. Science that was more complex than things like phones, televisions, cars, and other functional technologies that aided in daily life was clearly indulged in by people who were ignoring their callings. The primary function of sex was obviously reproduction, and it was something that only a man and wife should engage in, but once the man had his wife, he alone dictated everything that happened in the sexual relationship. No matter how depraved an act might seem, his wife had no choice but to obey her husband and grant him every demand, as long as it involved no other partners or outright denunciations of Christ. These were things that Pastor Jacobs understood to be true.

Pastor Preston patted Pastor Jacobs on the back and said, "It's great to have you here, Ron. Thanks for coming. And, last but not least, who do we have here?" Pastor Preston looked at a young woman sitting in the final chair.

She said, "I'm Catherine Hobart. My friends call me Cathy. I'm twenty. I currently attend Allen Community College, where I'm the president of our local Intervarsity group. As president, I've taken it upon myself to be as involved as I can be with my church and really lead by example for the other Christian students in my Intervarsity group. Tonight I thought I'd see what this is all about, and if you don't mind, maybe I could bring some other students to the next meeting?"

God granted all children the unmatched gift of being clean from sin at birth. It was up to those children, as they grew up, to keep themselves clean. And if a child could avoid sinning until death, or at least avoid committing too many sins and sincerely repent before death, then he or she would go to heaven. There were certain unforgivable sins, including murder, rape, and sex before marriage, that no amount of repenting would erase. Children were sacred. Having a child and introducing that child to Jesus Christ was the most important thing a woman could do in her life. It was what God made women to do. Science and the contemplation of things like the origin of the universe were wastes of time and human resources. The world would be much better off without science. These were things that Catherine understood to be true.

Once everyone was introduced, Pastor Preston said, "It's good to see we've got hope for the next generation through Christ. All right, everyone, thank you from the bottom of my soul for coming here tonight. I'm sure you're all wondering what exactly this group is all about. So where to start? I suppose we should start with the name. I'm calling this group the Anointed. Does anyone here know what that means?" No one made any indication that they did.

He said, "Fair enough. It's a kind of an obscure and old term. It basically means that you're consecrated, made holy, made sacred in the eyes of God, and that's what I want to do with all of you tonight." Pastor Preston went to a cupboard at the back of the room and removed a small vial of oil. He said, "In the olden times, Christian priests would pray over soldiers before battle and ask God to grant them strength to crush their enemies and drive Satan out of this world. They would also anoint the soldiers and their weapons to make them invincible. And to do this, they'd invoke the spirit of Christ into oil, and then they'd rub the oil on the soldiers and their swords and their shields and their armor. It would bond them together in the name of Christ, and it would make them impervious to any enemy attacks. Tonight I'd like to anoint every one of us, which is going to be very beneficial for the things I have planned for this group."

James looked around at the other people gathered there that night. Some were clearly uncomfortable with this idea. Brad specifically looked like he was thinking about objecting, but after looking around himself and finding no real perceived support for his objection, he remained silent along with everyone else.

Pastor Preston went to each member of the group, dipped his fingers in the oil, and made the sign of the cross on each person's forehead. James closed his eyes as he received his anointing, and tried to listen for God's voice as he felt the oil drip down his forehead onto his nose. He heard nothing, but it seemed as though he felt something deep within him stir and move in a way he had never felt before. He hoped this was the Holy Spirit moving within him and reasoned that it couldn't be anything else.

Once all were anointed, Pastor Preston moved back to the front of the group and said, "Dear Lord, I ask that you watch over these anointed few and guide them safely through their trials so that no harm may come to them while they are in your service. I ask that you use them as you use me, to do your bidding, and allow us to vanquish the dark forces that Satan would use against us and against your glorious kingdom. Amen."

They all repeated "Amen" and Pastor Preston continued, "Okay, I know what you're thinking: 'I got some oil on my head. Now what?'" They all laughed, some clearly happy to have a lightening of mood and a moment to acknowledge collectively, passively, that this was a little out of the ordinary compared to any other kind of church group they had ever joined. He said, "The reason I wanted to anoint you guys tonight—sorry, guys *and* gals—is that I feel we are truly at war with dark-side forces that are threatening our way of life. The dark one has been and always will be trying to destroy this world and all human souls that reside on it, but I feel we are living very near to the end times, which is when he is at his greatest power, and it's up to us to stay strong and fight with all our might against everything he set in motion. So why did I anoint you tonight? Because you are now soldiers of Christ Jesus, and you are in a war."

James looked around and saw that Brad and some others were getting a little uncomfortable again, but he wasn't at all. This made sense to him in a way that nothing he'd ever thought or felt about Christ had. He began to think that perhaps the reason he'd never heard God's voice before was that he'd been doing the wrong thing. He'd been living a life so far from God's plan, so far from his calling, that God didn't even know how to talk to him. He was a soldier, a warrior for God, not a floor sweeper. Maybe he had been too humble in his life, while God had planned for him to be brazen, to stand in the face of evil and fight against it in Christ's name. Thinking of himself in this way, James began to feel a new sense of purpose, and he knew that, just as Pastor Preston had said, his presence in that meeting was part of God's plan.

Pastor Preston said, "Come on, now, you're all soldiers! Getting anointed is a heck of a lot better than having to go through boot camp, isn't it? Can I get a hallelujah?"

A few of the attendees, James included, said, "Hallelujah."

Pastor Preston said, "That's it? God can't hear you all the way up in heaven. Shout it out. *Hallelujah!*"

This time everyone joined in. Pastor Preston said, "That's it. Hallelujah! Hallelujah! Soldiers of Christ, hallelujah!"

Soon everyone in the room was chanting "hallelujah" at a high volume. It gave James a new sense of power and pride. Pastor Preston said, "And now, my soldiers, it's time for our first mission, which is obviously completely voluntary, but I think it'll be fun for everyone. It'll be in a few weeks and we'll have doughnuts. It'll just be a good time.

"So here's what it is. As I'm sure you're all aware, one of Satan's most successful military campaigns in recent years has been his attack on the sanctity of marriage. Thank Almighty God that our glorious state hasn't fallen. But, as you know, our neighboring state can't say the same. Now, this doesn't mean that we can't take up the fight for our Christian brothers and sisters who live only a few hundred miles away. We have to be willing to go to where the fight is, instead of waiting for it to come to us, because by that time it might be too late. And on top of that, we're soldiers. Soldiers get deployed to wherever they're needed most. So we're deploying in two weeks, and then we're going to march."

Pastor Preston carried on, giving the details of the march, which he had planned to lead to the steps of a city hall in their neighboring state, where several gay marriages were to be officiated by the mayor. He urged every newly anointed soldier of Christ to act as a general for Christ as well and recruit as many people as they could to join them in this march, in this protest, in this fight to save marriage from the clutches of Satan himself.

Once the plan was outlined, Pastor Preston directed everyone to a sign-up sheet he had posted in the back of the room. James indicated that he would attend. He found this to be one of the most exciting moments of his life.

As he left the meeting, James overheard Brad and Gail discussing their uncertainty about what they had witnessed that night. They claimed to be Christian, but this was a little too much for them. James didn't engage with them. He couldn't understand how anyone could ever question anything done in Christ's name. Jesus had suffered and died for every sin man would ever commit, and all that was being asked in that moment was to drive a few hundred miles and stand in front of a building holding signs that championed the plan God had for us all. He knew in that moment that these people were hypocrites, and he dismissed them, knowing that God would deal with them in the end.

Before he went to sleep, James read the following, and he felt at peace: *Corinthians 11:13–15: For such men are false apostles, deceitful workmen, disguising themselves as apostles of Christ. And no wonder, for even Satan disguises himself as an angel of light. So it is no surprise if his servants, also, disguise themselves as servants of righteousness. Their end will correspond to their deeds.*

chapter
eleven

Karen woke up after sleeping through her alarm for fifteen minutes. In the past few weeks, her fatigue had become more chronic and more severe. As she sat up in bed, she was immediately nauseated. She could smell the grease from the eggs that Paul had obviously made for himself before leaving for work. As she stood up, she noticed that her underwear was wet.

Once in the bathroom she removed it and noticed a discharge coating the inside lining. She inspected it and found it was thicker than anything she'd ever seen, and without even bringing it to her nose she could smell that it was salty and metallic. Karen's disgust, mixed with the nausea she was already feeling, forced her to vomit in the toilet.

She drew a bath and stood naked in front of the mirror. Her breasts had definitely grown. Her stomach was now visibly betraying her secret pregnancy, and she could start to see a small line forming down the center of her stomach, from her belly button to her vagina.

In the bathtub, she felt her stomach and tried to imagine what exactly was happening inside it. She knew the facts. She knew there was a grouping of cells that had begun to specialize. She knew there were different organs and limbs and fingernails and hair and things that she considered to be human growing inside her. Despite her adamant stance that abortion was a perfectly viable means to end a pregnancy, she found herself wondering what this child would look like if it lived into adulthood. She allowed herself to think about it in detail.

Karen imagined that it was a boy. She imagined him having dark hair like her and Paul. She imagined him growing up to be of average height and build, wearing glasses. She thought he might have longish hair, curly, that would suggest a sense of happiness, a carefree attitude. And it was as this thought, about the psychological well-being of her unborn child, crept into her mind that she forced herself to stop thinking about it. She could let herself indulge in the idea of what this child might look like, but once she started imagining what type of adult he would become, she felt she was treading on dangerous ground. Instead, she ran some more hot water in the bathtub and convinced herself that her idea for the website was sound, that it was something the world needed, that it was quite possibly the most important thing she would ever do in her life.

She knew, however, that she wouldn't be able to keep the pregnancy secret for much longer. She knew she would have to tell the most important people in her life. She didn't know how her parents would react. She assumed they'd be confused, but that they'd help her if she needed them. Her parents were supportive of everything she did, and she saw no reason for that to stop based on the nature of the project she was undertaking. It was Paul who caused her the most concern.

She got out of the bathtub, toweled off, and went into the

kitchen for a glass of orange juice. As she drank it and thought about how best to tell Paul what exactly was going on, she noticed he left the creamer out on the counter. On an impulse, she poured some into her orange juice and found that it was delicious. She knew this was a side effect of the pregnancy.

Karen sat at the kitchen table, opened her laptop, and plugged in her USB device. As she sipped on her orange-juice-and-creamer mixture, she read over the web page she had made, trying to convince herself that she shouldn't make it live. She knew it would enrage people, but that's what she hoped for. In fact, the outcome she most desired was the kind of outrage that would lead to a public debate, that would force rational people to stop ignoring the religious right as inconsequential, that could shift the public toward a greater skepticism of religion.

She started thinking through how the conversation with Paul might go. She knew he never wanted to have a child, but thought that if she ever accidentally became pregnant and wanted to keep it, he would be supportive. But she knew this situation wasn't quite the same. To her knowledge, nothing like the situation she was about to create had ever existed. There was no blueprint, no tested strategy for how to break this exact news to this exact involved party. She resigned herself to this fact and tried to remain calm throughout the day as she ran some errands, ate lunch, and finally waited for Paul to come home from work.

When Paul came in, Karen was sitting on the couch with her laptop open and her website on the screen. She still hadn't made the site live and had planned to do so from a public computer, but as it appeared on Karen's screen, the site gave every impression that it was indeed live. Karen decided to show Paul the site and pretend for a moment that it wasn't her idea, that it was a real website made by some other girl. She said, "Hey, babe. You have to check this out."

Paul made his way to the couch, sat down next to Karen, kissed her on the cheek, and looked at her computer screen. He read the text that Karen had written and said, "Holy shit. That's pretty hard-core. Has this hit the news yet?"

"No, not yet. What do you think, though?"

"It's ballsy as fuck. I mean, fuck. It's really pretty nuts."

"Obviously, but on a philosophical level, do you agree with what she's doing? Do you find it cool at all?"

"Jesus. I thought I was going to walk in the door, grab a beer, and watch *Jeopardy!* I didn't realize I was going to be subjected to a philosophical debate as soon as I got home."

"Sorry. I just think it's really interesting, and I want to know what you think about it."

"It is really interesting—especially the part about not keeping any of the money and putting it in a trust fund for the kid, if she has it. That's the part that makes me think it's a real social experiment, not just some crazy person. I guess it's one of the smartest ways I've seen anyone use the Internet." He paused a moment. "Fuck. It's so good conceptually. Can you imagine having to go through that, though? She has to get shut down. I mean, is it even legal?"

Karen had not thought about this at all. She knew of no specific laws she would be breaking if she made the site live, but Paul's question gave her pause. She said, "Yeah. I mean, why wouldn't it be legal?"

"Shit, I don't know. Even if it's not, I'm sure as soon as this thing hits mainstream news outlets there'll be some kind of law passed or something—or, fuck, maybe whatever state she's in will ban abortion. You know how crazy those right-wing fuckers are."

"I'd love to see them try to ban abortion. I think that type of reaction is exactly what she's looking for, you know, something that forces the country to really dig in and say 'Abortion has been legal for a long fucking time, the argument is over, so shut the fuck up already.'"

"Well, if it's not a hoax, I think that's what might happen."

"It's not a hoax."

"How do you know?"

Karen lifted up her shirt to expose her belly.

Paul said, "Are you fucking shitting me right now, Karen?"

"No."

"What the fuck?"

"I know. It's a lot to take in."

"You're pregnant right now? Karen, you're having a baby? And this"—he pointed at her computer—"this is *you*?"

"Paul, please just stay calm and let's talk about this rationally."

"Talk about—wait, you're asking *me* to be rational? What about you? I mean, why are you waiting to tell me about this now?"

"I was just going to get an abortion, so I didn't tell you."

"Why wouldn't you fucking tell me you were going to get an abortion? I would have taken you and helped you. You know that."

"I know. I just . . . I didn't think it was worth worrying you about if I was just going to take care of it anyway."

"Holy shit, Karen. That's fucking crazy. But this is *way* more fucking crazy. So you obviously didn't get the abortion. Have you gotten any response about it? Do people know it's you, yet? Jesus fucking Christ."

"It's not live yet."

"Oh fuck. Okay. Fuck. I thought it was out there in the world already." He took a deep breath. "When did you come up with this?"

"I was on the way to Planned Parenthood, and it just kind of came to me. I thought I could do this for my dissertation."

"Your dissertation? Karen, you're fucking around with a life here."

"No, I'm not. It's not a life. It's just a thing in my uterus. It's not a life until it comes out."

"Don't fuck around with semantics—not with me. You know what I mean. I mean, *fuck*, Karen. And beyond whatever designation you want to give to the fetus you're now carrying inside you, you're fucking with your life and my life and—wait, is that timeline on the site accurate?"

"Yeah, give or take a week, I think."

"So you're two months pregnant and you never told me? I mean, I'm a fucking dad. Holy shit. What the fuck? I can't stop saying *What the fuck?* because I don't even know what else to fucking say. This is insane. I don't even know how to process any of this right now."

"I know it seems crazy, but I'm telling you now, before I make the site live, because I want you to know what I'm doing and I want you to be here with me through it."

"So this isn't a discussion, then? This isn't us figuring out together if you should do this or not? This is just you telling me that you're ransoming our unborn child on the Internet to prove some point about how fucked-up Christians are?"

"I wouldn't have put it quite like that, but, basically, yeah."

"Holy fucking shit. What am I supposed to do here? I mean, what reaction were you hoping for?"

"I hoped you'd think it was a really great idea and be supportive."

"Karen, it's a fantastic idea. It's a fucking once-in-a-generation cultural-rallying-point type of idea. A moment-that-changed-everything kind of idea. But you're making the idea real. There are so many other factors that come into play when it's more than an idea. Have you really thought this through?"

"I think so."

"The shit I was talking about earlier is the tip of the iceberg. I mean, abortion being outlawed is just one possibility. You could go to fucking prison."

"For what? I'm not doing anything illegal."

"They'll find something, Karen. They'll make a new law. Abortion really pisses people off, in a way almost nothing else does, and that can make people do all kinds of shit."

"But isn't that why it has to be done?"

"To piss people off?"

"To make people understand how absurd the pissed-off people are."

"I think you're going to piss off more than just the Christian wackos."

"So are you saying you don't think I should do this?"

Paul put his hand on hers and said, "You know I'd never ever tell you what to do. You've always been someone who thinks in ways that most people never understand. It's one of my favorite things about you. So if you feel like you have to do this, then you have to do this. It's your decision, obviously."

"Yeah, I know, but I'm not asking for your obligatory feminist support here. I want to know what you think."

"Well, beyond the potential fallout if you get discovered, what about the fact that if you get the money and have the baby . . . we'd have a kid out there in the world? What if I wanted to keep the baby and raise him or her?"

"Would you want to?"

"I don't know. Probably not. I mean, we've talked about how we never wanted kids, ever. I'm still of that mind. But this puts things in a different perspective for sure. They always say the moment you see your baby being born changes how you feel about all of that shit. What if you have the kid, and it changes the way you feel about it?"

"I don't think it will. I've thought about it a lot, and I'm committed to the idea. If I got the money I'd have to give it up for adoption, or it would go against the premise I'm setting up for my dissertation."

"And you don't think people are going to find that attitude a little cold? A little heartless?"

"Fuck what other people are going to think. I want to know what you think."

"Honestly, I think it's a really fucking brilliant idea, if I'm being objective here. But I can't really be objective. I mean, I just can't be. I wish someone else in the world was doing this, but not you, not us."

"But no one else *is* doing it."

"Couldn't you just write about the idea in your dissertation and come up with some theories about how the world might react or something?"

"I could, but that would be a pile-of-shit dissertation. It might get me my PhD, but it wouldn't get out in the world. It wouldn't change the way anyone thought."

They sat in silence for a minute or so. Paul's mind was racing. He had thought many times about what would happen if Karen accidentally got pregnant. He had prepared himself to drive her to a doctor or to Planned Parenthood. He had prepared himself to pay for an abortion. He had prepared himself to bring Karen home and care for her as she recovered physically and psychologically. He knew that would be a terrible ordeal to endure as a couple, but he thought he would be able to handle it if it happened. This, however, was something far more traumatic. Even the best-case scenario—which, in his mind, would be that the monetary goal was met, and then Karen would have the baby and give it up for adoption—was terrible. There was, in Paul's mind, no good outcome where he and Karen were concerned.

She said, "When you saw the site before you knew it was me, you thought it was as good as I did when I first came up with the idea. This could be the most important thing I do in my life. I want you to be in it with me. One of the reasons I love you as much as I do is that for as long as we've known each other, we've seen the world pretty much the same. And it might not seem like that's so rare, but it is. Every person has access to the same information about the world and the universe and reality, and almost none of them come to the same conclusions about the nature of any of it. But we always have. If anyone can get what I'm doing, I know it's you."

"Yeah, I definitely get what you're doing. I just don't know if I can handle doing it with you."

Karen wasn't expecting this answer from Paul. She assumed it would take him some time to analyze what was happening, but once he did, Karen felt sure that he would agree with her and be enthusiastic about helping her see it through. She said, "What does that mean?"

"I don't know, Karen. This is a big fucking deal. This isn't like you asking me to go pick out a couch for the apartment or something. You're going to be vilified if people find out who you are. People are going to think you're the next coming of fucking Hitler."

"But you won't think that, will you?"

"No. Obviously not. I love you and I love you because you think of shit like this. But I'm sitting here right now thinking about all the bad that might come from this, and I'm not real sure I want to be your Eva Braun."

"Come on. It's not remotely that bad."

"You're putting a price on a human life. No one, no matter what their politics or religion or philosophical leanings, likes that, including me."

Paul walked to the door, grabbed his jacket, and said, "I have to clear my head for a while. I think I'm going to go down the street and get a beer or something. I just need to think."

"Okay."

Paul said, "I'll be back in a while," then left.

Karen sat on the couch staring at her computer. She hoped he could come to some understanding of what she was attempting, but she knew that if she really was to move forward with this, she would have to accept that some things in her life would be irreparably altered, not the least of which would be her relationships with those closest to her.

chapter twelve

James woke up at 6:00 A.M. No one was meeting at Woodstone until 9:00 A.M., but he was too excited to sleep. The thought of doing what he considered to be the first real work in God's service of his life was almost too much for him to bear.

He got out of bed and went through his normal morning routine. As he was combing his hair, he looked at himself in the bathroom mirror, running his fingers over the spot on his forehead where he had been anointed. He felt different that morning. He felt like he had purpose beyond anything he had known. Even though he knew God was always watching him, he could really feel his presence there in the bathroom, shielding him like armor.

On his way to Woodstone, James went to the grocery store and bought several kinds of potato chips, sodas, some premade sandwiches, and some napkins. He knew that simply going on this mission for Christ was all that had been asked of him, but he wanted to do more than what was asked. He wanted to show God that he was ready to hear his voice, to receive a command directly from him, and, most important, to obey it without hesitation.

He arrived at Woodstone a few hours early and sat in his car reading the Bible until Pastor Preston pulled up, fifteen minutes before the rest of the group was scheduled to show up. James got out of his car with the sacks of groceries he brought and greeted Pastor Preston, who was excited by James's enthusiasm for the task at hand. Pastor Preston took a box of doughnuts from his car, unlocked to doors to the rec room at Woodstone, and held the door open for James as the two men walked inside.

Once inside, Pastor Preston looked over the sign-up sheet to see that a few more people had committed to their mission over the days that followed their initial meeting. He said, "Well, it looks like we'll have three or four people joining us. It might not seem like a lot, but when you've got Jesus Christ on your side, every soldier is an army. Sorry, what was your name again?"

James told Pastor Preston his name and took no offense at the question. He understood the Pastor to be a busy man who was constantly under the order of God. A name slipping his mind from time to time was to be expected. The two men engaged in a brief conversation about what James did for a living, where he lived, and for how long each of those things had been the case, and then Cathy Hobart arrived. She poked her head in the door to the rec room and said, "I smell doughnuts."

As she entered the room, Pastor Preston shifted his attention to her and said, "Cathy. Great to have you out this morning. How's school going?"

She said, "Fine, thanks. We're about to start finals, so I'm a little bogged down with studying, but I'm never too bogged down to serve Christ."

Pastor Preston said, "That's the spirit. Pun intended," and

they both laughed. James forced a chuckle, although he found nothing humorous about it. It just seemed like the correct response in the given situation. Cathy got a doughnut as two more people arrived. Pastor Jacobs and Brenda Tammer entered the rec room, and Pastor Preston said, "Well, I think we're all here. So everyone get a doughnut, or—sorry, James, right?"

James nodded.

Pastor Preston continued, "James here was generous enough to bring some other snacks and sodas and things. You guys have some breakfast. I'm going to go get the keys to one of our vans, and I think we should be on the road within fifteen minutes or so."

Pastor Jacobs said, "I've got the signs in my Range Rover. My wife and my little girls were working on them all week. I couldn't be more proud."

Pastor Preston said, "Now, that's what it means to be a Christian family right there."

Pastor Jacobs said, "Amen to that, brother. Amen to that. Should I get the signs now or wait until you pull the van around?"

Pastor Preston said, "Oh, right. Uh, I can just pull the van around and we can load them in," then left the rec room to get the keys to the van that would carry the Anointed on their first mission for Christ.

In the van, James sat next to Cathy in the seat the closest to the back. He could see the top sign in the stack of signs behind him. It read, "God's law will never legalize gay marriage." He wondered what phrases were on the other signs, but not enough to reach over the backseat and look through them. He'd see them all soon enough.

He knew he had more than three hours to pass, so he brought along a Bible, which he read from for the first few minutes until Cathy asked him, "So have you ever done anything like this?"

James told her that he hadn't. He told her that he was aware that several states had begun to legalize marriage between two homosexuals, and although he didn't support this trend, he hadn't yet done anything to voice his concern in public. Cathy said, "I haven't, either. I've wanted to for a while now, but my parents always thought I was too young. This is my first ever protest for Christ. You mind if I Instagram us?"

James told her that he didn't mind at all, so Cathy took a picture of them together in the back of the bus, and as she was posting it to her Instagram account with the hashtags #anointed, #soldiersforchrist and #protectingmarriage, she asked, "Do you want me to tag you in it?" James explained to her that he didn't have an Instagram account. He didn't see the point.

Cathy said, "The point is so that your friends can see what you're doing. It's especially good for things like this, because they can see that you're setting a good example as a Christian. I could help you make an account right now if you want." James explained that he didn't have too many friends who would care about what he was doing. He cared, and that was enough for him.

Cathy said, "Okay, cool with me," and then she posted the picture.

James spent the rest of the trip listening to the various conversations the other people had, answering questions about himself when he was asked, and singing a few devotional songs that Pastor Preston had brought along on his iPhone. They were in the middle of one of these songs when Pastor Preston pulled into the parking lot across the street from the city hall, where some protestors had already gathered on the steps. He said, "All right, soldiers, this is it. Game faces on. Grab a sign from the back, and let's soldier up for God."

With that, everyone got out of the van and made their way to the back, where Pastor Jacobs handed out signs. James's sign read, "A marriage certificate won't save you from hell." Pastor

Preston held a sign with a simple design of a red X over the word *Faggot*. James thought vulgarity and crassness were always unnecessary, and in this specific case obscured the real message they were trying to convey in their protest. It was easy, he thought, for the public to get the wrong impression of what they were doing. He wanted to raise the public awareness of just how far Satan's influence was spreading—in this case, all the way to the heartland. Nonetheless, James followed Pastor Preston with the rest of the Anointed as they carried their signs to the steps of the city hall, where the mayor was presiding over the wedding of two women.

James and his group found a spot behind some barricades, beyond which protestors were not allowed. Pastor Preston said, "Okay, guys, we're not trying to get arrested or anything, so we can't go past this point, but we can scream as loud as we want to. Let Jesus hear us up in heaven. Keep marriage between a man and a woman! Keep marriage between a man and a woman!" James, Cathy, the rest of the group from Woodstone, and a few others joined in. One man who showed up a few minutes later had a megaphone to lend to the cause.

As they chanted, James watched the two women on the steps of city hall. As the mayor pronounced them legally married, they cried and embraced one another. They were genuinely happy. James knew that Satan's influence was chiefly to blame, but he couldn't help thinking how strange it was that all people had access to the same basic understanding of Christianity, or at least to the knowledge that Jesus Christ died for our sins, and yet some chose to exist outside of his rules. Some chose to live lives that were an affront to his love, knowing that they were damning themselves in the process. He just couldn't understand how anyone would make such a choice, but he resigned himself to the idea that it wasn't for him to understand.

As they continued to protest and wave their signs in the air, the man with the megaphone started to get louder and louder.

The next couple to be married, two men, looked in the direction of the megaphone before their ceremony began. The man with the megaphone said through the device, "I hope you enjoy your honeymoon in hell, faggot!"

God made different races for a reason, and dating or marrying outside your race was a sin. So too was any romantic relationship beyond a single man and a single woman. Once married, a woman was to obey every command given to her by her husband, just as was outlined in the Bible. If a woman expressed any interest beyond those deemed acceptable by her husband, she was considered a sinner and should repent. Science was necessary only for necessities in the modern world, like transportation and some very basic medicine, but beyond that, God would provide anything a person might need to survive. It was a man's duty to have as many children as possible and raise them with the same beliefs he held sacred so that the right way to live wouldn't be forgotten. These were things that the man with the megaphone understood to be true.

Upon hearing the man with the megaphone shouting in their direction, one of the grooms-to-be stepped down from the city hall steps, despite his fiancé's objections, and walked over to the barricades where James and the rest of the protestors were standing. The man with the megaphone said, "What's the matter, you got a problem with free speech, faggot?"

The groom-to-be said, "Not at all. What I have a problem with is a redneck piece of shit screaming about the sanctity of marriage when he probably fucks his cousin and his sheep behind his wife's back."

God was love. That was all anyone really needed to know about God. All religions throughout human history had been wrong, because they were products of the societies that existed in the times of their creations and as such they were subject to the influences of social stigmas, political objectives, and financial pressures of those same times. God, the Creator, loved all his or her children equally because he or she created them. Science was another one of God's creations, which he or she loved just as much as the living creatures throughout the cosmos. Raising a child was a vital part of being human, and the ability to adopt a child was more proof that God loved his creations so much that he gave them ways to explore every aspect of being human, even if their innate biological desires would prohibit them from experiencing one of the most important aspects. These were things that the groom-to-be understood to be true.

The man with the megaphone became enraged and said, "This is America, not San Francisco, you cocksucking faggot!"

The groom-to-be said, "San Francisco is in America, you stupid piece of shit, and has it occurred to you that you probably have a gay cousin or brother? Or son?"

The man with the megaphone looked at one of the police officers standing near the barricade, who had a smile on his face, and said, "Are you going to let this faggot talk to me like that?" The police officer shrugged his shoulders and the man with the megaphone said, "Well, I'm not," then jumped over the barricade and swung his megaphone at the groom-to-be, who shoved him back into the protestors and punched him in the face. The police tried to move in, but some more of the protestors had already joined in the fight, punching and kicking the groom-to-be, as well as his fiancé and some of their supporters. It was quickly turning into a brawl.

James quickly and silently prayed to God for some sign to let him know what to do. He wasn't afraid of getting injured or even arrested. He knew that no wound he could incur would be sacrifice enough to match what Jesus did for him, and he knew that no law of man would ever be equal to the law of God. In that moment Pastor Preston said, "My Anointed, this is the battle we came here for. Show God that we are his soldiers." With that, Pastor Preston started swinging his sign around wildly, and James took this to be the sign he was looking for.

He jumped the barricade and tried to defend himself as he helped pull the man with the megaphone back toward the group of protestors. In the process, James was punched in the face and hit twice in the back with something hard, though he couldn't tell what it was. He fell to his knees from the blows to his back, and then stood to see where his attacker might be, but within seconds of standing back up, a rock sailed through the air and struck him in the temple, knocking him unconscious.

James woke up in the back of an ambulance. Pastor Preston and Pastor Jacobs were with him. Pastor Preston said, "You all right, son? You took a nasty shot to the dome back there, but you were a hero. You dove into the mass of those homosexual sympathizers, and you dragged one of our own, a fellow Christian, to safety."

Pastor Jacobs said, "It was as if God was moving you to action. I really think we might have seen a miracle here today."

James asked them if anyone was arrested, and Pastor Preston said, "Funny you should ask that, because there was one arrest. It was the homosexual who started the fight with the man you saved from probably being beaten to death. And it's already on the local news that a homosexual lost his temper and started a brawl on the steps of city hall. Honestly, it couldn't have gone any better for us. Here, look at this."

Pastor Preston held up his phone for James to see. He had Cathy's Instagram account open. Her most recent photo was of James dragging the man with the megaphone back from the brawl. Under the image were the hashtags #ChristianHero and #RealManOfGod.

James couldn't help smiling a little bit. As he lay there in the back of an ambulance on his way to the Des Moines County Hospital, he silently spoke to God. He told God that he had learned something about himself at the protest. He understood that sacrifices would be required of him, and he had learned that he was ready for more. He could handle a larger burden. All God had to do was ask him to shoulder it, and he would.

James asked Pastor Preston if he had a Bible with him. Pastor Preston said, "Of course I do, son. Would you like me to read something from it?"

James requested Peter 4:12. Pastor Preston opened the Bible and read: "Beloved, do not be surprised at the fiery trial when it comes upon you to test you, as though something strange were happening to you. But rejoice insofar as you share Christ's sufferings, that you may also rejoice and be glad when his glory is revealed."

James thanked Pastor Preston, and then the Pastor said, "No, son, thank you."

chapter thirteen

Karen still had no straight answer from Paul. Every night, when he came home from work, he would tell her that he was still thinking about it. She felt that this was a good sign, that he hadn't passed a negative judgment outright. Every day that he claimed to still be thinking about the situation, Karen thought, could be bringing him one day closer to accepting her decision and agreeing to go on the journey with her. With or without his support, she knew there were practical steps she needed to take in the service of her plan. As she got into the elevator at the Robertson Medical Plaza, she didn't know which of those steps she was more nervous about: her first ob-gyn visit or the conversation she had to have with her supervisor.

Karen had been going to the same ob-gyn since she was in her late teens. Her name was Niral Prasad. From time to time, on prior visits, she would think about how strange it was that this woman, who had started out as a stranger to her, had seen her vagina more times than some of the men she had dated. Despite this fact, Karen didn't feel like she really knew her ob-gyn on a personal level, and she didn't think divulging her plan to her was a good idea.

Karen waited in an examination room and looked through her texts. There was none from Paul. In the few days after she told him about her plan, he had become less communicative. She assumed he needed some space to figure things out for himself and decided not to bother him about it. She did have a text from Tanya that read, "Have you heard from Paul yet? Also, Mexican food tonight?" Karen replied, "No. Yes," and then her doctor walked into the room.

Dr. Prasad said, "So, I understand you're pregnant. Congratulations. This is a very exciting time."

There was one God. That God existed in everything: in the earth, in the air, in animals, and in people. It was up to every human being to honor that God by following a few very simple rules for living. Among them were being honest, treating other living beings with compassion and mercy, having patience in all situations, and being as generous as possible. Every living thing was imbued with a soul, and that soul kept recycling after the death of the vessel in which it was housed until it had achieved enlightenment through experience. Science and technology were wonderful human creations that helped people do everything from the mundane to the miraculous. Having a child was something to be honored and celebrated because it meant that another soul was beginning its next journey in its own unique evolution of spirit. These were things that Dr. Niral Prasad understood to be true.

Dr. Prasad said, "So how far along do you think you are?"

"I'm not exactly sure, but I think somewhere around fourteen weeks or so."

"Fourteen weeks? That's pretty late to be having your first visit to me."

"Well, I wasn't sure until about ten weeks in, I guess, and then I—" Karen was on the verge of telling Dr. Prasad that she'd thought she was going to have an abortion, but she caught herself. She continued, "I just wanted to make sure that I actually was pregnant, you know, and that I was going to stay that way."

Dr. Prasad said, "It's very common to feel that way. Many pregnancies do terminate in the first trimester, which is why it's recommended that you don't announce anything to family and friends until you pass the twelve- or thirteen-week mark, which it seems like you have. But all that said, you should definitely be coming in at least every four weeks from here on out. Okay?"

"Okay."

"Now, we need to do a few things here today, since it's your first pregnancy visit. I'm going to need some urine, some blood, and we're going to do a trans-vaginal sonogram. If you really are fourteen weeks, you're going to be able to actually see your baby. We won't be able to see the sex for another four weeks or so, but—"

"Uh, I actually kind of just want to make sure everything's okay health-wise with the baby and with me. I don't really want to see it."

"Oh. All right. That's a little . . . Would you mind me asking why?"

Karen knew that the real reason was because she needed to maintain an emotional distance from the situation, and that seeing the baby growing in her, seeing the child that was equal parts her and Paul, would make that more difficult than it needed to be. She said, "I'm just kind of superstitious about it, I guess."

"Oh, well, you know there's no reason to be, but obviously you don't have to see the baby if you don't want to. I can just take a look to make sure everything's as it should be. So which do you want to do first? Blood, urine, or sonogram?"

Karen gave blood, urinated in a cup, and then made her

way back to the examination room, where she disrobed, put on a medical gown, laid down on the examination table, and let Dr. Prasad place her feet into stirrups. Dr. Prasad had examined her vagina many times throughout her life, using various instruments and on some occasions, with nothing more than her fingers. The device Dr. Prasad produced for this examination was unlike anything Karen had seen before. It was long and phallic and had an appearance that struck her as far more sexual than clinical. Dr. Prasad put a condom on the device as well as some lubricant, making it even more sexual, and then inserted it into Karen's vagina. Karen could feel it pushing against the back wall of her vagina, which caused a slight amount of discomfort. Dr. Prasad said, "How are you doing?"

Karen said, "Fine," and turned her head away from the screen where Dr. Prasad was looking at the image created by the ultrasound wand.

Dr. Prasad said, "Do you want me to tell you what I'm seeing, or is that also something you don't want to know?"

Karen said, "Uh . . . I guess just tell me if anything's out of the ordinary—you know, if there's something I should worry about."

Dr. Prasad said, "Okay."

After almost a minute, Dr. Prasad removed the ultrasound wand and said, "Everything looks fine. You can get dressed and meet me in my office at the end of the hall to discuss your next steps," and then left the examination room.

Karen got up, put on her clothes, and looked at the screen that just a few seconds before had displayed an image of her unborn child. She tried to stop herself from thinking about what it looked like, but she couldn't help it. She wondered.

Back in her office, Dr. Prasad told Karen that everything was fine. The baby was perfectly healthy, and her initial estimate of fourteen weeks was pretty accurate. Dr. Prasad said, "We'll have your blood and urine work back in a few days, but I'm going to prescribe you some special prenatal vitamins anyway. Since you came in a little later than we like to see most moms, I think it's best to just get your iron up to where it should be as soon as we can. Have you noticed anything strange or painful that you think I should know about?"

"I'm getting cramps. I'm constantly tired. The morning sickness has started to wear off, but some things still make me a little sick to my stomach. My hair is falling out a little. I have a weird discharge in my underwear some mornings, and my back hurts almost constantly."

Dr. Prasad laughed, "I'm sorry to say, that's all one hundred percent normal and there's more to come. Eventually you'll have more of that discharge. Moles on your body might start getting bigger. That nausea will eventually turn into ravenous hunger. Actually, that should start happening very soon, so you have to be careful to eat healthy. Gestational diabetes is sometimes a concern if you eat too much sugar or fatty foods."

Karen said, "Okay, so pregnancy is even worse than I thought."

Dr. Prasad said, "I don't mean to make it sound like a nightmare, but the truth is, it's tough on your body. There are ways to make it more bearable, but it's going to be something of an ordeal. I like to be honest about that. But in the end it's always worth it."

Karen said, "We'll see."

Dr. Prasad said, "Obviously, if you have any questions, feel free to call or make an appointment anytime before your next scheduled appointment, which we should set for another four weeks from now."

On her way from Dr. Prasad's office back to UCLA, Karen reminded herself that it wasn't too late to get an abortion. It wasn't too late to end all this. She wouldn't have to go to any more obgyn appointments. Her body wouldn't have to undergo any more changes. Paul wouldn't be forced to make whatever decision he would ultimately make. Everything could go back to normal, to the way it was before she decided to do this. That was her last thought as she pulled into a parking spot in the same garage where she always parked at UCLA. As she walked across campus toward Professor Noone's office, she saw a booth set up near the student union with a sign that read, "Sign a Petition to Support Intelligent Design Being Taught in Public Schools," and she knew she had to go through with her plan.

Once she was in Professor Noone's office, he said, "So, I'm assuming you're not here to ask for another extension, Ms. Holloway."

She said, "No, no more extensions. I have an idea, and I think it's really, really good."

"And do you think *I'm* going to think it's really, really good?"

"I don't see how you can't."

"Well, that's about the most confident lead-in to a dissertation presentation I've ever heard. I'm all ears."

Karen opened her laptop, brought up the web page she had made, and turned the screen around so Professor Noone could read what she had written. She watched his face to see if she could gauge his reaction as he was reading it, but he gave no indication. Instead, he finished reading the page, closed Karen's laptop, and pushed it back across his desk toward her.

She said, "So . . . what do you think?"

"Karen, this is really a fantastic idea."

"You think so."

"It's phenomenal. All that time you took to think of this was worth it. At its core I think it presents an incredible philosophical quandary, and I think you can turn it into a fantastic dissertation. I've always personally been extremely interested in the problems with religious doctrine, when adhering to it means potentially ignoring or even defying certain principles of the same religion. So I gather you're using this hypothetical situation to speculate on what American society might do if something like this were real?"

"Well, I'm definitely writing about how America would react to this, but the situation isn't quite hypothetical."

"Are you serious?"

"Yeah."

"Do you know this girl?"

"It's me."

"You're pregnant? Right now?"

"Yeah."

"Oh my god. Karen, I don't know about this. Is that already on the Internet?"

"No. Not yet."

"I appreciate that you've waited until you talked to me about it."

"Well, it wasn't just you. I told my boyfriend about it, too. I understand that this will affect more than just me."

"It's none of my business, really, but is he the father?"

"Yeah."

"And what did he say about it?"

"He's still thinking about it. Look, Professor, I think this is important. This is what we were talking about—doing something that actually makes people think differently instead of just writing some ridiculous paper that no one reads."

Professor Noone took a deep breath and said, "Well, this certainly would be more than a ridiculous paper that no one reads. As I said, I think the idea is brilliant. I've spent most of my adult life in philosophy, teaching, studying, thinking, and I've never seen something like this come across my desk. It's very daring, it's interesting, it's thought-provoking—and I'm just as curious as you must be about the public reaction. But I just can't sign off on this in good faith."

"What? Why not?"

"You're proposing to hold the life of a child in the balance for the purpose of what is essentially an experiment. As a representative of the Philosophy Department, I obviously can't support it."

"Because you're afraid you'll lose your job?"

"My job has nothing to do with this, but that could certainly be at least one of the repercussions should you actually go through with this. I imagine you'd be expelled as well."

"You'd expel me for this?"

"I wouldn't, but the dean might. This could become the kind of issue that's too big for me to stay in front of. Even if you manage to conceal your identity through the entire event, which I personally think is unlikely, your dissertation will be read by everyone on the PhD panel—and then you'd be on your own. I couldn't do anything to protect you. And if you were expelled, you obviously wouldn't finish the PhD program, making the entire endeavor fruitless for you."

"Fruitless? If I do something that forces people to look at how hypocritical Christians are and it actually changes things, then how is that fruitless—even if I don't get my PhD from this school?"

"Karen, you can write about this as an abstract idea, and it would still have an impact here and, I think, in the academic community at large. The idea is so strong, I don't see why you actually need to do it."

"Because real people don't care about ideas."

Professor Noone sighed, and said, "Look, I obviously can't stop you from doing this, but I am going to strongly encourage you to write about it hypothetically and save yourself from, at the very least, potentially destroying your career in academic philosophy before it even begins. You're extremely bright, Karen. I'm trying to help you, because I think you could be sitting in my chair one day, or any other chair at any other school for that matter."

"Maybe I'm not sure I want to be sitting in a chair, Professor."

Karen left Professor Noone's office without a doubt in her mind that she had to go through with her plan. She had always despised the falseness of the academic world, but now when she was faced with the choice between yielding to it or cutting herself off from that world entirely, the choice became much clearer. She knew she was on the verge of something immense. She knew that Professor Noone was right: She could very easily write the theoretical version of this for her dissertation, get her PhD and slowly make her way through the academic world until she was a tenured professor at a college somewhere, maybe even a great college. But she also knew that eventually she'd be sitting across from a student who would have a proposal for a dissertation that was threatening in some way to the falseness of it all. And she knew she'd think back to the time when she had the chance to do something great, something groundbreaking, but she didn't. She knew she'd always wonder what her life would have become if she'd taken the chance. She didn't want to wonder. She wanted to know.

When Karen got home, Paul was there waiting. He said, "Hey."

Karen said, "Hey."

He said, "So I've thought about this. A lot. And I . . . I don't even know how to say this. Fuck. I love you, Karen, but I can't do this."

"What do you mean, you can't do this?"

"I mean, I can't be supportive of this whole thing. It's crazy. I can't do it."

"Okay, so what does that mean? You're just going to sit by in protest or something while I do it?"

"No. It means I'm moving out. I just can't be a part of this."

Karen could feel tears coming. She said, "Are you fucking serious?"

Paul, too, started crying, "Yes. I'm serious. This is a fucking huge thing, Karen. Jesus Christ. It's our baby, and you're treating it like it's just a . . . I don't even know, but like it's not our baby."

Karen said, "But it's *not* our baby. It's not a baby at all. I was going to get an abortion. You'd be okay with that, right?"

"Yeah, of course."

"Well, one of the two outcomes in this is still an abortion, and the other is adoption, so I just don't understand why you think you have to move out."

"Because this is fucking insane. How do you not see that?"

"I know it's kind of extreme, but it has to be to prove the point."

"Well, then, you're going to have to prove your point without me. I just don't want any part of this. It feels wrong, and if I feel like this now, how am I going to feel when you actually put that site on the Internet, when people start hating you, when you start getting more and more pregnant—when, at least for me, it is a baby? Karen, I'm sorry."

By this point, both Karen and Paul were sobbing. She had never believed that her desire to do something meaningful with her life would lead to the end of a relationship with the man she had grown to love more than anyone else. Paul, too, found the situation more than odd. One of the things he loved most about Karen was her intellect, and her unyielding rejection of modes of thought, such as religion, that she understood to be useless. But in this instance, for Paul, her intellect seemed to be treading on something sacred between them. Karen's idea had triggered a level of inconsideration that Paul had never witnessed from her, and he concluded that she cared about her idea more than she cared about him or about their life together. That was the realization that forced his decision to leave.

"So that's it? Five years together and you're just throwing it all out the window?"

"I could ask the same thing of you."

"I have to do this."

"I know, and I wouldn't ask you not to do it for me. And even if I did, I know it wouldn't matter. Your mind is made up, so I don't really have a choice. I'm sorry."

Paul hugged her one last time and kissed her on the cheek, then said, "I'm going to stay at Dave's tonight, and I'll come get my stuff in the next few days if that's okay."

Karen couldn't speak. She just nodded. Paul took a few steps toward the door and said, "I don't know what else to say. Good luck, I guess. I love you, Karen, and I hope that however this all ends up is exactly how you want it." Then he left.

Karen sat down on the couch, still crying. She took out her laptop and read over the site that was stored on her USB storage device. The pain she felt at Paul's departure began to turn to rage. She felt as if no one would understand what it was she was attempting to do, not Professor Noone and surprisingly not even Paul. Their refusal to be involved in her plan only fueled her motivation to go through with it. As she wiped the tears from her eyes, without going to an Internet café or back to one of the computer labs on campus, using only her own laptop in the quiet of the apartment she now lived in alone, Karen made the site live.

chapter fourteen

Although James was familiar with the Internet and knew how to navigate it, he primarily only used it to check his email, which was always work-related, or to browse a few Christian websites, ChristianMingle.com included. So as he walked into Woodstone for Sunday service he wasn't exactly sure what everyone was talking about, but he could tell that most of the conversations were about the same thing, and it seemed like something extremely upsetting.

As he walked down the hallway, Cathy Hobart stopped him and said, "Hey, how's the head doing?"

James explained that he had had a headache for a day or two, and the bruises where he was struck with the rock still hurt a little, but otherwise he was doing fine. She said, "That's good. I still can't believe how awesome you were. Seriously, so cool. So what do you think of that website?"

James told her that he didn't know which website she meant. Cathy said, "Are you serious? It's, like, the biggest news story in the country right now. Do you not read the news or anything?"

Before James could answer her, they both heard the tone indicating that the Sunday sermon was about to begin. Cathy said, "I guess we should get in there. I'm sure Pastor Preston will be talking about it. Maybe if you're around after, we can discuss. I'd love to know what you think."

James watched Cathy walk away and, for the first time since he'd met her, wondered if maybe God had put her in his life for a reason. He wondered if maybe she was his soul mate. She was younger than he would have imagined his soul mate to be, but he knew that age and time were meaningless in God's eyes. If Cathy Hobart was his soul mate, her age wouldn't matter. James decided that he would remain open to the possibility but not do anything that would force the issue. God would reveal his plan when he felt he should and not before. James vowed to be patient as he took his seat with the other members of Woodstone's congregation.

Pastor Preston took his place behind a podium at the center of the pulpit. He stood for a few moments and looked out into the crowd silently, as though he wasn't exactly sure how to begin this Sunday's sermon, as though something was weighing so heavily on him that he needed to conjure a deeper inner strength in order to address it with his fellow Christians.

Eventually he said, "Brothers and sisters, the events that have taken place in the past week are beyond terrible, beyond sinful. They are condemnable. They are damnable. They are all that is dark and evil in the kingdom of man. They are, without question, the work of Satan himself. And, my dear brothers and sisters, I'm afraid that they are evidence that the end times are upon us."

Pastor Preston took a pause to let his last words sink in. When the whispers multiplied and became audible to everyone in the room, he continued, "For those of you who may not know exactly what I'm talking about, this ultimate act of evil was committed late last week." He pointed a remote control at the multimedia screen behind him, and an image of a website appeared on the screen, the words too small to be read by anyone sitting more than a few rows back.

He said, "This girl, this anonymous girl, made this website here, and I know it's probably tough for some of you in the back to see what it says, so I'll explain it to you. This girl was granted the greatest blessing the good Lord Jesus Christ can bestow on a woman. She was blessed with a child. And what did she do when she found out the good news? Did she celebrate? Did she give thanks to God? Did she pray that her baby be healthy? No. No, she didn't, brothers and sisters. Instead she made this website. On this website she claims that Christians are hypocrites. She claims that we're not really interested in protecting the life of a human child. She claims that what we really want to do is control women. Now, you know and I know and the good Lord above knows that's simply not true. Sure, it was Eve who ate the apple, but, brothers and sisters, that was all part of God's plan. We accept that and we move on. Now, this girl goes on, on this website, to say that if Christians are really interested in protecting all unborn children, then we should have no problem donating one hundred million dollars to her. And, if we don't, she's going to have an abortion."

There were some audible gasps from the congregation. Pastor Preston continued, "Oh, yes. One hundred million dollars or she's going to murder this innocent child. She goes on to say that she's not going to keep any of the money, that she's going to put it all in a trust fund for the baby. Right. I'm sure we can all count on this girl being honorable and keeping her word on that. But she claims that if she does get the hundred million dollars, she'll have the baby and give it up for adoption, which is the only good thing that could come from this—that child being raised by someone else."

Pastor Preston had worked up a sweat, and he took a moment to wipe his forehead with a handkerchief. He continued: "Everything, brothers and sisters—everything—is brought into existence by our Almighty God for a purpose. And I have to believe that this girl and this website have been brought into this world for a purpose, and I don't think that purpose is for her to make a hundred million dollars. You know what I think the purpose of all of this is? In my heart of hearts, and to the core of my Christian bones, I truly believe this a test. It's a test of every Christian in this country and even on this earth. Oh yes, God is testing us. He wants to see if we've learned anything, if we've been paying attention. He wants to see if we're good Christians, steadfast and strong in our faith, or if we can be easily swayed by a trick of Satan. Make no mistake, my brothers and sisters, our reaction to this could be rewarded by God if we make the right choice. But if we don't, well, then, there will be a punishment to follow. There certainly will be. So what do we do? How do we assure the reward and avoid the punishment? This is a good question, and it's one I've been grappling with for the past week. Once you recognize a test from God, you have to figure out how you pass the test. And to figure that out, I think you have to look in your heart, and you have to do what's Christian, and if you do that, there's no way you can fail.

"That's right; if you do what's Christian, there's no way that you can fail."

James sat silently, taking all this in. This girl had created a scenario he found so detestable, so unbelievably evil, that he wouldn't have thought it possible. He agreed with Pastor Preston that it could only be the work of Satan himself, and it made sense to him that it must be a test. Why else would God have allowed it to occur? He found himself wondering, though, what was the correct response, what was the Christian thing to do? If all Christians met her financial demand, they would save a child. But if they refused to give her the money, they would be combating a terrible evil in the world. Each option seemed to have its merits.

Pastor Preston continued, "Now, this is obviously a complicated situation, and it's difficult to know what the Christian thing is to do. As of this morning, you can see right down here on the website, she has more than two million dollars already donated. I know it's hard to think about that helpless little life ending if we don't give her every penny she's demanding—but, brothers and sisters, that's what Satan wants us to think, wants us to feel. Satan is very, very good at finding your weakness and using it against you. But we have to be strong, for a few reasons here. Reason number one is very simple. What this girl is doing with this child is spiritual terrorism. That's right, I said it. She's a spiritual terrorist, holding that tiny soul hostage and making demands. Now, last time I checked, we're living in America. One nation under God, and that doesn't mean Zeus and that doesn't mean Allah. That means one nation under Jesus Christ. And I'm pretty sure America doesn't make deals with terrorists. I'm pretty sure America sends SEAL Team Six in and puts a bullet through the heads of terrorists. Just ask Osama bin Laden. Reason number two is a little more complex, but I've given it a lot of thought. So this girl is a spiritual terrorist. It's easy to understand that she's evil, but what about that baby? What about that innocent soul who got thrown into this situation without asking for it, without having any chance to live? Well, brothers and sisters, that baby is facing only two possible outcomes. If we don't give this spiritual terrorist the money she's demanding, then she will have that abortion—and, as terrible as it is, as much as my mouth sours with the taste of the word, we all know that that little baby will go straight to heaven, and God is a much better parent than anyone here on Earth could ever be. What better reward is there for that child than to send him or her straight to the loving arms of Jesus Christ?"

James thought about this. It made sense logically to him, but in some way it still seemed like it meant supporting an abortion, which made him uncomfortable. If something could be done to save the life of this child, shouldn't it be done at all costs? He remained unconvinced that this was the correct course of action for every Christian on the planet.

Pastor Preston continued, "So that's one thing that might be true for this baby. But there might be another thing that's true. It's possible, brothers and sisters, that Satan has done more than just conjure this evil situation to get us mad and to get us second-guessing ourselves and to get us talking about sin in a way that makes it seem like maybe it's not a sin. It's possible, brothers and sisters, that—and if these are the end times, which I think they are—that this is how Satan is trying to usher the Antichrist into the world. Remember that, above all else, Satan is a trickster. He uses us against ourselves. He tricks us into thinking that what we know to be true is a lie, and accepting what we know is a lie as truth. He exploits our weakness and makes us think there's only one course of action. And I'll admit to you right now that I'm weak when it comes to protecting children. I'm the weakest person in the world when I see a child in need, especially an unborn child that can't defend itself. But what if that's not a child at all? What if that child has no soul? What if that child, brothers and sisters, is the Antichrist? I mean, isn't that just what Satan would do—try to trick the Christians of the world into literally paying some charlatan to give birth to the Antichrist?"

The congregation openly began discussing this possibility among themselves. James immediately felt that this was a better explanation. It made perfect sense to him. And the realization that the Antichrist was on planet Earth, waiting to be born, was energizing. James felt that whatever God's purpose was for him was tied to this event, to this child.

Pastor Preston continued, "So, brothers and sisters, what are we to do as Christians in this situation? I say to you that we are to do nothing. We are not to give her a single cent, and we are to allow her to end the life of the demon growing inside her at this very moment. Satan may think he can pull a fast one on us, but we're Christians, brothers and sisters. We have Jesus Christ on our side and it's pretty tough to fool him. Satan might be able to fool us. We're just human beings. But he can't fool the big guy. He can't fool Jesus. So all we have to do is listen to Christ, and He'll tell us what to do.

"And I know some of you may be thinking to yourselves that we can't just let this girl get away with this, and I agree with you. But, trust me, she'll be taken care of. She's a coward. She's doing this anonymously. Can you imagine that? Can you imagine being a Christian anonymously? I can't. I'm proud of who I am and of everything I do in the service of the Lord. Cowards, though? Cowards hide in the shadows, behind lies and tricks, just like this girl, this coward. And if you'll turn with me to Revelation 21:8, you'll see what happens to cowards. You'll see that she's not going to get away with this. The word of God says, 'But as for the cowardly, the faithless, the detestable, as for murderers, the sexually immoral, sorcerers, idolaters, and all liars, their portion will be in the lake that burns with fire and sulfur, which is the second death.' Brothers and sisters, this girl is going to burn in hell. Amen."

The rest of the congregation repeated, "Amen."

As James walked out of the auditorium and into the parking lot, Cathy caught up with him and said, "So, what do you think?"

James told her that he agreed with Pastor Preston, that this had to be the work of Satan, and that the child was very likely the Antichrist. He told her that nothing else seemed reasonable to him given all the details.

She said, "I know. It's really crazy—I mean, exciting, but also really crazy, that we're living in this time right now. I've never felt so Christian in my life."

As James looked at her, he saw something in her eyes, some spark, some excitement about her love of Jesus that moved him. He realized he felt compelled to ask her to have dinner with him, and although he cautioned himself to take it slow, he reasoned that God must have a reason for filling him with the motivation to ask her out. God must be moving him to action, he thought, because it was part of his plan. So James asked Cathy if she'd like to get dinner sometime, and Cathy said, "That would be great, really, but I already have a boyfriend. I'm sorry."

James apologized for being so forward, and Cathy said, "No, you don't need to apologize. You didn't know I had a boyfriend, and if I didn't, I'd totally go out to dinner with you. I hope it's not weird or anything now, and we can still be friends, because you're, like, one of the only real Christians I've met in a while." James assured her that nothing was weird between them and that their friendship wouldn't change. He felt the same way about her that she did about him. She seemed like a true Christian in ways other people James knew did not. There was no hypocrisy with Cathy, no double standard.

On the drive home, James told himself that he was trying to make decisions for himself that were outside of God's plan for him. Nothing else could explain why Cathy already had a boyfriend. James made a vow to God as he pulled into his parking spot that he would never again make a decision for himself without praying about the issue intensely and waiting for God to give him some sign to let him know what action he should take. He made sure to include in the vow the promise that he didn't need to hear God's voice or anything that selfish. James just asked that God help him understand what it was that he was supposed to be doing to honor God and to fulfill his plan.

He went inside, turned on his computer, logged in to his ChristianMingle.com account, and canceled his membership. He reasoned that God didn't need a website to deliver his soul mate. God had been delivering soul mates to human beings for thousands of years before the Internet even existed. James cursed himself for not having realized this sooner.

chapter fifteen

Karen watched Tanya as she looked at the website and waited for her reaction. She felt like she had already lived this exact same moment with Paul. She wondered how many more times she'd have to live it. When Tanya finished reading she said, "And this is why he broke up with you?"

Karen said, "Yeah."

Tanya said, "Karen, I don't even know what to say to any of this. I mean, obviously I was happy when you decided not to get the abortion, but this is just . . . It's not right. I know I'm your friend and I'm supposed to support you through everything, but if I'm being honest, I'm on Paul's side here."

"Well, I need you to be on my side. I know it's asking for a lot. Paul couldn't give me that, but I need somebody who can or I'm going to crack here."

"Maybe you should crack. Maybe that's telling you something. Maybe you shouldn't do this."

"I am doing this, Tanya. When Paul left me, all I did was try to convince myself not to do this, to go back to the way things were before, so that I could get him back. I came as close as I was going to come to shutting it down, but I obviously didn't. The site's live."

"Have you told your parents?"

"No. I don't want them involved. I don't think they'd get it at all."

"I don't get it at all."

"I know. I know. I'm not asking you to do anything except be there for me when I need you. You know, to go to the doctor or to help me get groceries when I start getting really pregnant or just to talk to me when no one else will."

"You probably know this about me, Karen—that I'm obligated to help you if you ask me, because I'm a Christian, and even though you're doing the most un-Christian thing I could possibly imagine, I know it's not my place to judge you."

"So you'll help me?"

"I guess so."

Karen hugged her friend and cried. She said, "Thank you so much, Tanya. I fucking love you."

"I love you, too. I hate what you're doing, but I love you. And I know I always tease you about how you're going to hell, but you better repent for this one or you really are. I have to get back to study for a test. I'm going to pray for you and for your baby, whether you want me to or not."

"Do whatever you have to. I might have to call you later tonight."

"Why?"

"Paul's coming over to pick up some of his stuff. I don't know how I'm going to handle it."

Tanya said, "I'll be up late, so call if you need to," then left.

*　　*　　*

Karen finished eating a pint of ice cream as she checked her site and saw that the total dollar amount collected had reached a little over five million dollars. She'd known the idea was good since she came up with it, and she assumed it would become national news, which would force the percentage of the population who considered themselves pro-life to take some kind of stance. Knowing all of this, Karen still found it extremely surreal to be staring at the hard evidence of her actions. Five million dollars was a lot of money. It was still nowhere near her ultimate goal of a hundred million, but it was significant, and there was still a lot of time before her deadline. She began to wonder what would happen if the goal of a hundred million was reached, how it would affect the country, how it would affect her, how it would affect the child's life.

She closed her laptop and went to the bathroom to take a shower. Paul was supposed to arrive soon, and even though they were officially over, she couldn't help wanting to look presentable when he got there.

In the bathroom, she stood naked in front of the mirror, looking at her body. This was a habit that Karen succumbed to every day, but more and more she felt like she was looking at a stranger, at an alien who had replaced her.

In the shower, she rubbed her stomach and tried to imagine what it would look like at the final stage of pregnancy. She wondered if she would even make it that far, if the donations would reach her goal. As she moved her hand over one of her breasts, she became aroused. She had read that at some point during pregnancy a woman's libido becomes more intense. She moved her hand from her breast to her vagina and rubbed her clitoris slowly just to test how aroused she actually was.

Less than three minutes later, standing under the running water of her shower, she had masturbated to orgasm. As she dried off she became aware that she had never masturbated in the shower standing up, as she had just done, and she was also still thinking about sex despite having just had a satisfying orgasm.

She got dressed and headed back into the living room, where she opened her computer back up and checked the donations on her site again. Checking the number had become an obsession of Karen's since launching the site. When she had trouble sleeping because of the pregnancy, sometimes she stayed up for hours, hitting the refresh button and imagining the person who had just donated a dollar or five dollars or ten.

Since launching the site she'd heard nothing from Professor Noone about any expulsion or even reprimand, so she assumed that there was no reason to contact him. Karen decided that until any kind of real opposition from him or the other members of the philosophy school's faculty materialized, it was best to lay low and go on with her experiment.

Karen had also started a detailed journal of the process she was outlining in her dissertation, which she was working on daily. The work she was doing made her feel like all of this was serving a purpose, an empirical and intellectual purpose. She found it difficult to maintain this conviction sometimes, especially when she started thinking about Paul and what this entire ordeal might mean to the other relationships in her life, but the work made it seem worth it. Karen knew that ultimately her life was meaningless, and the best thing she could hope for was that before she died she would have done something that made people think deeply about what she felt was a great hypocrisy. She knew that she could die happy if at some point in her life she had had a hand in causing people to be more critical of religion, of speeding along its demise, which she knew was eventual but which she desperately wanted to occur in her lifetime.

When Paul knocked, Karen shut her computer and answered the door. It was strange letting him into the place as a guest, but she knew this was a part of breaking up that had to be endured.

Paul said, "You were right," and gave Karen some hope that

maybe he was going to admit he was wrong. Maybe he was going to admit that he made a mistake and maybe he was going to move back in.

Karen said, "About what?"

"About this thing being huge news. It's on every website, every news channel. They even talked about it on *The View* today."

"Are you serious? What'd Sherri Shepard say?"

"I don't remember."

"Shit. I'll have to find that online."

"Yeah, you'd like it. There are a bunch of tweets you should look at, too. Kim Kardashian's was pretty good."

"I saw it. What a fucking idiot."

"I just like how she thinks anyone gives a shit about her opinion on this."

"I know, but honestly, the more people like her talk about this, the better."

"I really don't think you need it to get much bigger. There's not a person with an Internet connection or a TV who doesn't know about it."

Karen hated how easy it was to talk to Paul, how easy it was to fall into old patterns. In those brief seconds of small talk it almost felt like they weren't breaking up, like they were talking about someone else.

She said, "Have you told anyone that you . . . that you're involved in this?"

He said, "I'm not involved in this, Karen. I'm not involved at all. That's why I'm moving out."

"I know, but you know what I mean."

"No. I haven't told anyone. I know we're breaking up, and I know this is a shitty situation, but I still love you. I probably will for a while, and I don't want people knowing this is you."

"Why not?"

"Karen, I know it took either massive balls to do this or massive stupidity—and I've never known you to be stupid at all, so

I assumed it was balls—but are you seriously asking me why it would be bad for your identity to get out there?"

"I mean, I know it's a big news story and everything."

"It's not just a news story. You're shitting all over the majority of this country's religious beliefs. I'm pretty sure they think you're going to burn in hell, and they're probably all too happy to send you there A-S-A-fucking-P."

"Come on. The only people it will piss off that much are the lunatic-fringe Christians, and even they know killing is a sin. I'm sure they fear pissing off their God more than they hate me."

"Just be careful."

"I will."

"So . . . I just need to get my computer stuff and the rest of my clothes, I guess. You can have the furniture and anything else I helped pay for that was for the apartment."

"Don't you need furniture? You can have some stuff if you need it."

He said, "I don't really think I can deal with using the things we used together," then started to cry a little bit, which made Karen cry as well.

She hugged him and he hugged her back. They stood crying in the living room, just hugging each other and crying for a minute or so. They both felt that they would very likely never meet a person with whom they would be more compatible than the one on whose shoulder they were crying. They both felt that the end to this relationship was avoidable. They both felt that they were losing something irreplaceable in the other person. But Karen knew what she was doing was bigger than personal comfort and happiness. It was affecting the world.

Paul eventually pulled back, wiped his eyes, and said, "Okay, I'm getting my stuff and getting out of here."

Karen followed him into the bedroom where he started putting his clothes into a plastic trash bag. It was sad to see, but she felt she owed it to their relationship to witness every moment—

especially the final one, for which she knew she was responsible. There was some penance in it. As she stood over him and offered to help, she smelled his shampoo. It was a smell that had always reminded her of sex, and she found that she couldn't stop herself from imagining Paul on top of her, sweating as he was sliding his penis into her. Even as aware as she was of the facts of the situation, that she was watching the man she loved pack his clothes in what was likely the last time she would ever see him, all she could think about was having sex with him one last time.

She said, "Um, I know this is going to sound insane and it's probably just my hormones from being pregnant and everything, but do you want to, uh, have sex one last time?"

Paul looked up from where he was kneeling in the closet, stuffing his trash bag full of clothes and said, "Are you serious?"

Karen said, "Yeah. I'm really fucking horny right now."

Paul said, "Are you really serious?"

Karen said, "Yes."

Paul put the trash bag down, stood up, and kissed Karen. She unbuckled his belt, unzipped his pants, and pushed him back onto the bed. She slid his pants off and performed fellatio on him until he was erect, then took her own pants off, slid her panties to the side, straddled him and slid his penis into herself. He said, "Jesus, you weren't kidding."

She rode him, rocking her hips back and forth with his penis inside her as quickly as she could. Karen had always enjoyed sex, but this was something different. Beyond the normal pleasure she experienced, this time it felt like an itch was being scratched, one that was so deep she couldn't find its exact location. And the orgasm it produced was one of the best she'd ever had.

She climbed off Paul once he finished and said, "I know that was weird, but thank you."

Paul said, "It was pretty weird. Now I have to pack the rest of my shit and leave. That's even weirder."

She said, "I know. I'm sorry, but that . . . I really fucking needed that."

He said, "You know it's not too late to stop this, right?"

She said, "Don't. It is too late. I'm doing this, Paul. I've already done it. It's out there in the world now. Even if I wanted to take it back, I couldn't now."

"But you could. Your site did what it was supposed to do. People are talking. You could just take it down. No one would ever know it was you, but they'd still be talking about it."

"I can't do that. I have to see it through. This is important, and I understand why you don't want to be here for it. I do, seriously, and I don't hold it against you or blame you at all, but you have to understand why I'm doing it and that I can't quit until it's done."

He said, "And what after it's done?"

She said, "I don't know. What do you mean?"

He said, "I mean, after it's done and you've done this crazy thing, you just go on with your life, find some other guy, get pregnant again, have another abortion ransom website?"

She laughed. Even in the worst situations Paul could always make her laugh. She'd miss that. She said, "No. I'm hoping to never get pregnant again. But when it's over, it's over. I'll turn in my dissertation. Based on how the media is treating this, I'll probably be able to publish it, maybe expand it for a book or something, and I'm assuming it'll start my career as a philosopher who actually means something to the world. I mean, when was the last time a philosopher was seen as an important contributor to culture, or to anything for that matter?"

Paul said, "To publish a book, you'll have to go public with your identity."

Karen said, "I know. Once it's over and things calm down, I think it will be easier to do."

Paul said, "I know. You're right. I know that objectively. It's just hard for me to think of the rest of my life without you. But I just can't do this with you. I just can't."

She kissed him on the forehead and said, "I know," then put her pants back on and went into the living room, leaving Paul to collect the rest of his things alone. She didn't feel like they were breaking up, like this was the last time she would see Paul. She hoped that once things were over, once this was done and its effects had taken hold, maybe there would be a chance to reconcile. If the financial goal was met, however, then Karen knew that Paul's child would be somewhere in the world, living a life that might never involve him. She didn't know if he could ever forgive her for that. She had hoped from the beginning of this that the financial goal wouldn't be met. She had hoped for this outcome for a variety of reasons. It would prove her point. She wouldn't have to go through the agonizing experience of child labor. And she wouldn't be responsible for bringing another life into the world. But in that moment the only reason she hoped for that outcome was so that she and Paul might be able to work things out.

Eventually Paul emerged from the bedroom with a few bags of clothes and a small cardboard box of various items, including books and an iPod. He said, "I got everything."

Karen said, "Okay."

He said, "I just really can't believe this is the last time we're ever going to see each other."

She said, "It doesn't have to be."

He said, "I think it does. Goodbye, Karen. I love you and I hope this all works out the way you want it to."

She said, "Thanks," and watched Paul walk out the front door. Karen smelled her hands. She'd had them wrapped in Paul's hair when they were having sex. They smelled like him. She inhaled deeply, in case she'd never have the chance to smell it again, then flipped her computer back open to check the current donation total on her site. It was unchanged, but she did see that she had a few emails.

There was one from her mother, asking when she and Paul

were coming to visit. Her mother insisted that she and her father should see more of Paul, because they believed it was only a matter of time before he would be their son-in-law. Karen deleted the email without responding and checked the next one. It was from someone Karen didn't recognize. The suffix was cnn.com.

It read, "Hello, Ms. Holloway. We've been covering the story of your website for a few weeks now and we'd love to hear your side of the story if you'd care to comment. Please reply as soon as you can, as we are planning on running a story that includes your name within the hour. Thank you for your time. Sincerely, James Shoemaker."

Below the email was the CNN logo and general contact information for the network. Karen had no idea how they'd discovered that she had created the website, but they had, and she felt that this very probably was not a good thing.

chapter sixteen

James woke up Friday morning, showered, brushed his teeth, and then checked his email to find out his work schedule for the weekend. He was usually required to work two nights out of the three from Friday through Sunday, as dictated by his supervisor. He preferred working Friday and Sunday nights so that he could get enough sleep Saturday night to be well rested for church on Sunday morning.

He opened the PDF file that contained his schedule and found that the days from Friday through Sunday were blacked out. At the bottom of the schedule was a note that read: "There will be no weekend work this week. Dillard's is laying a new floor. Work will resume on Monday. The new schedule will be out Sunday night."

James closed the file, logged out of his email account, then sat back in his chair. He hadn't had a weekend off in a very long time. The last one he could remember was when the entire mall was closed because of a flood. He wondered if this was a sign from God but found it hard to decipher the possible meaning. After praying for some help or guidance in knowing how he should use his weekend off, he heard nothing and came to no greater understanding. It was in this silence, this lack of response from God, that James realized the answer was obvious. God had cleared his schedule so that James would be able to listen for his voice without interruption.

James got up from his chair and started making a mental list of the things he'd need to buy at the grocery store for his weekend in. He completed the list as quickly as possible, excited and anxious to begin the three days of focused concentration that were ahead of him. But as he put the list in his pocket, got his car keys, and went to his front door he stopped. He was disappointed in himself, on the verge of disgust. He realized that if God eliminated his job for those three days, it must have been because God didn't want James to be distracted at all. God would supply anything he might need over those three days, and he admitted to himself and to God that he had fallen victim to arrogance. If only for a moment, James thought that he knew better than God what he would need for that weekend, and he sought to supply it for himself. He apologized to God, put his car keys back on the table by his front door, ripped up the list, and took his jacket off before sitting down on his couch in the living room. If God didn't want him to have any distractions, then he wouldn't have any. He wouldn't watch television. He wouldn't check his email or answer his phone. He wouldn't buy food and he wouldn't eat. He wouldn't even sleep. He would just pray and listen as closely as he could to the sound of nothing, until God decided to fill that nothing with the sound of his own voice.

James sat on his couch and looked out the window. He could see some cars in the parking lot. He noticed a few people coming and going, a cat walking near the dumpsters, some birds flying overhead, and an occasional airplane. After roughly ten minutes of looking out the window, James realized this was just as much a distraction as going to the grocery store would have been, so he closed his curtains and sat on his couch staring at the wall and listening as intently as he could for any sound of God's voice.

He could hear his neighbor's television, but not clearly enough to make out any words. He could hear people talking in the parking lot below his apartment, every now and then, but not clearly enough to understand what they were saying, either. He could hear music coming from cars as they passed by. He could hear washers and dryers in the laundry room turning on and off, and he could hear the low electrical hum of his own refrigerator. None of these things was God's voice, however, and he began to wonder if God's voice was loud enough to be heard through the ambient noise of the world. He realized, even as he thought this, that he was being absurd. God could obviously make his voice as loud as He wanted. So he dismissed the notion that maybe he should unplug his refrigerator.

He looked at his wall, and as the hours passed he counted the small inconsistencies in the paint. They made tiny bumps and indentations that he never noticed before. James watched the shadows crawl across them, and he couldn't help seeing shapes and faces in them. He looked at his phone's clock and saw that it was a little past noon. He had been sitting on the couch listening for God's voice for four hours. Hunger had crept up on him sometime during the morning, and by lunchtime James could feel his stomach starting to gurgle and churn. This was just a distraction, though, one that had to be put out of his mind. He forced himself to think of the pain that Jesus had endured in the final days of his life. It was far more than just hunger from skipping breakfast. James apologized to God for giving his hunger even a second of attention.

When thirst set in, he thought about getting a glass of water, but felt shame at the thought of giving up so easily, after only a few hours into the three days God had given him. He knew that God would provide him with water if he needed it, and he knew that God would reward him only if he was diligent, if he followed God's plan. So he put the hunger and the thirst out of his mind and he sat.

James closed his eyes so he wouldn't be distracted by the sight of anything, and he thought about what God must have been doing in heaven at that moment. In his mind's eye, James saw God sitting on his gleaming golden throne, looking down through the clouds. God was watching him and deciding whether he was ready to be spoken to. James imagined Jesus there, too, at his father's side. He thought that, although God spoke to different people all the time, each time was a moment of great import, because every person had a part to play in his plan. The moment a person heard God for the first time, and learned of his or her role in his plan, was the most important moment in that person's life. God knew this, and so those moments must have been equally important to him.

With his eyes still closed, he began thinking about all the events in his life that had led him to that moment sitting on his couch waiting for God to speak to him. He knew that all those events were part of God's plan. The various foster homes, the teasing and rejection in most of the schools he had attended, the abuse he had suffered at the hands of his peers as well as his caregivers—it was all part of something he knew was far too complex for him to ever understand, and yet he knew he was an integral part of the functioning of whatever that thing was, whatever God had designed for not just him, but for all humanity.

His memory settled on a specific event in his life. It was the time he first truly understood just how great God could be. In the seventh grade, all of the students in James's American history class had been partnered together by the teacher. The pairings were arbitrary but mandatory. The partnerships required that the students paired would sit with their desks pushed together throughout the school year, helping each other with assignments and doing class presentations together on various subjects. James was paired with a girl named Natalie Chambers. She was one of the popular girls in the seventh grade, and James remembered initially dreading his required interactions with her. Most of her friends openly made fun of James for being strange or quiet or any of the submissive personality traits he had developed as the result of inadequate foster care and constant moving. But James was surprised to learn that Natalie wasn't like her friends. She seemed to be genuinely nice to him, and she never made him feel bad about himself.

They developed a relationship in which James found a great sense of worth. He had only ever had acquaintances throughout his life, and, although he and Natalie never spent time with one another outside class, he considered her a friend. And, beyond the friendship, he found that she was the first girl for who he formed romantic feelings. So, when the spring dance was announced, he waited after school one day near the parking lot exit where the students were picked up by their parents. When he saw Natalie walking out, he asked her if she'd like to go to the dance with him.

She was polite but refused him, claiming she had a boyfriend. She told him she was sorry, and that if she didn't have a boyfriend, she would have loved to go to the dance with him. James considered this a victory, and for the rest of the night, even though Natalie had turned him down, James felt good. For possibly the first time in his life, he felt like he was normal.

That night, James had prayed to God that his actions wouldn't alter the relationship he had with Natalie. She was really the only thing he looked forward to at school, and he genuinely hoped nothing would change between them. As they sat down next to each other the following morning, James was relieved to find that his prayers had been answered. Natalie was just as polite and nice to him as she always had been. They were still friends, and for that James was grateful.

Leaving school that day, he was happy. He knew that if God wanted him to have a girlfriend, a girlfriend would appear for him, and Natalie simply wasn't meant to fill that role. As he walked home, thinking about what the girl God chose for him would be like, three older boys approached him. They didn't go to his middle school. They claimed to be in the ninth grade at one of the local high schools, and one of them claimed to be Natalie's boyfriend. It was this boy who threw the first punch. Then the rest joined in. They threw James to the ground, kicking and punching him while Natalie's boyfriend called him a faggot and told him to stay away from his girlfriend or he would find James and attack him this way every day.

When they were finished, Natalie's boyfriend spat in James's face and threw his backpack over a fence into the backyard of a nearby house. He could hear the boys laughing as he lay there crying. With no other recourse, he prayed to God for retribution. As an adult, he realized that this kind of prayer should only be used in the direst of consequences, but in the seventh grade he had lacked the understanding to restrain himself. So he conjured in his mind Leviticus 24:20: *If a man injures his neighbor, just as he has done, so it shall be done to him: fracture for fracture, eye for eye, tooth for tooth; just as he has injured a man, so it shall be inflicted on him,* and he asked God to uphold this biblical law.

As he watched the boys cross the street, still laughing at him, a car struck two of them, including Natalie's boyfriend. Not knowing what to do, and feeling guilty that he had somehow caused the accident, James ran all the way home. He found out the next day that both of the boys would be fine. Their wounds were superficial, some bruises and bumps, not a single broken bone, much like the injuries that James suffered at their hands. James saw no way that those boys could have avoided serious injury after being hit by a car—except for divine intervention. God had answered his prayer. And from that day forward James knew, in a concrete way, that God was capable of anything and that he was listening.

As the afternoon of the first day of James's three-day weekend stretched on, he tried praying and asking God to speak to him. He assured God that he was ready, that he was listening, just as he knew God had listened to him on that day in seventh grade. Even in his assurance he felt foolish. He realized that God knew him better than he knew himself, and he stopped praying immediately. He apologized to God for having been so arrogant as to tell God what he already knew, what he himself had created. James reminded himself that God had created every atom in his body, every thought in his mind, and every emotion he would ever feel. It must be insulting to God, he thought, when people told him that they were ready to hear his voice. God knew when they were ready, and he must have known that James wasn't ready yet or he would have spoken. He vowed to remain silent for the duration of the three days, and he vowed never again to tell God what God already knew.

The rest of the first day was long. James became very hungry and thirsty that evening, but he wanted to prove to God that hearing his voice meant more to him than the discomfort of fasting. He knew plenty of people had gone through far worse than giving up food and water for three days in God's service. An image of Jesus on the cross materialized in James's mind. Jesus was writhing in pain, but his face was at peace, and he was glowing with holy power of the divine. James thanked Jesus for his suffering and for saving himself and the entire human race.

Eventually the shadows on the wall grew long and then bled into the darkness of night. James could hear people returning to their apartments from work. He heard the man who lived next to him unlock his door and then lock it again behind himself before turning on the television in his living room. James didn't know this man, but he saw him from time to time. They'd exchange pleasantries every now and again, but they'd never had a conversation that lasted more than a few seconds. James wondered why he had never talked to this man at length or about anything of import. He lived only a few feet from this man and knew nothing about him. He vowed to God that he would be a better neighbor after this weekend.

He listened to his neighbor for a few hours before he heard the television go silent and the door unlock and lock again, followed by his neighbor's footsteps heading off into the night. James wondered where he was going and what the night held for him. His neighbor was roughly his own age, so it stood to reason that he was going out to a bar to meet women. He wondered if his neighbor was Christian. He decided he would ask him the next chance he got.

As the first night wore on, he could hear his downstairs neighbor, a girl who was also around James's age, having sex. He felt ashamed for listening, but he knew she wasn't married based on her lack of a ring, which he noticed the first time he saw her, and James thought that it was necessary for a good Christian to be aware of the world of sin so that he or she could avoid it. When she and her partner finished, they stayed awake talking for an hour or so. James couldn't make out what they were saying, but at one point he heard them laughing. Laughter after committing such a sin made James more than uneasy. He was disgusted.

He eventually felt his eyelids getting heavy, but he fought off sleep. Sleep, like food and water, was just one more of the basic human necessities James had vowed to give up during these days to prove to God that he was ready to hear him. He was tempted to lie down on his couch, but he knew that temptation was likely the Devil's work. Most Christians made the false assumption that the Devil worked on a large scale, that he was responsible for only the largest-scale sins, like the terrorist attacks on September 11 or shootings at schools, but James knew better. He knew that Satan was certainly responsible for the worst atrocities in human history, but he also knew that the Devil's most heinous work was done on the small scale. It was the little temptations to which people were more likely to give in that eventually accumulated and corrupted a person's soul until they no longer had a relationship with God. And the worst part of that satanic strategy was that the temptations were so small that most people didn't even notice them until it was too late.

It could be anything from tempting a person to cheat on a diet until they woke up one day obese to tempting a person to cheat on their spouse until they woke up one day and were HIV positive. In this case, James knew that Satan was tempting him to recline on the couch, then he'd tempt him to close his eyes, and then he'd wake up the next morning having missed his opportunity to hear God's voice. He rebuked Satan's attempt by going into his bathroom and splashing cold water on his face. James remembered staying awake through the night a few times at different church camps in his youth, but he hadn't done it as an adult. It was more difficult than he remembered, especially with no other outside stimulation to hold his attention. But he knew that the promise of God's voice was all the stimulation he needed. He didn't want to disappoint God, so he did some jumping jacks to get his blood pumping, and then returned to his living room and took his seat on the couch again.

Listening closely to the world around him, James created small games to keep himself awake. He'd count the number of passing cars in multiples of seven. He'd trace the indentations on the top of his mouth with the tip of his tongue and try to count how many distinct shapes there were. He'd stare at the wood grain in his coffee table and try to determine how many individual trees were used to make it, by the placement and direction of the rings he could make out.

Eventually the sky outside began to lighten. The first night was nearing its end. James went to his window and looked out at his apartment complex's parking lot. His eyes were tired, and he had some doubts about his ability to stay awake for another forty-eight hours, but he cast them out of his mind as he saw the sun peeking above the tree line in the distance. He couldn't remember the last time he'd seen an actual sunrise, and it was clear to James that this was God's way of recognizing his efforts, of letting James know that he was doing the right thing.

James closed his eyes and let the sun hit his face as it rose in the early morning. He felt its warmth, and he knew that this was the embrace of God. It seemed unlikely to James that anyone else was up at that hour, enjoying this sunrise as he was, and so it stood to reason that this specific sunrise was designed by God just for him. It was the handshake before the conversation to come.

As the morning of the second day wore on, hunger, thirst, and fatigue tested James at new levels. He knew he had peanut butter, jelly, and bread in his apartment. It would be very simple to prepare himself a sandwich and a glass of water. But he fought off the urge. He couldn't let Satan win.

By noon of the second day, if James stared at one spot on the wall long enough, he was able to see small white spots at the edges of his field of vision. He knew this was induced by the lack of food, water, and sleep, but he took some pride in it. He kept reminding himself that plenty of others, Jesus included, had suffered far worse in the service of God. He could do this. He would do this.

Early on Saturday afternoon, James's next-door neighbor returned to his apartment, leaving James to wonder where he might have gone for that long, where he might have slept. Within a few minutes James could hear his neighbor's television, and this time he could make out every word of what was being said. It was some kind of news program and they were discussing the website that Pastor Preston had mentioned in his sermon the prior Sunday. James hadn't given it much thought since that sermon. He decided that his strategy would be to ignore it totally. This was, he estimated, the best strategy against a satanic attempt to foul the world. But he welcomed the chance to have something to occupy his mind other than forcing himself to stay awake, and he reasoned that God wouldn't have made the volume loud enough for him to hear if he wasn't meant to listen.

The news anchor was reporting that the identity of the girl who made the site had been discovered. Her name was Karen Holloway, and she was a PhD student in UCLA's Department of Philosophy. She had yet to give an interview about the matter, but the news anchor promised that they would have an exclusive one-hour conversation with her the following night, Sunday. The anchor went on to report that this girl was being both condemned for her actions by religious communities worldwide and idolized as a hero of feminism and secularism by smaller groups of people. James found it difficult to understand how anyone could view what she was doing as heroic. Even beyond the religious aspects of his objection, James thought that all people should have a basic human level of disgust for what she was doing, based on the involvement of an unborn child. At some point the anchor moved on to another story about American troops being officially drawn down in Afghanistan or some place near Afghanistan, and James lost interest.

He couldn't stop thinking about Karen Holloway and what she was doing. He knew that ultimately God would see her punished, but he wished that this punishment would be far more immediate. He was confused as to why God would even allow something like this to happen at all and then he reminded himself that God worked in mysterious ways. It was not for any human being to understand what he does, or when or why he does it. It was only to be accepted as his divine plan and not questioned. God had some specific purpose for Karen Holloway's website, and that purpose would be revealed when God decided it was time.

Eventually James heard his neighbor leave again, but he failed to turn off his television before doing so. James first found this terribly inconsiderate, but then he realized that this must be part of God's plan for him, so he began to listen very closely to everything being reported on the news. Reports on wars, disasters, murders, police brutality, and worldwide civil unrest seemed to James like clear evidence that the end times were close at hand, and he began to understand why it was that God had guided his neighbor to leave the television on. James felt that God was giving him a special warning, a context that would help whatever message God had for him make perfect sense.

Aside from the stories of the various types of strife and misery in the world, the story of Karen Holloway and her upcoming interview on the network seemed to be the news item discussed the most. Her story seemed to push through the others, taking on a central importance. For James, though, Karen Holloway's story was linked to the other stories. Her actions were evil and spiritually damaging to society, and James was surprised that none of the reporters made the connection between her actions and the other news reports.

The second night came and passed, but James's neighbor didn't return, leaving James to wonder again where he might have stayed. His disappearance, however, meant that his television droned on, exposing him to a full night's coverage of Karen Holloway and her website, with news reports and commentary in constant rotation. By the time the sun rose on the third day, James was in a state of extreme hunger, thirst, and exhaustion. He stood at his window and felt the sun on his face, as he had the day before. He closed his eyes and imagined God's warm embrace as the light hit his face. It was difficult to open his eyes after closing them. But he did open them, and when he did, the sun looked more glorious than it ever had before. The colors were richer and brighter. The sky itself seemed to hum and pulse. The clouds moved faster than usual, and he thought he could see angels shining in the far distance above them.

The smell of someone cooking bacon in his apartment complex snapped him out of his visions. His stomach ached, but he had become used to the pain. It was almost comforting to him. He knew that pain was just an obstacle to God's voice, and the more intense it became, the closer he was to hearing God speak.

He was dizzy as he walked back from the window to his couch again and he felt that his lips were dry and cracking. But like the hunger, James knew this pain to be evidence of his spiritual journey to God over the course of these three days. As he sat back down on his couch he realized something that should have been obvious to him but that he had overlooked. God had given him three days. He knew there was nothing left to chance in God's plan, nothing arbitrary. He was reminded of Luke 18:33: *They will flog him with a whip and kill him, but on the third day he will rise.*

This was in reference to Jesus's resurrection. James knew he wasn't as important as Jesus, but he thought it was logical that God would use the period of three days to prepare a person for change. Jesus's body had remained entombed for three days before he rose again, proving his divine nature and ascending to heaven where he remained by his father's side for eternity. James saw himself in this way. He had remained entombed, in a way, in his apartment for three days, awaiting his transition into a new realm, a new understanding of the world and his place in it. In his exhaustion he felt more certain than ever that God would speak to him on this third day.

The hours stretched on and James listened to his neighbor's television as the various reporters counted down to their network's exclusive interview with Karen Holloway. James was curious to hear it, curious to see what possible reasoning she would give to justify her actions. He would listen carefully, though, so as not to allow Satan's thinking to take hold in his own mind. He was certain that this interview could be nothing less than Satan's attempt to poison as many unsuspecting minds as possible with his foul propaganda.

The shadows grew longer as the afternoon faded, but James didn't question why God had not yet spoken to him. He knew it would happen before the sun set, because it had to happen on the third day. It simply had to. He looked at the clock on his phone and saw that it was 5:49 P.M. The interview with Karen Holloway was to begin in eleven minutes. James moved on his couch to the spot where he could best hear his neighbor's television and settled in, welcoming the pain in his stomach and the dried skin on the top of his mouth. As he scraped his tongue across the back of his teeth he heard it: the voice of God.

God's voice sounded remarkably like his own, like the voice he would hear when he was making mental lists of things to buy at the store, or of things he needed to do at work, or very like the voice he heard in his mind when he read from the Bible. James didn't expect God's voice to sound so similar to his own, but he didn't question it. All people were made in God's image, after all.

God told James that he had something very important to do with his life, and it had to be done soon. Despite not having had a drink of water or anything else in three days, James began to weep. James understood his tears to be a miracle. As they rolled down his cheeks, James listened to God tell him that he had created James to perform an errand that was crucial to the survival of the human race. This errand would involve self-sacrifice, and it would be difficult to understand, but it should never be questioned, and it should never be shared with anyone else. It should only be blindly obeyed.

James dropped to his knees and prayed to God with as much focus as he could summon. He told God that he would do whatever was required of him. He begged God to use him in whatever manner he chose. God told him that he was to go to California. God explained that this was only the first of several things he would be required to do in the service of this divine errand. Several more signs and instructions would be delivered to James as he needed them along the journey. Go to California. That was the last thing God told James.

As the voice from his neighbor's television warned that there were only seven minutes left before the interview, James fell to his floor with tears of joy and amazement in his eyes. He said one final prayer to God, telling him that he would do what he was asked, he would carry out God's plan no matter what the personal cost to himself. And then James slept.

chapter
seventeen

Karen Holloway looked at herself in the mirror of the greenroom at CNN in Los Angeles, where she was waiting before being interviewed by Anderson Cooper. For a brief moment her anxiety subsided and her nerves faded when she noticed that her hair and face looked better than they usually did. The makeup people and stylists had touched her up, but beyond that, she felt she was looking better than she had in a long while. She wondered if this was the glow of pregnancy that she'd heard about, and although the prospect of what she was about to do still made her nervous, she was glad that at least she would look good doing it.

Tanya, who was there with Karen, said, "You look fine."

Karen said, "I know. I actually think I look pretty fucking good."

Tanya said, "I still can't believe your parents aren't here for this."

Karen said, "I didn't want them to come. When my name got leaked, that phone call was bad enough. I couldn't have my mom here right now telling me that I'm making the biggest mistake of my life—not right before I go on TV."

Tanya said, "But at some point you have to have more than just a phone call with them."

Karen said, "I know. I know. But not right now. I need to focus on this. I know it sounds stupid or arrogant, but I think what I'm about to do could potentially be really important."

Tanya said, "It doesn't sound stupid or arrogant. I think you're right. I think what you're doing is pretty terrible on a moral level, but it's undeniable that people are interested. Whatever you're going to say tonight, there will be a lot of people listening."

Karen had thought a lot about whether this interview was a good or a bad idea, but she eventually decided it was better to have more exposure and be able to explain herself to the public than it was to remain silent and allow all the media conjecture about her to continue. Her identity was already in the world, and putting a voice to it seemed to be only beneficial.

The day before, she'd been emailed a series of questions that she might be asked during the interview. So she stayed up late, formulating her answers and memorizing the various talking points she wanted to be able to mention if possible. By the time she left for the interview, she felt as ready as she could be for her first appearance on national television.

A producer came into the greenroom to tell her it was time to go to the set. After Tanya gave her a hug and wished her luck, Karen followed the producer outside, where someone clipped a microphone onto her collar, and then she was led to the set. As she sat down across the table from an empty chair, she took a deep breath. She knew this moment was in some ways more important than whatever would happen with the site and the money.

Anderson Cooper stepped out onto the stage and introduced himself to Karen. He said, "Hi, nice to meet you."

Even if God wasn't real, most people in the world believed he was, so the effect of God on humanity was still very real, and that was something worth understanding. Science and the growth of knowledge were important, but no more or less important than the various forms of human artistic endeavors. Sexuality was one of our most primary motivations, but certainly not the only one, and it was something no one had any control over in their lives. Discrimination based on these preferences was still very much a part of American culture, and although this discrimination was fading, it wasn't fading fast enough. Raising children, like sexual orientation, was merely a preference that varied from person to person, and sex was linked to this preference only in the most basic concrete sense. These were things that Anderson understood to be true.

Karen said, "You too. This is all a bit surreal to me."

Anderson said, "Well, what you're doing is all a bit surreal to a lot of people. I'm going to try to make this as easy as possible for you. I really think you deserve to have your voice heard in this, and I want you to be able to get everything out that you want to get out."

Karen said, "Thanks. That's great. I mean, that's all I could ask for."

Anderson said, "You got some of the questions from one of my producers, but we'll also be throwing in some Twitter questions at the end. We'll stay away from any of the outright offensive stuff, obviously, and keep it strictly to valid, fact-based questions or things that are more philosophical in nature—you know, just the pertinent questions."

Karen said, "That sounds fine to me."

Anderson said, "Good. Also, I know someone probably already told you this, and I'm sure it won't be a problem, but we're live, so no *fuck*s or *shit*s or anything like that. We have a delay, so you'll get bleeped anyway, but it's always better if you don't have to get bleeped." Then he sat down in the chair across from Karen.

A producer came out and informed them that they had one minute to air. Karen watched Anderson Cooper look over his notes. She looked out and saw camera operators looking into their monitors. She saw people running back and forth in the shadows of the studio. She wondered if this was what every show was like for them. She wondered if they cared at all about the interview that was about to take place, or if it was just one in a long line of interviews that came and went with only fleeting impact. She wondered if most of the world felt that way. Then the lights came up on the stage, and a producer started to count them down. It was happening.

Anderson Cooper looked into the center camera and said, "Good evening. Tonight we have an exclusive interview with arguably the most controversial person in America, maybe the world. Karen Holloway, the UCLA philosophy student who has issued an online challenge to the Christian right of America, is here with me tonight. She's currently pregnant, and she claims that if she doesn't get one hundred million dollars in donations through her website, she'll have an abortion. If she does meet her financial goal, then all the money will be put in a trust fund for the child, who will be given up for adoption. The public have had very different reactions to Karen and what she's doing. She's certainly been vilified by the Christian right as well as by many other activist groups, including many women's rights groups, despite how she says she's doing this in the name of women's rights. Others have praised her as a champion of feminism. Tonight we hear her side of the story, in a special live interview here on CNN."

Anderson Cooper turned to Karen and said, "Karen, thanks for being with us tonight. I know the past few weeks for you have probably been a little crazier than you're used to."

Karen said, "Yeah. I never really expected anyone to find out who I was."

Anderson Cooper said, "Well, let's start there. Many people

have criticized you for trying to remain anonymous. They've claimed it was an act of cowardice. Is that true? Were you afraid to have your identity known publicly?"

Karen said, "I'm sitting on your show right now doing this interview. I don't see how that could be interpreted as fear of my identity being known or cowardice of any kind. The reason I wanted the entire thing to be anonymous is that I wanted the idea, the experiment, to live and die on its own merits. I didn't want my identity to get in the way of people seeing just how hypocritical the pro-life movement is in this country. Whatever people were thinking or feeling about this whole thing, I didn't want to become the focus of those feelings. But that seems to be exactly what's happening anyway."

Anderson Cooper said, "To some degree I think you're right, but your site has generated a little over seven million dollars, and looks to keep generating money, so even if some of the attention is focused on you, people are still paying attention to the site and the conversation you've started."

Karen said, "That's true."

Anderson Cooper said, "And at the current rate of donations coming in, does it seem to you like you're going to hit your projected goal of one hundred million dollars?"

Karen said, "It's impossible to say. The donations have slowed down a bit, but I think there's also a lull in things like this between the beginning and the end. We saw it with the Affordable Care Act. When the clock starts counting down the last few days, I'll be very interested to see what happens. Because I know that within the most prominent evangelical churches in the country, there are two camps emerging. One camp is urging their congregations to donate whatever they can. They're actually sticking to their pro-life philosophy. But the other camp, which I think is the majority of Christians in this country, both evangelical and not, has denounced me and claims that a donation to my site is the wrong thing to do. Which obviously proves my point."

Anderson Cooper said, "And what is that point exactly?"

Karen said, "Well, it's just like I said on my site. The Christian right in this country isn't really pro-life at all. They're anti-woman. I'm doing something that's completely legal in our country. I'm exercising my right as a woman, to choose to have a child or not, and for under a dollar each, the pro-life Christians of this country have the ability to make sure that this fetus is carried to term and given a good home, not to mention set up for life. This child, if born, would obviously never have to worry about money in his or her life. But if they fail to meet the goal, then I think it proves they aren't really interested in human life, they're far more interested in attempting to control women, by limiting their choices and imposing their own religious mandate on as many people as possible, which is one of several hypocrisies at the root of Christianity. And ultimately I hope that exposing that hypocrisy will help nudge people in the direction of ending religion."

Anderson Cooper said, "And if you do end up getting the hundred million dollars, will you have any hand in deciding who adopts the baby?"

Karen said, "Well, I'd personally love to see the child go to a gay couple, but I've opted to remove myself completely from the adoption process. Statistically, the child is much more likely to go to a Christian family—which should be further incentive for the Christians in this country to donate."

Anderson Cooper said, "If your financial goal is met, and you have the baby and give it up for adoption, will you want to be a part of the child's life in any way?"

Karen said, "Not at all."

Anderson Cooper said, "Why not?"

Karen said, "I decided a long time ago that I didn't want to have kids, and I think this fetus, should it become a child, would be far better served by parents who really want to have a child."

Anderson Cooper said, "And what if the child, at some point, gets curious and wants to meet you or wants to be in your life?"

Karen said, "That's a more difficult question. I wouldn't want to deprive the child that opportunity to know me or meet me, but I think I'd try my best to stay completely removed."

Anderson Cooper said, "But do you think you'd even be able to do that? This child, assuming you actually have it, will be a public figure of some sort for his or her entire life. You very likely will be as well. It seems like it would be pretty difficult for either of you to not at least be aware of the other as your lives progress."

Karen said, "I don't know if that's true at all. I think if you don't want to be a public figure, it's very easy not to be. I obviously can't speak for whatever kind of person this child might or might not become, but I know myself, and I have a much stronger desire to see my work's effect in the public than do I have any desire to see myself as a celebrity of any kind."

Anderson Cooper said, "Okay. Let's get to another point you've made, which is that your goal isn't just to prove that the Christian right is hypocritical, but also to nudge people toward the end of religion. Do you really think that's even possible?"

Karen said, "The end of religion, and the belief in mythologies and fairy tales, is inevitable. We're already seeing it happen in this country. Every time a new poll comes out about the beliefs of the younger generations, we see that fewer and fewer people affiliate with any organized religion, and more and more people are self-described agnostics. If we know anything from history, it's that social and technological progress never stops. The belief in a God was something that was beneficial for a very long time for us. When we couldn't explain why it rained, or what the stars were, it was easy to conjure the idea of a big guy up in the sky who made everything. But today we know that's not the case, and as technology explains more and more of the universe, and as we move forward socially, becoming less and less tolerant of discrimination against women and homosexuality and other things religion discriminates against, I personally think the writing is on the wall. I mean, women are the largest group of subjugated people on the planet. Even in countries like America, where things are relatively good for women, we still make only seventy-five percent of what a man makes for performing the same job at the same level. It's still socially expected for a woman to give up her last name upon marriage. And obviously our culture still protects its young men far more than its young women where rape and sexual assault are concerned. And the idea that any of that is okay comes from religion. It comes from the notion that a woman must be subservient to the man, just as it says in not only the Bible but most foundational texts of major religions. And because we allow religious freedom, we feel the need to lend credence to these views. If you discriminate against any group in this country, all you have to do is claim that it's because of your religious affiliation, and you're beyond reproach. And this isn't just about women. Obviously religion has always allowed for open discrimination against homosexuality, race, and a wide number of other things. Religion just doesn't serve the same purpose it used to—or any purpose, really. Religion is the last bastion of discrimination. I think we'll all be better off when it's gone."

Anderson Cooper said, "But the counterargument to that is that religion, specifically if we're talking about Christianity here, is that it gives guidelines by which people live their lives—and that in turn helps to ensure order and certain moral values in our society."

Karen said, "Although that seems like a valid argument, it's not. All of the religious laws—in the case of Christianity, it's the Ten Commandments—are subject to context. Take the commandment that I think we'd all agree is the most ironclad, the one that pretty much everyone agrees on: *Thou shalt not kill.*

After Osama bin Laden was killed, your network aired footage of Americans celebrating in the streets. Not only did Americans, most of whom are Christian, not care that a murder had just been committed, they celebrated it. Now, as an atheist, I have no problem with Bin Laden being killed. I think it was a good thing to do. The world is better without him. But if you're a Christian, whether or not you agree that the world is a better place because of his death, that commandment should obligate you to protest his murder, which violates a direct order from your God. But I think you'd be hard-pressed to find one in ten Christians who would actually support that stance. So in that case even *Thou shalt not kill* gets thrown out the window.

"And it obviously doesn't stop with Bin Laden. You have Christian governors in states like Texas and Oklahoma, both of whom are devout Christians, executing people in prison left and right. You have plenty of Christian members of the military killing people every day in the Middle East, and you have Christian citizens here supporting those killings. And I'm not arguing that it makes them bad people to support our military actions. I'm arguing that it makes them bad Christians, or not even Christians at all. Most people aren't as religious as they think. And that's okay. Ultimately, if I could have one idea sink into the culture as a result of what I'm doing, it's that. It's okay to reject religion openly. Most people already are, in one way or another, but they still identify with the religion they were indoctrinated into when they were young. If there's no other reason to reject religion, people have to understand that science and technology are really our only hope for the future—especially in a time when we're facing things like climate change and overpopulation. And I don't think you can have a religious scientist."

Anderson Cooper said, "Well, I think there's evidence to the contrary. There are plenty of scientists who are also religious. Francis Collins, the scientist who mapped the human genome, is famously religious."

Karen said, "There are absolutely religious people who practice scientific techniques, but they're not scientists. An actual scientist who has devoted his or her life to the pursuit of truth via the scientific method—I'm talking about making a hypothesis, gathering evidence through experimentation, and drawing a conclusion about that hypothesis—could never logically come to the conclusion that a god exists. There's literally no factual evidence. To believe in a god, you have to be the type of person who believes that the world and existence is fantastical, that it has mythological elements that are not only real, but more important than the physical elements we can actually interact with and measure. A real scientist simply wouldn't be able to do that. So, while you can have religious people practicing certain aspects of science, you can never have a scientist who is religious."

Anderson Cooper said, "That's kind of a semantics issue, isn't it?"

Karen said, "I think semantics matter—and I'd guess most people do, too. After all, I'm on this show right now because of semantics. My position is that there's a fetus growing in me right now, which has no legal right to life because it's not yet a person. Many other people would claim there's a human being growing inside of me right now that has the same right to life that you or I do. In some way, semantics is what this entire thing is about."

Anderson Cooper said, "Fair enough. I'm sure you're aware that some Republicans in Congress have used what you're doing to reinvigorate their attempts to make it more difficult for women to get abortions in their states, and in some cases it seems that they're making more progress than they have in a while. Does it, in any way, make you regret your decision to do this, the fact that you might actually be responsible for setting abortion rights back in some places?"

Karen said, "Well, I don't regret what I'm doing, and I don't actually think I'm in any way responsible for setting reproductive rights back. The trend in conservative states to put restrictions on Planned Parenthood and other clinics was ongoing far before I launched this site. Certain states have the unfortunate luck of being run by people who don't actually want to do the most good for the most citizens. States like Texas have their laws made by old, rich white men doing what they think is in their own best interest. Beyond the horrible way they've treated the women of their states, where reproductive rights are concerned, they've systematically made it far more difficult, if not impossible, for most minorities—women included—to even vote. Their moves to restrict voting rights are obviously designed to ensure that they stay in power, and to prevent opposing views from being represented in government. To overcome a situation like that, I think it takes something like what I'm doing—a moment that forces people to say to themselves, *Wait a minute, we can't let this happen anymore.* I think the harder certain politicians push against reproductive rights, the more of a fight they're going to have on their hands. And if I have something to do with starting that fight, then I couldn't be happier. No regrets at all."

Anderson Cooper said, "What do you think of the people who are calling you a spiritual terrorist?"

Karen said, "Not much. I don't believe in spirits, so I guess I don't accept the idea that I could be performing a terrorist act against spirituality. It's like calling me a unicorn murderer. I'd lump them into the same category as the people who think I've been sent to Earth by Satan to give birth to the Antichrist. I'd say it was laughable if it wasn't a crystal clear example of what I'm trying to expose—the Christian right's agenda to control women. I'm a woman who is taking absolute control of my body and my rights. Their immediate reaction is to invoke Satan and compare me to a terrorist. And it's those same Christians, who call me a spiritual terrorist and claim that I'm the mother of the Antichrist, who are urging their congregations not to donate. They use their religion to justify allowing this abortion to happen, the same religion they claim requires them to protect every unborn child's life. They can't have it both ways."

Anderson Cooper said, "I'm curious about this next question. How has this affected your personal life?"

Karen said, "Not very well. I guess that's accurate."

Anderson Cooper said, "Can you be a little more specific?"

Karen said, "Well, I had to talk to my parents about it once my identity was revealed, obviously."

Anderson Cooper said, "And how did that go?"

Karen said, "Again, not very well. They're not too happy with me. Ultimately I think they support me, because they know this is something I feel very strongly about. At least I hope I made that clear to them when we talked about it. But like any parents, I think they just want what's best for me, and they see the obvious potential for this to be very stressful."

Anderson Cooper said, "And what about the father of this baby?"

Karen said, "It's not a baby. It's a fetus at this point. But, to answer your question, he's, uh—he's sadly one of the relationships that hasn't survived through this process."

Anderson Cooper said, "Do you think he'd want to be a part of this child's life if you were to have the child?"

Karen said, "I can't speak for him, except to say that he doesn't want to be a part of any of this, and I'm respecting his decision by not making his name public and not involving him."

Anderson Cooper said, "Do you know if he's watching this interview?"

Karen said, "I don't." For the first time in the interview, Karen could feel her emotions overriding her intellect. She knew this would be one of the questions she was asked, so she was prepared for it, but the thought of Paul sitting in a new apartment somewhere watching this interview made her sad—because they were no longer together, but also because the image of the man she loved watching her on television as she was forced to speculate on his feelings about her decision seemed emasculating, and she never wanted to think of him that way.

Anderson Cooper said, "Okay, we've got a few questions now from Twitter."

Karen said, "Okay."

Anderson Cooper said, "The first question is from @joshpaulthorpe. He asks, 'Have you ever been pregnant before, and if so, have you had abortions before?'"

Karen said, "I'm not sure about the relevance of that question, but the answer is no."

Anderson Cooper said, "All right, @Revoredo6 tweeted, 'Does it comfort you or anger you to know that people all over the world are praying for you?'"

Karen said, "Neither. I obviously don't believe that whatever entity these people are praying to exists, so it's a waste of time, but it doesn't anger me. I think anyone and everyone should be allowed to spend their time however they like. I would say, on the issue of prayer in general, though—or, maybe it's more accurate to say, if you're a person out there who's praying, then I'd like to say this to you: If you think your god is listening to you and has the power to do anything, and you've never prayed for an end to human misery, war, disease, hunger, or anything of that ilk, then you're deplorable. If you have prayed to your god to end these things, then your god is deplorable. Either way, prayer seems to me like a waste of time."

Anderson Cooper said, "Moving on. @ChristianWoman7 asks, 'If someone else was doing what you were doing, would you donate to her website?'"

Karen said, "No, I wouldn't. I'm not pro-life in any way, and although I'd think what she was doing was interesting, I wouldn't donate."

Anderson Cooper said, "Let me ask you this: Do you think

you've received money so far from anyone who doesn't consider themselves pro-life, or from people who are outside of the Christian right?"

Karen said, "I can't be sure. It's obviously completely possible. I'm sure there have to be people who aren't Christian who have donated, but I personally can't see why anyone who was pro-choice would donate money, outside of a kind of celebrity-culture interest in what's going on, which is something I wanted to avoid through anonymity. They certainly wouldn't be donating on philosophical grounds."

Anderson Cooper said, "All right, and one final question from Twitter. @AprilLavalleyLaw asks, 'What's to stop other girls from copycatting this for their own financial gain, instead of for a social experiment?'"

This was something Karen had never thought about, and she paused before answering, "I guess at the moment nothing is stopping them from doing it. I think, though, that this is kind of a self-regulating idea. I have to believe that if someone else did this, and it was expressly for the purpose of making themselves money, very few people would give them money, and any girl who attempted something like this would very quickly find out that it wasn't worth the effort. And beyond the first girl who attempted it after me, I'd think no one would donate any money anyway. The idea will lose value with each successive attempt."

Anderson Cooper said, "I think you're probably right about that. Karen, thank you for sitting down with me tonight. I have to say that no matter what people think of what you're doing, it definitely seems that you've thought this out and that you have a purpose behind it all. I'm sure everyone, myself included, will be following this story to its conclusion, whatever it might be."

Anderson Cooper then turned back to the center camera and said, "My guest tonight has been Karen Holloway. I'm Anderson Cooper. Thanks for watching, and good night."

As Karen and Tanya drove back to Karen's apartment that night, Karen asked her friend what she thought of the interview. Tanya admitted that it was very good, that Karen came off as likable and intelligent. Karen checked her site from her phone and saw that in the course of the interview, a little more than a million dollars had come in.

chapter eighteen

Despite sending Pastor Preston several emails asking for an urgent meeting, James Dobbs had to wait a full week before he could see the minister. As he sat in the foyer of Woodstone Church waiting for Pastor Preston, who was fifteen minutes late, James thought about how much time he had spent in that church and in that town. He was nervous about starting what he expected to be the most important journey of his life, but he was excited. He knew that what he was about to do was important and needed to be done, not just for himself but for everyone on the planet. He felt that somehow this church had played a role in forming him as a person God had finally recognized as worthy of this task, worthy of carrying out his role in God's plan. James had many good memories in Woodstone, and he knew he would miss it after he left.

Pastor Preston was talking on his cell phone when he came

through the front doors. He said, "I know it's more expensive, but I think it's worth it. That's right. Black leather, with the same color black for the trim around the dash. Yeah. Okay, next Tuesday. It better be ready. I'll have one irate wife on my hands if it's not. All right, bye." Pastor Preston hung up and moved over to James as he said, "They've screwed up the interior of that car twice now. But you know what? I forgive them, because I'm a Christian, and I understand that things like this are just tests from God to see if we have the patience and love that he wants us all to have." He shook James's hand and said, "Okay, now, I got your emails. Seems like there's some important stuff going on, and I'm happy to consult you spiritually on anything you might need help with. That's what Jesus put me on this earth to do. Just let me get this coffee down, come into my office, and let's hear what you need to tell me."

James followed Pastor Preston into his office. He'd never been in it before. The walls were covered with pictures of Pastor Preston with various celebrities, Sarah Palin, Chuck Norris, and Kirk Cameron prominent among them. A glass case on one wall was full of trophies from various church-sponsored softball teams and choir groups. On the wall immediately behind Pastor Preston's desk was a giant painting of him and his wife holding hands as Jesus hovered above them, shining light down on them from his open hands. James wished he could have a relationship with a girl like Pastor Preston had with his wife.

Pastor Preston drank a last sip of coffee, threw the cup in the trash can next to his desk, sat down and said, "All right, now, let's do some work of the spirit. Before we start, let's join hands." James gave his hands to Pastor Preston, who bowed his head, closed his eyes, and said, "Heavenly Father, please fill me with your everlasting understanding and wisdom in this moment so that I may do what you have put me on this earth to do. Please help me guide the soul of this young man who sits with me in his hour of need so that he may do your bidding and carry out your holy plan. Amen."

James repeated, "Amen."

Pastor Preston said, "So, James, I know you know this, but I just want to take this opportunity to tell you again that you're really one of the rising stars here at Woodstone. I haven't had much time to talk to you after our rally the other week, but seriously, and I mean this with all of my heart, you're an inspiration, son. Truly. Christ sees what you do, and you should feel very, very good about that."

James thanked him for his compliments, and then Pastor Preston said, "So I'm more than happy to listen to whatever you want to tell me, and I'll do my best to help you however God sees fit. So what's the urgent thing you wanted to tell me about? Something with a new job opportunity? You're thinking about buying a new car? Don't tell me this has to do with a young lady? Not to toot my own angelic horn, but I'm very good with matters of the heart where they cross over with matters of the spirit."

James told Pastor Preston that it was none of those things. He explained to Pastor Preston that the sermon he gave on listening for God's voice was transformative for him. He told Pastor Preston that he had never heard God's voice in his entire life, and never really thought that it might have been because he wasn't an active enough listener. He told Pastor Preston that circumstances had come to be which allowed him three days off from work, and he felt that the number three had biblical significance in reference to Jesus rising from the dead on the third day after his crucifixion. He went on to tell Pastor Preston that he had used the entirety of those three days to remain awake, listening for God's voice, because he was certain that God had cleared his work schedule specifically for this purpose. He finished his story by telling Pastor Preston that on that third day without sleep, food, or water, he had indeed heard the voice of God, and that God had revealed a plan that he wanted James to follow—a purpose for his life.

Pastor Preston said, "That's incredible. Honestly, I couldn't be happier for you. Between that and our rally with the Anointed, it seems to me like you're entering your spiritual prime. We never know when or where God will choose to speak to us, but you were listening, and that's all he wants. So what did he say to you?"

James apologized to Pastor Preston for not being able to give him any details about the nature of his conversation with God. He told Pastor Preston that the conversation was private, and at God's behest he was unable to reveal anything. And even beyond that, God himself didn't reveal anything beyond the first step of his plan to James.

Pastor Preston said, "I see. Well, we each have our own relationship with God. I understand that more than most, I think. But if you didn't come here today to speak with me about what God told you, then what exactly do you need my help with, son?"

James explained he needed some help carrying out the plan, and he assured Pastor Preston that the plan was of great importance to everyone, not just him.

Pastor Preston said, "Of course. I'd be more than happy to help any of God's children follow their path, especially someone like you who is so obviously devoted to an unwavering Christian life."

James explained that his plan would very likely require many things, and that most of them he knew would be provided by God as they were needed. But the first thing he needed, the thing that would enable him to initiate the plan God set out for him, was very simple, and it was something he knew Woodstone could easily help him with. He told Pastor Preston that he needed enough money to get to California, the place that God told him he had to get to, the place where he would be used in the service of God's ultimate plan. He went on to say that he didn't need much money, and he was happy to travel by bus if it was easier for the church financially.

Pastor Preston said, "And what's in California, James?"

James explained that God hadn't told him exactly what he

would have to do in California, but that even if he had, James still wouldn't be at liberty to say. God did tell him not to divulge the details of the conversation with anyone. The reason he needed to go to California was between him and God.

Pastor Preston said, "I see. Well, James, I guess the best thing I can tell you is that sometimes we want to hear God so badly, and we strain so hard to hear his voice, that we think we heard him when we really didn't. It's kind of like when you're so hot that you get the chills. When it's a hundred degrees out, and your air conditioner is on the fritz, and you want to feel a little breeze so badly, sometimes you feel things that aren't there. The same thing can happen with God's voice. And I understand how devout you are. I know you're not just trying to get a free trip to California out of the church, and I know you've been waiting to hear his voice and you will, son, but I don't think he told you to go to California."

James couldn't understand why Pastor Preston was questioning the validity of his conversation with God. Of all people, he assumed Pastor Preston would be as excited as he was about the event and more than happy to help in any way he needed. James tried to explain a second time as clearly as possible that he really did hear God. There was no mistaking his voice or his message. He reminded Pastor Preston that he had always told his congregation that the reason Woodstone was created was to help those who are truly faithful, and James was definitely faithful. He asked Pastor Preston how he could rationalize turning away a member of the Anointed when that member was asking for help carrying out God's plan.

Pastor Preston said, "That's a good question, James. I'm a pastor. That means I've been called on by Almighty God to spread his word, to gather those who follow in the teachings of his son, Jesus Christ, and to be used as he sees fit. I talk with God every day, James, and I know how he works, and I don't mean to take anything away from the experience you had. But take it from me, as someone who has had much more spiritual experience than you, if he wanted me to help you go to California, then why would he have told you nothing else about the trip? That just doesn't make sense. And besides that, why would he have had a whole conversation with you, knowing that you'd come to me to ask for help, but then not tell me you'd be coming? Wouldn't he have spoken to me, as the minister of his word?"

James reminded Pastor Preston that God works in mysterious ways, and that no one should question his motives or his actions or presume to know his plans.

Pastor Preston paused for a moment. The logic of James's argument was difficult to deny. He was aware that he himself had delivered several sermons making that very point. He eventually said, "You're right about that, James. I certainly don't know everything God knows about his plans. but I can tell you that in all my years as pastor of Woodstone, I've never sat in this seat and had a member of my congregation ask me directly for money to take a trip, and just as you believe that you heard God telling you to go to California, I can hear him right now telling me that I just can't help you get there. So, while it's obviously impossible for me to know everything about your relationship with God, I can tell you that I know mine better than anyone, and right now I have to obey his command. If God does intend for you to take this journey, it seems like he might have some lessons to teach you along the way that he knows you can only learn by doing it yourself, without help from anyone but him."

James took what Pastor Preston said at face value. Then James asked Pastor Preston, since he was in direct contact with God at that moment, if he could ask God how James was supposed to get to California.

Pastor Preston said, "Okay, I suppose I can do that. Almighty Father, can you please help this young man on his way and deliver to him the knowledge and resources that he needs to carry out your heavenly plan?"

The two men waited in silence for a few seconds before Pastor Preston said, "I'm sorry son. He's silent."

James lowered his head. Pastor Preston could tell he was disappointed, and said, "Listen, James, don't let this get to you. Sometimes God makes our journey more difficult to teach us a lesson. And even if you don't end up getting to California, God will still favor you, and he will still love you, because you're one of his children."

James reminded Pastor Preston that he had no choice in the matter. He had to get to California. He had to carry out God's plan. There was no alternative. He told Pastor Preston that he would do whatever it took to get there.

As James stood and walked out of Pastor Preston's office he turned back and he told the Pastor that no matter what would come to pass, he would forgive him for turning him away when he needed help the most, just as Jesus did with Peter.

chapter
nineteen

Karen woke up, and before she brushed her teeth or showered, she rolled over and checked her laptop, which was sitting on her nightstand. The donations were up to a little more than nine and a half million dollars. After spiking during the interview, in the past week the money had been slowing down. She caught herself thinking about the very real possibility that she might have to get an abortion. Although that was the outcome she wanted, the outcome that would prove her point, she couldn't help thinking that all this work would seem like a waste if the pregnancy was terminated. As soon as the thought crossed her mind, however, she rejected it as the work of her hormones.

She sat up and scratched her breasts. They had become itchy with regularity as they grew in size. As she reached down to scratch her stomach, which was also increasing in size, creating visible stretch marks near her belly button, she felt something jarring inside. It was unmistakably a kick. She quickly put her hand over the spot where she felt the movement and waited for several seconds, but it did not repeat. She gently rubbed her stomach and hoped she wouldn't have to endure many more experiences like that. She could sense her resolve weakening in the face of some innate maternal instinct. Despite her rational understanding that she didn't want this child, didn't want to be a mother, Karen's ability to view the child as merely a tool in her experiment was getting strained. She knew that things would become far more complicated than they already were, but there was nothing to be done about that.

Her first step out of bed was difficult. Her back hurt, her feet and hands were slightly swollen, and one of her legs was numb. Karen had taken to sleeping on her side in order to mitigate some of these symptoms of the pregnancy, but now it seemed that even this strategy was yielding her no viable results. She reminded herself to ask her doctor on the next visit about sleeping techniques that might help her through these advancing stages of the pregnancy.

She showered, brushed her teeth and her hair, and urinated for the second time since she woke up. Then she put on her most flattering maternity dress. She hated the maternity clothes she'd had to start wearing due to her increased size. They were just another symbol to Karen of the ills of pregnancy, another identifier of her inability to be normal because she was a woman carrying a fetus.

She got in her car and drove to UCLA, where she had been summoned to meet with a board of advisors, including Professor Noone. On the way there she listened to NPR, which was running a story about her. As Karen listened, a woman who ran a Planned Parenthood clinic in Texas explained that while she supported Karen's right to launch her project, and applauded her for standing up to the right-wing extremists who wanted to control women, she felt that Karen's website challenge would ultimately make getting an abortion in her home state even harder than it already was. She explained that laws had already been passed, largely by the white Christian men who dominated the Texas state legislature, that were designed to make it virtually impossible for most Planned Parenthood locations and other medical abortion providers to stay open. She claimed that Karen's website had prompted a discussion in the legislature that could potentially spur the state government to redefine personhood as beginning at conception, which would render even the morning-after pill illegal.

This argument had become more prominent in recent weeks. People who claimed to be on her side, who claimed to understand and support her efforts, were becoming more vocal about the website's potential detrimental effects on the availability of legal abortions in states with conservative governments. Karen had no sympathy for their complaints, though. She felt that people who had a problem with the way things were being run should take a stand of their own. She knew that committing herself to this cause would fuel a new debate about abortion, to a level that it hadn't seen since *Roe v. Wade,* and that's what she wanted. She was tired of conservative, religiously motivated legislators chipping away at women's rights in America while rational citizens and politicians, who were in the clear majority, did nothing. She had come to despise liberal supporters of abortion rights as they accepted the implementation of endless new hoops and burdens when it came to securing legal and safe abortions. She knew the people she would anger by doing this would use it as leverage to push their agenda, and she wanted that. Karen thought that if pro-life activists pushed it far enough, rational Americans would finally push back, and with luck they would push hard enough that the argument would be resolved for good. But the NPR story, and other recent stories she'd heard, suggested that this might not be the case.

As she parked her car at UCLA, she noticed that she had been followed into the garage by campus security. She got out of her car and asked, "Do you need something?"

The security officers explained that they didn't need anything, but they'd been alerted to her arrival and wanted to make sure she got to her advisory meeting safely. Karen hadn't thought she'd need an escort, but when she came out of the garage, she was glad she had one. Students were lined up and down the walkways and streets that ran through the campus. Some were supportive of her, holding signs and wearing T-shirts with slogans like "Karen for President" and "Girl Power," along with pictures of Karen's face. Others, though, held signs reading, "You and Your Baby Will Burn in Hell," and "Your Mother Should Have Aborted You." This group screamed at Karen as she walked through campus, and their screams set off responses from her supporters. She hoped her presence on campus wouldn't cause a riot, but that seemed possible. As she made her way to her meeting, she became aware for the first time that she had become a celebrity, which was the last thing she wanted.

Security escorted her through the crowds and into Dodd Hall, where she was asked to wait outside a conference room. She knew what the meeting was about. The discovery of her identity and her CNN appearance must have attracted the attention of people at UCLA higher up than Professor Noone. She guessed that the meeting was to determine whether she'd be allowed to stay in the PhD program. She had seen other students get kicked out of the program, but usually for lack of attendance or failure to meet deadlines. On rare occasions, a student might be asked to leave based on some extracurricular behavior that was a breach of the school's code of conduct. But she had done none of these things. To her knowledge, she had given the university no legitimate grounds to dismiss her.

A few minutes later, an assistant showed her into the conference room where Professor Noone was waiting with the dean of the philosophy school and two other professors whose classes she'd taken. She sat down across the table from them, and Professor Noone said, "Thanks for coming in, Karen."

Karen said, "I didn't think I had a choice."

The dean, whom Karen had met several times at various philosophy school functions over the past few years, said, "I don't know if that was meant to be a joke, but this is no laughing matter, Ms. Holloway."

Whether a God did or did not exist was irrelevant to humanity. The only relevant thing where God was concerned was the debate over its existence, and the continued intellectual pursuit of the idea of God. The universe was vast, but it was unlikely that we would ever get to see much of it, or truly interact with any of it, beyond the small speck of dust we called Earth. So while every intellectual pursuit obviously had some inherent value, the sciences of space were not as important to the human race as those of Earth, which included biology, geology, chemistry, and mathematics, but also philosophy. Philosophy was the most valuable of all sciences. It was what gave us guidelines by which we could exist and think. It was what ordered our thoughts, from the first terrified instincts that enabled us to survive as we crawled out of the primordial ooze, into great volumes of knowledge and understanding of the world around us. Any other pursuit, although potentially worthwhile in its own right, simply wasn't as important or meaningful. These were things that the dean of the philosophy school understood to be true.

The dean continued, "We obviously called you here today because of recent events that have come to our attention concerning your—how should we call it—experiment?"

Karen said, "Okay."

The dean said, "While we applaud the idea, we have some misgivings regarding your application of the idea. Our Department of Philosophy isn't merely a place at which students can achieve their PhD status. It's a family, and we must decide at all times whether the people in that family are upholding the same principles that we are, and that this school has for so many years. I can tell you that some of us here on the advisory board felt you should be dismissed from the program without a second thought. They felt that what you've done is immoral, beyond justification. I can also tell you that some of us did not feel that way. Some of us chose to insist that this is a school of philosophy, and that if we didn't at least give you an opportunity to argue your own position, we'd be acting against one of the most fundamental aspects of the science we've all chosen as a profession. So, Ms. Holloway, you are here today to make us understand why you are doing what you are doing. And I sincerely hope this is something you can do."

Karen knew in that moment there was almost nothing she could say to save herself. She knew the dean was very likely among those on the board who wanted her dismissed without an argument, and that ultimately his vote, if they even put it to a vote, would carry the most weight. The dean was old, and he was traditional, and in some ways she thought he was just as bad as the close-minded conservatives she was fighting against. She thought about walking out without saying another word. But this was her only chance to explain herself to Professor Noone, and he was a good advisor and the person who was responsible, at least in part, for her decision to come to UCLA in the first place. Some part of her was sorry for doing this against his advice, and she wanted him to know that. And if there was any slight chance that she could remain in the program, she thought it might be by appealing to the board members' sense of academic curiosity. Perhaps there was a chance, however small, that she could remind them of how they felt when they were young philosophy students trying to do something that mattered.

She said, "First of all, I just want it on the record that Professor Noone warned me not to do this. I acted against his advice, and he shouldn't be held responsible in any way."

The dean said, "Understood."

She said, "Okay. Well, let me explain how I came to the decision to do this. I've had a tough time figuring out what my dissertation would be. I've had a few extensions, but not because I was being lazy or because I didn't know enough to grind out a standard dissertation, the kind of thing you've all read a hundred times before. I was hesitating because I wanted to do something that would matter—not just here at UCLA or even in the broader world of academic philosophy, but in the real world."

The dean said, "Well, you've certainly got the world's attention with this stunt. Whether or not it will matter remains to be seen."

She said, "I understand that. When I was applying to PhD programs, I came to UCLA because of the work of some of the faculty here, Professor Noone included. It was work that was important, that wouldn't just sit in a library somewhere, but that might actually change the way people think and experience the world. To me, that's what philosophy really is. It's presenting ideas to the world that they've never seen or thought about before—ideas that force people to think differently. And when you do that, you change the world."

The dean said, "We understand that, obviously. But you could have just as easily presented this idea or this scenario theoretically, in a paper, and there would have been no problem. Instead, you insisted on putting this idea into action. You've taken it far out of the realm of academia, out of the realm of thought. You've crossed the line from intellectual discourse into conduct, and it's your conduct that has given us cause for alarm—and quite possibly put yourself at personal risk. If your advisor warned you against pursuing this idea, why did you feel you had to carry it out?"

Karen said, "Well, the idea originally came to me when I found out I was pregnant. I honestly don't think I would have arrived at it otherwise. And the first time the idea popped in my head—and I'm sure you've all had this experience—I immediately felt like it was important, it was good, it was possibly the best thing I would do in my life. I knew that without action, without making it real, it would be lost in the shuffle of academic papers and journals. I just didn't feel like I could let that happen. I knew that the idea by itself wasn't enough."

The dean said, "But I assure you, it *was* enough. I agree with you—we all do, in fact—that this idea is significant. It demands discussion. But making it real almost perverts the purity of the idea. The debate has become about you now, Ms. Holloway, not about your ideas."

Karen said, "I know, and I'm sorry for that. My plan was to remain anonymous, specifically to preserve the purity of the idea. But the idea was so big that I got sucked into it. Once it became national news, it was really only a matter of time before someone figured out who I was. Would it have made any difference to you if I would have remained anonymous? I mean, if you had known and the rest of the advisory board had known, but not the world?"

The question seemed to surprise the dean. He said, "I'm not sure, to be honest. I would never have approved this, if that's what you're asking."

Karen said, "It's not what I'm asking. I'm asking something different: If I had done this, if the site was live and people were donating millions of dollars and the public debate was happening just as it is now, but my identity was still unknown—and then I revealed myself to you and the board—would that make this any different?"

The dean said, "I suppose it would."

Karen was infuriated by the dean's response, which she had foreseen. She said, "So then this is all just about public perception of the school. It has nothing to do with my work at all."

The dean said, "That's not true."

Karen said, "Of course it is. If you would have been all right with me doing this in secret, what else could this meeting be about? It's because you can't have the UCLA Department of Philosophy associated with what might be considered a controversial idea. This, by the way, is exactly why I didn't just write a paper. People out there in the world would never even have known about this. The debate that's now going on across the country would never have happened. I would have written a paper, some of you would have read it, I would have gotten my PhD, and that would have been it. But now it's out there. It's in the world. And I think there's some part of you that hates not having control over it. Maybe that's really what this is about. I don't know, but I do know this: I didn't get into philosophy so that I could become one of you, sitting across this table, telling students that philosophy should be explored safely within the confines of academia. I got into it to make people think differently. And that's what I'm doing right now. Are any of you?"

The dean said, "I think we've heard enough. Thank you for your time, Ms. Holloway. Professor Noone will contact you shortly with our decision on your future as a PhD candidate here at UCLA."

Karen walked out into the hallway, still furious. The hypocrisy of academia was frustrating to her. She knew the work she was doing was more important than anything the people on that advisory board had done in the past two decades. If she did get kicked out of the program, she decided, she'd wear it as a badge of honor.

On the drive home, she tuned to an '80s station, hoping to avoid hearing anyone else passing judgment on her. Between the oldies, though, even the DJ made a few comments about her. There was no escaping what she had become.

As she pulled up to the apartment she once shared with Paul, she got an email from Professor Noone. It read, "Karen, I'm sorry to give you this news over email, but the advisory board has decided to dismiss you from the program. The board concluded that your actions are inconsistent with the type of candidate we support in the UCLA philosophy program. You'll get a formal notice shortly, but I felt you should know as soon as possible."

Even though this was the outcome she had expected, Karen was still stung by the news. She wondered if she could salvage any kind of career after being kicked out of a PhD program. She had never really wanted to be a professor, necessarily, but that was the obvious career path for someone with a PhD in philosophy. She hoped that some school out there would accept her and let her finish her PhD, but maybe not. Maybe they were all unwilling to see their students' work live in the real world, not just in books and papers.

She pulled into her parking spot at her apartment building, got out of her car, and started calling Tanya to tell her what happened. Before she could hit the call button, however, she heard someone a few feet away yell, "*Slut!*"

God was good all the time, and he created men and women to live on the earth and to seek happiness through him. God created women to bear children and to care for men. The universe and anything beyond Earth was unimportant because it wasn't mentioned in the Bible. Sex was something that should occur only between one man and one woman, and always at the man's behest. A woman was to obey any command given to her by her husband. Any disobedience was a sin for which the man had a God-given right to punish her. Children were sacred and pure, especially girls, and they should remain that way until their wedding day, when God blesses them to protect them from the sins they are about to commit in order to consummate their marriage. These were things that the stranger understood to be true.

Karen turned and saw a man standing on the grass near one of the windows of her apartment. He said, "You're going to burn in hell, you filthy slut."

Karen hurried to her door without responding. She was scared that she might be attacked, but the man stayed put, and she was able to get inside and lock the door behind her. When she looked out her window, the man was still there, looking in at her. He said, "You won't get away with what you're doing. You know that, right? God punishes those who are impure."

Karen closed her blinds and called the police. By the time they showed up, the man was gone. She gave a detailed description of the man, and when she asked if the police could leave someone outside her door for protection, they told her that if they posted an officer outside every woman's door who had a guy calling her a slut, they'd have no one left to stop the real crimes. Before they left, they suggested she buy a gun.

chapter
twenty

James Dobbs counted out all the money he had in the world, some of which he had made from selling most of his belongings in a yard sale. In total, he had a little more than twelve hundred dollars. This was enough, he thought, to make it to California if he was frugal. Once he got there, he felt certain that God would provide him with whatever else he might need to fulfill his role in God's plan.

As he put the money in his pocket he looked at the things that were left over from his yard sale, the things no one had bought. There weren't many items. A set of pots and pans, an alarm clock, a framed print of a quote from the Bible—Mark 12:31, *You shall love your neighbor as yourself*—a few pairs of shoes, and four packs of unopened dental floss. He felt bad throwing these items away, but he knew they would be of no use to him from that moment on.

He put the items into a box and walked toward the community dumpster in the back of the parking lot of his apartment complex. As he approached it, he saw his next-door neighbor approaching it as well, carrying a bag of trash. As they met at the dumpster, James held the lid open for him to toss in his trash bag and his neighbor said, "I saw you out here earlier. Yard sale, huh? Just doing some spring cleaning or are you moving?"

God was ruler and creator of everything. Jesus Christ was his son. Neither of these entities cared if you were straight or gay or how you voted or about anything else other than how you treated other people. The universe was vast, and somewhere in it, God must have created other forms of life. The purpose of these other forms of life would likely never be known to humanity, which would likely never even encounter it. Sex was something that could be indulged in for fun or for procreation. The beauty of it was that it was so versatile, and this was the way God had made it. Children were good, and necessary to further the human race, but not everyone should have them, and in some cases, remaining childless was the most honest decision a person could make. These were things that James's neighbor understood to be true.

James explained that he was going on a trip and he didn't know how long he'd be gone, so he had sold some of his belongings for extra money to help him fund his travels.

His neighbor said, "Oh. Are you keeping the apartment?"

James told his neighbor that he wasn't keeping the place, because he didn't know how long he'd be gone or if he'd ever come back, but he didn't know who was moving in after him. He submitted his notice to the building manager and that was that. He further explained that he also quit his job.

His neighbor said, "Wow, clean break and a fresh start. That actually sounds really nice, man. I think most people wish they could do something like that. Well, for what it's worth, I know we didn't really get to know each other or anything, but you were a great neighbor, man. About the best anyone could ask for. Quiet and everything, you know?"

James thanked his neighbor and told him that he was sorry they never got a chance to sit down and have a conversation. He thought that they might have gotten along pretty well, maybe even become friends.

His neighbor said, "Yeah, probably. So when are you leaving? Are you around tonight? Maybe get a beer or something?"

James told his neighbor that he was leaving as soon as he finished with the trash. He was looking forward to the next chapter in his life and he couldn't wait to start. Then, as James raised the box with the leftover items toward the dumpster, he saw the framed print of the quote from Mark 12:31. Feeling that this might be another sign from God, he took the framed print out of the box and asked his neighbor if he'd have a spot somewhere in his apartment for it.

His neighbor said, "Uh, yeah, I think I could find a spot. You sure you don't want to just take this with you, though? It's nice. You can hang it up in your next place."

James became immediately nervous. Perhaps he'd overstepped, or perhaps this man wasn't even Christian. James asked him what his spiritual affiliation was.

His neighbor said, "Oh, I'm Christian. Don't get me wrong, I think it's nice, and it's very nice of you, too. I just didn't want to take something that seems to be kind of important to you, you know? I mean, if it's something that was personal to you, you should keep it."

James was relieved that his neighbor was Christian. He explained that he felt it was fitting he should give it to his neighbor, especially because they didn't really know one another. It made the act even more reflective of the true meaning of the passage.

James's neighbor accepted the gift and said, "Well, thank you. I'll definitely put it up in my kitchen tonight."

James told his neighbor that would make him happy, and that

he'd think about it when he was on the road. Then James lifted the box and tossed the other remnants in the dumpster.

His neighbor said, "Well, thanks for this, really. It was way too nice of you. Have a safe trip and good luck with whatever you're doing next."

James thanked him and wished him well. His neighbor walked back up into his apartment and James made his way to his car. He had nothing now except his car, his phone, and the money in his pocket. He had no plan beyond getting to California—he had decided to head for Los Angeles unless God directed him elsewhere—and he had no means of supporting himself. He knew he should have been nervous, but he wasn't. Instead James felt free and exhilarated. He felt free from the normal burdens that most people are shackled by. He had no more reason to worry about his bills or his job. Like a knife freshly sharpened and lying on the butcher's block ready to be used, James felt honed to a point by God himself. He knew God was watching every move he made with great interest, and he wouldn't disappoint him.

As James pulled out of the parking lot he took one last look back at the complex. He had spent his entire adult life living in that one-bedroom apartment, and there was some small part of him that was sad to be leaving, but he knew that was just the Devil trying to make him second-guess what he knew he had to do. He got in his car, turned out into the street, and headed for the highway. As he did, he said a prayer thanking God for this opportunity and promising God that he wouldn't fail.

chapter
twenty-one

Karen got out of her car and looked in the backseat, where she kept a few boxes of things and some clothes. She thought briefly about taking some of them out, but her back and hips were sore, and she hoped her father would help her later. She turned from her car and looked up at her parents' house. She hadn't lived there since she was in high school, and although she had no intention of moving back in with them, she did feel a strange sense of unwilling nostalgia creeping in. She forced herself to purge the idea, which would be a setback in her life. Staying with them now was just something she had to do given the circumstances. Her apartment was no longer safe.

As she knocked on the door, she began to dread the conversation she knew she'd have to have with her parents. She didn't know if it would happen immediately or the next morning or a month after she'd been living with them, but she knew she'd have to sit down and answer their questions. She hoped, though, that for a time they'd just be happy to have her back in the house.

Her mother was usually the one who answered the door at their house. She remembered that from her childhood, and had always wondered how those roles had developed between her parents. This time, though, they answered the door together. Her mother, Lynn, hugged her, already crying, and said, "My baby girl, are you all right?"

God was something that each person could define for themselves. It wasn't necessarily a sentient entity that created everything, but maybe it was some kind of unifying energy that flowed through everything. Certainly there was something that every person carried inside, which conveyed a spirit or an animated quality that other animals didn't share, and this was too subtle and complex to be rationalized away as a simple product of the physical organ known as the human brain. Although human beings were a part of the natural world, we were set apart in a real and significant way. Sex wasn't sacred, but if it was in the context of a relationship with a person you cared about deeply, it could be much more than just a physical act. Children were not special or unique, but the relationships you developed with them were, and raising a child correctly was far more important than simply having the child. These were things that Karen's mother understood to be true.

Karen's father, Robert, hugged her next and said, "You know, we're going to have to talk about things. Get inside. Dinner's on the table. Let's eat, and then we can talk. Give me your keys, and I'll get whatever you have in the car."

The idea of God was interesting and if implemented properly, had obvious benefits where the organization of societies was concerned. But never in history had it been implemented properly. It had only ever been used as an instrument of discrimination and subjugation. The universe was largely unknown, and it seemed increasingly likely that its nature would never be fully understood by humanity before we destroyed ourselves in one way or another. But the pursuit of that understanding was still of value. Sexual interaction was necessary for the furtherance of the species, and the psychosocial components of it seemed to have become more important in modern society than the function. This was neither good nor bad, simply the way things were. Having children was a serious decision that should be made only after significant thought and planning. If a child was conceived through accidental means, abortion was certainly a viable option, but so was keeping the child and finding ways to do the best you could in the service of providing that child a life with all the benefits possible, as he had done with Lynn when she became pregnant with Karen. These were things that Robert understood to be true.

Karen said, "Thanks, Dad. There are a few things, not much, just some boxes and clothes." Then she followed her mother into the kitchen, where dinner was waiting.

At first they ate quietly, with all participants reluctant to start the conversation. Her mother seemed hesitant to address the obvious issue, though she certainly wanted answers. Finally, her father took the initiative and said, "So, what exactly is going on? We haven't heard from you except for one short phone call since all of this started happening."

Karen said, "That's not true. I've sent texts when Mom has texted me."

Karen's mother said, "That's not what we're talking about. You know that."

Karen took a deep breath and said, "Okay. I guess I'm doing a kind of experiment. That's really about it."

Karen's father said, "An experiment? That's what you're calling this? Karen, you just showed up at our door with a car full of clothes because you don't feel safe at your place anymore. How is that an experiment?"

Karen said, "I actually think it's a good sign. It means that what I'm doing is affecting people."

Karen's mother said, "It's affecting us. We saw you on TV, your interview. We're so worried about you."

Karen said, "Don't worry about me. I'm all right."

Karen's father said, "You're clearly not. Paul's gone. You got expelled."

Karen said, "How did you know about that?"

Karen's mother said, "It was on the news."

Karen's father said, "And how long do you think you can stay here before we've got weirdos lurking around in our bushes?"

Karen said, "Mom, Dad, I'm really grateful that you're letting me stay here. I'm not going to take that for granted. No one knows I'm here, and I'm going to be careful about when I leave and where I go. It will be fine. And then, once this ends, I'll go back to my place and things will go back to normal."

Karen's father said, "I don't know if you've really thought this through, honey. Things probably won't ever go back to normal for you. You're a national figure now—hell, a global figure, I'd guess. And if you end up having this baby, that child will be a national figure for his or her entire life and you'll be tied to that story for the rest of yours."

Karen said, "Well, I doubt I'm going to get the money. The donations have started to slow down. So you don't have to worry about it."

Karen's mother said, "Why are we not talking about the thing we should be talking about here? Why are you doing this at all? Did we do a bad job raising you or something?"

Karen said, "Mom, no, of course not. You did a great job. I know you guys might disagree with what I'm doing, but I'm doing something that I feel needs to be done, something that's important to me. I'm not asking you to be okay with it. I know you're not, but I am asking you to help me because I'm your daughter and I need help."

Karen's father said, "We're obviously helping you. You're staying with us. And we understand that this is important to you. But

I think what your mom is getting at is, why do you even feel the need to do this?"

Karen said, "Because this country is fucked up. The way women are treated is terrible, and it's getting worse. That, and because I just felt like I didn't want my life to be wasted at school doing meaningless work that no one cares about. I wanted to do something that would get people thinking and maybe even change the way they think."

Karen's mother said, "You've always been a troublemaker. Even as a little girl. There was this cute little boy you used to play with who lived next door to us when you were very little. He used to tell you that he was going to marry you, and you'd tell him you were never getting married to anyone. One day he showed up to our door with one of those candy rings and told me he was going to ask for your hand in marriage that day and he wanted my blessing. So I gave it to him, and I let him out in the backyard where you were playing with our old dog, Molly. He walked up to you, got down on one knee, held out that ring, and asked you to marry him. Do you remember what you did?"

Karen said, "I don't remember any of this. I remember you telling this story a million times, but I don't remember the actual event at all."

Karen's mother continued on without pausing to register Karen's comments. She said, "You said, 'I'd never marry anyone who would kneel for anything.' Then you took that ring from him, put it in your mouth, and crunched off all of the candy in a few quick seconds while he sat there with his mouth hanging open. You handed him back the plastic part of the ring, with no candy left on it, and he started crying. I was watching from the doorway and I laughed pretty hard at the time, I'll admit it. But I knew we were in trouble from that day forward."

Karen laughed and said, "I think I'd still do the same thing today."

Karen's father said, "I think we all know that your mother and

I are never going to fully get why you want to do this, but we're here for you and we just want you to be safe and careful."

Karen said, "I will be."

They ate dinner without any further discussion of Karen's website or how it was affecting her life. They talked instead about what Robert was doing at work and what Lynn was planning for some new additions to their home. When they finished eating, they watched television together for a few hours until Lynn and Robert went to bed and Karen was left alone.

Before she unpacked her things, she went outside into her parents' backyard. They lived far enough out of the city that the sky was darker, and the stars were brighter than she was used to at her apartment. She remembered as a child spending hours in that backyard, lying in the grass looking out into space and wondering what might be out there. Her favorite thing to imagine was some other creature on some other planet lying down in some alien version of a backyard, looking out into their equivalent of the night sky and wondering if anyone was looking back. And then she'd imagine a million more planets with a million more creatures doing the exact same thing. Even as a child, Karen understood that the universe was vast and rich, and she lamented how she would very likely never get to see all the mystery and beauty that it held. She would very likely never even get to see all of the mystery and beauty held even on her tiny speck of dust called Earth.

After a few minutes of contemplating the endless possibilities of the universe, and forgetting why she was staying with her parents, Karen went back inside to settle into her bedroom.

It was strange being back in the room where she grew up. It hadn't really been changed since the day she left for college. The room had been dusted and vacuumed over the years, but her parents had never turned the room into anything else. They'd never felt the need to use the space for anything other than the memories it held.

Karen looked at pictures of herself from high school and tried to remember the events they captured. She hadn't thought about the boy she went to prom with for a very long time. In high school she was the president of the feminism club, which had only two other members. She regularly openly debated boys about the irrelevance of sports and sports culture. She tried to convince any girl she saw wearing a boy's letterman jacket that it was a symbol of his ownership over her. She made better grades than everyone else in her class, and took pride in it. And she could regularly be found in the cafeteria during her lunch period talking with female teachers about the inequality of pay between themselves and their male counterparts. Karen was certain that no boy would ask her to prom, and she was fine with that. Not only would she view it as a personal victory if no boys had the courage to ask her, not a single boy stood out in her mind as a worthy candidate anyway. So when this boy in the photo, whose name she could no longer remember, asked her to prom, she was shocked enough that she accepted. The boy, who sat next to her in calculus, was smart, and seemed well-intentioned enough, and prom was a rite of passage that Karen felt she should experience, if only to make her more informed in denouncing it.

She had viewed the idea of prom as purely platonic, but her date had other ideas. As the night wore on at their table, where they remained the entire night because Karen refused to dance, he told her that he'd had a crush on her for the entire year and he'd just been too afraid to talk to her because she was so intense. She remembered laughing at him, and she had always felt bad about that. He asked her if she wanted to go to an after-party a friend of his was throwing because his parents were out of town. She agreed, resigned to carry out this experience to its conclusion, to fully engage in prom.

Once at the party, she quickly became aware that it wasn't really a party. Four other couples were there at the house, along with three six-packs of beer. Shortly after Karen and her date arrived, most of the couples went off to find their own secluded spot in the house, and he suggested they do the same. Karen told him that she had no interest in having sex with him that night, and he argued that they should. He wasn't forceful about it, instead trying to appeal to her logical sensibilities to get what he wanted. She thought it was amusing then, and still did, but she also realized how lucky she was, that it could have been much worse.

He told her that if she actually was interested intellectually in the full experience of prom, as she'd said a dozen times that night, then logically she should also want to engage in the most common culmination of such a night. He further argued that, even if it was bad, it would only strengthen whatever final negative judgment she would pass on the tradition as a whole. And if it was good, that that would give her at least one element of the night that she actually enjoyed, and that would be a victory in itself.

It was a sound argument, but Karen refused him bluntly, and the two of them shared a beer while they listened to another couple have sex very loudly in the next room before she asked her date to take her home. At the time the experience was absurd to Karen, but now in retrospect it was very sweet in its simplicity. She knew she'd never again in her life have an experience that simple.

She went to a dresser and started putting some of her clothes away, trying to ignore the pain in her lower back. She noticed one of her favorite pictures of her mother in a tiny frame on top of the dresser. It was taken the day before Karen was born. Her mother, Lynn, was smiling, standing in their backyard with the sun shining behind her and her hands on her belly. She wondered if her mother and father had ever thought about aborting her, or if they'd known from the beginning that they wanted to have a child. They never had a second, and she always assumed she was an accident they couldn't bring themselves to correct, and Karen always felt some guilt about that, even though she knew it was irrational.

She moved the picture from the dresser to her nightstand and looked at it as she lay in bed, resting on her side in an effort to ease the cramps she was starting to feel in her legs. Her mother had always described it as a picture of the last day the world was "Karenless." She knew that eventually the world would be without her again, but before she left it, she was determined to change it.

chapter
twenty-two

James had been driving for much longer than he ever had before in a single trip. It was starting to take its toll on him physically. His shoulders and legs were sore, his eyes were getting heavy, and the landscape was less and less stimulating as he moved through the Oklahoma Panhandle and into the Texas Panhandle along Highway 54. Everything was flat, and there were few buildings in the small towns he passed through. James thought that this was God's way of preparing him for whatever he would need to do once he got to California, of removing any distractions so that he could mentally strengthen himself. James knew that once he arrived in California he would have to remain vigilant against Satan's efforts to distract him from whatever the subsequent steps of God's plan would be. Worse yet, he knew that Satan might try to trick him into believing in a false goal. God hadn't yet revealed his entire plan, and James suspected that Satan might see this as an opportunity to make him fail. After all, James was carrying out God's will, which would necessarily be counter to Satan's own plans for humanity. He would encounter distractions of all kinds. There would be confusion. There would be temptation. And once he got to his ultimate goal in Los Angeles, once he was close enough to be a serious threat to Satan's own plans, there would likely be hopelessness and despair. James knew he would have to overcome all of this in order to succeed for God. He thanked God for giving him this time in the beginning of his journey to focus, to clear his mind and purify his spirit.

James felt his stomach churn and realized he hadn't eaten since he got in his car and started driving. The pain in his stomach reminded him of what he'd felt at the end of the first day of his fast. He remembered the pain fondly, but he was glad he wouldn't have to continue feeling it for two more days. He had brought no food with him on his trip, because he knew that God would provide for him. James began thinking about finding a grocery store, but then he saw what he took to be a sign from God. It was a Dairy Queen sign just off the highway in Dalhart, Texas.

No other fast-food restaurant would have had the same personal meaning to James as the Dairy Queen, and he knew that God knew this. When James was young, his first foster family had been devoutly Christian. His foster father was strict and physically abusive, though he always justified the abuse with the Bible. James couldn't understand this rationale as a child, but as an adult he reflected on the times his first foster father would whip him and his foster brothers and sisters with a car antenna, and understood that pain can sometimes be a better teacher, a better expression of love, than anything else. But as a child he had found this impossible to understand.

While he was with that foster family, Dairy Queen was his favorite place. James had a Sunday School teacher who was kind to him, and she would take all the children from her Sunday

School class to Dairy Queen every Sunday. She'd buy them ice cream and encourage them to get to know one another, and it seemed that she chose to express her love and obedience to God through compassion and understanding. It was a brief reprieve from his foster father, and the caring his Sunday School teacher showed him was unique in his life at the time. As a result, Dairy Queen was the place he most closely associated with happiness as a child. It was the place where he felt closest to God.

His foster father's temper was not confined to his wards, however, and eventually the man beat his wife so badly that he was sentenced to some time in jail and their foster children were all removed and dispersed to other foster homes. He wasn't very close with any of his foster siblings, but he sometimes wondered where they ended up and if they felt the same way about Dairy Queen as he did.

As he walked through the front doors, the familiar smell of the soft-serve machine and the grease from the fryers transported him right back to those Sundays. He ordered the same thing he always ordered as a child: a double cheeseburger, fries, and a Heath Blizzard. Every bite was justification that what he was doing was what God wanted, and it filled him with excitement at what God might have in store for him on the rest of his journey.

He looked around and noticed that he was the only person in the place besides the staff, which included a young cook who was very likely a local high school student and the older lady who had taken his order. It was late, and glancing at the store's hours posted on the door, James saw that they were about to close. He looked at the older lady who was wiping down a table near him and apologized for keeping them in the store later than they had to be.

The older woman said, "Nonsense, young man. You eat your dinner and stay here as long as you like. We have to clean up anyway, and I don't mind having some extra company."

God was innately good, and individual happiness was his

greatest gift to any person. Science and the study of space and planets were fine, but those things weren't for most people. Most people couldn't have a true understanding of science, so those endeavors were best left to those who could grasp them. Being kind to one another and making life pleasant were what most people should focus on. Sex and love were for the young. After a certain age, after having enough experiences, life eventually became about finding something to pass your time while you remembered the things that made you truly happy. Having children was essential, because it was easier to remember your own youth if you surround yourself with young people. These were things that the old woman understood to be true.

James thanked her and wondered if she was an angel. He knew it was certainly possible that God would send angels to help him along in his journey. If she wasn't an angel, he hoped he would encounter one or two on his journey, and he looked forward to recognizing them.

After finishing his meal, he said goodbye to the older woman and told her that he appreciated everything she had done for him, to which she responded, "I just gave you dinner, son. You needed it and I gave it to you. Anyone else would have done the same." James took this overtly humble response to be further evidence of her possible divine origin. As he walked out into the parking lot and started wondering where he would sleep, he gave a brief thought to going back inside and asking the angel if she knew of anyplace to stay for the night, but he thought better of it. He didn't want to insult God's generosity by asking for more. God would provide him what he needed as he needed it. So he got in his car and got back on the freeway, looking for a divine sign. No more than a minute farther down the road, he saw a sign for the Corral RV park and pulled off at the next exit.

Once he got to the RV park, certain that this was where God intended him to spend his first night on the road, James found that they were closed. There was a small building in front of the park labeled "Office," but it was dark and the door was locked. James was silently asking God if he had misinterpreted anything, if he was meant to have gone somewhere else, when a man emerged from a nearby RV and lit a cigarette. James asked him if he knew where the supervisor was, or if there was some way to contact him.

The man said, "I think they're closed for the night. I doubt you can make a reservation or anything for tonight, if that's what you're looking for."

If there was a God, then humanity was better off without him. Any creature that had absolute power over everything on planet Earth clearly only wanted to cause us all pain and misery in some of the most sadistic ways possible. The universe was vast and mysterious and beautiful, but no human being would ever get to experience it. The knowledge of such things was only the taunting insult of a paradise we could never experience. Instead most people would spend their lives performing a job they didn't care about and wondering if anything in their life would ever have real meaning for them. Ultimately they would conclude that there was no meaning. Sex was the only thing worth living for, but the trappings of a regular relationship were too high a price to pay for it. Taking small vacations with a prostitute in an RV was the only thing that could keep a man sane. Children were not only disgusting and inconsiderate, but they were also evidence of the futility of life, of the disposable nature of everything, the inherent obsolescence in each and every person's excuse for a life. These were things that the smoking man understood to be true.

James told the man that he was trying to find a place to stay for the night. He explained that he'd been on the road for a long time, and he had no problem sleeping in his car, but he wanted to find a safe place, not just the side of the highway. The smoking man said, "Well, you can see my RV here. It's an Airstream Incognito, on the smaller side, but I accidentally booked a full-size spot here for tonight. Your car could probably fit right behind me if you wanted to pull in for the night."

The stranger's generosity surprised James, but it solidified his understanding of just how invested God was in him and his journey. Clearly God had sent two angels from heaven to help him on his first night of the journey. James kindly accepted the offer and pulled his car behind the RV as the stranger finished his cigarette.

James asked the stranger how long he'd been on the road and what his final destination was. He hoped the answer would reveal some hint from God about what the next day of his own journey would hold. The stranger said, "Today's the first day of a little road trip I've been planning for a month or so. I try to get out in the RV at least three or four times a year. Clear my head. And I don't really have a final destination. Back home I guess. I just drive around for a few days, see the sights, meet some people like yourself along the way, and then head back home."

James understood the stranger's home to be heaven. He didn't want to pry too much further, as he felt that God would have instructed the angel to be secretive where details were concerned. He knew that God wouldn't want to give him every piece of information he needed, but rather to allow James to learn some things for himself. He silently thanked God for sending him two angels in a single night, and then he thanked the stranger again.

The stranger said, "You're more than welcome. It's really no trouble. We might be out of here tomorrow pretty early, so if I don't see you in the morning, good luck on your own trip, wherever it takes you."

The stranger threw his cigarette butt on the ground, stomped it out, and headed back into his RV. James couldn't help smiling about the small bit of information that the angel had let slip. He referred to himself as "we." For James there was only one way to interpret that. Not only was this stranger an angel, but God was present as well. God wasn't just up in heaven looking down on James. God was also there with him.

James got into his car, reclined the seat, and breathed deeply. He rolled down his window and let the night air into his car. He could feel God in the way the air felt heavier than normal for that time of year. He could smell God in the faint lingering smoke from the angel's cigarette. He could hear God in the cars passing by on the highway. He could sense that all this was part of God's plan, in a way that he never could before.

He opened his sunroof and looked up at the stars. The night sky had always fascinated James. It seemed so vast and so endless. He didn't understand how anyone could look up at the heavens and not know, beyond the shadow of a doubt, that a great and awesome God had made it all. He didn't dwell on how every star was just a ball of hydrogen floating in space like our sun. He didn't wonder what other planets might be locked in their own orbits around those stars. He never thought about what forces might be at work holding it all together. He only took in the immensity of it, and imagined the greatness of the God who created it all.

He closed his sunroof, got as comfortable as he could in his driver's seat, and fell asleep wondering what other angels he would meet on his trip to California.

chapter twenty-three

Karen's mother, Lynn, agreed to accompany Karen to her next doctor's visit, which would include an ultrasound that would be capable of revealing the gender of the fetus. Assuming Karen probably wanted to know as little about her unborn child as possible, Lynn had not asked her daughter if she planned to find out, but as they drove, her curiosity got the best of her. She said, "I don't really know how you're feeling, or what you're thinking about all this right now, and I don't really even know if you want to talk to me about it, but I'm going to ask you anyway. Do you want to know if your baby is a boy or a girl?"

Karen said, "It's not a baby. It's a fetus. And, no, I don't want to know."

Lynn was silent for several seconds before saying, "Okay. You know the doctor is going to know when she does the ultrasound, right?"

Karen said, "I know, but I don't want to know."

Lynn said, "Okay. Okay," and remained quiet for several more seconds before asking her daughter, "Would you care if the doctor told me?"

Karen said, "Why would you want to know? It's really likely that I won't be having this baby. The money is really slowing down, and unless it picks up there's no way it's going to hit the goal. That's the reason I don't want to know. Are you sure you do?"

Lynn said, "I'm not sure. I'm not at all. But . . . Look, I'm about to open a whole can of worms here. Do you want to have this conversation now?"

Karen knew her mother was anxious to have a real talk about the whole thing, which she had been denied since this all began. Karen had been feeling somewhat guilty about this, and now she finally gave in. She said, "Yeah, it's fine. Let's do it. We have to at some point."

Lynn said, "Okay. I'm not going to get mad or chastise you. I would have in the beginning, when your father and I first found out this was you, but I'm past that. I guess I just don't understand why you couldn't refund the money after you prove your point, either way, and then have the baby anyway and raise it yourself."

Karen said, "Because I don't want to have a baby."

Lynn said, "I know. You've always said that. But let me tell you something, and this is not me trying to coax you into having grandbabies for me. When you're forty, and you look back on this moment in your life, you're going to have regrets if you don't have this baby. It's that simple."

Karen said, "You know what? I might. You could be completely correct. But I'm not having the baby, Mom. I can't. I just can't. There's so much other shit wrapped up in this, I wouldn't even know where to start."

Lynn said, "Yeah, this is complicated, no doubt about that. But it will be far more complicated for you later in life if you don't have it."

Karen said, "Okay, just for argument's sake, let's say I have this baby, no matter how everything turns out. That kid would be at least as much of a public figure as I am right now. I don't think that's fair, you know, to bring a kid into the world with that burden right off the bat."

Lynn said, "And you think aborting the baby is fair?"

Karen said, "For me, this fetus is just a means to an end. Obviously, if the site hits its mark, then I'll have the baby, and it will get to live. And maybe it will even get to live in anonymity, if whoever ends up adopting the kid wants it that way. That's about as fair as this kid could hope for, I guess. But let's get back to your original premise here, where I have the kid and raise it myself. At what point do I tell him or her why people are always taking its picture and why it's always being talked about and why so many people in the world hate its mom? Is that a tenth-birthday conversation? *Listen, little Johnny or Jenny, I accidentally got pregnant, and then I decided to use you, when you were a fetus, to prove that the religious right in this country is filled with a bunch of misogynist assholes who want to take away women's rights at every turn. I was fully prepared to abort you, but once I proved my point, I didn't. Instead I had you, kept you, and now your entire life will be a sideshow attraction.*"

Lynn said, "It doesn't have to be like that, and you know it."

Karen said, "I think it has to be pretty close to that. In a best-case scenario."

Lynn said, "I just find it very hard to accept that you could actually have this baby, my grandchild, and give it to someone else to raise."

Karen said, "I really don't think that's going to happen, Mom."

Lynn said, "Really? Then why are we going to a doctor right now to get an ultrasound?"

Karen said, "Because I'm fucking pregnant. Jesus Christ. You know I need to have a doctor take a look at me to make sure everything's okay with me, with my body. This isn't just to take pictures of the baby."

Lynn said, "So you do think of it as a baby, then?"

Karen said, "Jesus fucking Christ."

Lynn said, "Sorry. This is just hard for me and your father, too, you know?"

Karen said, "I know, and I'm sorry you guys got dragged into this. I never wanted anyone to know it was me."

Lynn said, "How were you going to keep your dad and me from finding out that you were pregnant? We were going to see you sooner or later, weren't we?"

Karen said, "I was just going to be really busy with my dissertation for a while."

Lynn said, "So you were going to lie to us?"

Karen said, "Yes, Mom, I was going to lie to you to avoid conversations just like this one. I was trying to focus on the bigger picture."

Lynn said, "The bigger picture is your family, Karen. That's always what the bigger picture is. I know you think what you're doing is important, and it's going to change people, but it might not. Even if you get the money, or don't get the money, or whatever you think you want to happen actually happens, do you think the world will really be that different? And even if it is different, will it be different in the way you intended? The world moves at a slow pace. If you try to change it too much, it will reject you."

Karen said, "Jesus, Mom, thanks for the pep talk."

Lynn said, "Honey, I'm just saying that when you look back on all of this, years from now, you might realize it was all a lot of pain and suffering for not much of a result. Once it ends, people will go back to their lives, and eventually they'll all forget about it. But if you have a son or a daughter, you'll get to watch them grow into a person. And I just can't tell you"—and now she was starting to cry a bit—"I just can't tell you how rewarding that is."

Karen said, "Mom, don't cry."

Lynn said, "I can't help it. I remember the day we brought you home and your dad and I had a conversation about who we thought you'd be when you grew up."

Karen said, "I know. You've told me this a hundred times."

Lynn said, "I thought you'd be a ballerina because you were born with long legs, and your dad thought—"

Karen said, "He thought I'd be a race car driver, because I'd squeeze his fingers until my knuckles were white. I know. You were both wrong."

Lynn said, "Yes, we were wrong, but that's not what matters. What matters is that you grew into this incredible person, and we got to see that happen. For both of us, there's not one thing we did that's more important than raising you. And I just want you to have that experience, too."

Karen said, "I get it. I really do. But try and see it from my perspective. For me, doing this, doing something that forces people to think and maybe even change their minds about something, is just as important to me as having a kid was to you and Dad. I understand what you're saying, Mom. I always have when baby shit comes up. But I just don't feel the same way, and I'm asking you to respect that."

Lynn said, "You know we respect you, honey, but this is something that's beyond respect."

Karen said, "I know. It's my life, and I'm trying to do what I think is best."

Lynn said, "It's not just your life, though. That's the thing I think you're not really taking the time to see. You're living with us. You're affecting our lives, too."

Karen said, "If it's an inconvenience, I can get another place. I just don't want to be somewhere where my name's on a lease so that weirdos can find me."

Lynn said, "That's not what I meant. You're not inconveniencing us. We're happy to have you back. I meant that this isn't just about you, because what if those weirdos show up at our front door or the cameras or whatever? We're part of this, too, now. And what about Paul? I know he can't be doing too good. You guys broke up, or whatever happened, but I know you still love each other, and no matter what happens with the baby, that will still be true. I guess I'm just asking you to think about all this, because when you're old, whether you have a child or not, you're going to have lived with whatever the fallout is from this. That could be bad."

Karen said, "I know, Mom. I know. But it's worth what I'm doing."

Lynn said, "Okay, honey. If you really think that, then okay."

As they turned onto the street where Dr. Prasad's office was, they saw the crowd immediately. It was a smaller crowd, but it was similar to what Karen experienced the last time she was on UCLA's campus. There were two groups outside of Dr. Prasad's building—one supporting Karen and one protesting. And there were more signs, many of them directed at Dr. Prasad, with phrases like "Prasad is a Baby Killer," and "You Don't Have to Perform the Abortion to Kill a Baby."

Karen noticed one sign that showed her own face next to Hitler's and read, "God Kills All Antichrists." Although Karen found the sign amusing, she also began to understand for the first time that these people had a visceral hatred for her. They saw what she was doing as the equivalent of murdering millions of people. They truly believed that she was working with, or for, the Christian Satan. She wondered what people of other religions might think of what she was doing. There had been very little commentary about it online from other religious groups, and nothing as vitriolic as what the Christian groups were writing about her.

The two groups had positioned themselves on either side of the driveway leading to the building's underground parking garage. Three police officers were keeping the groups separate and corralling them onto the sidewalk so they wouldn't spill out into the street. They were also prohibiting them from going into the building.

Lynn said, "This is what I was talking about. This is nuts."

Karen said, "It's what I was talking about, too, Mom. When's the last time you've seen anyone this invested in an idea?"

As they drove into the parking garage, someone spit on the car's driver's-side window. Lynn said, "I'm not real sure they're invested in anything but hating you at the moment, honey."

Karen and her mother made their way through the building and into Dr. Prasad's waiting room, where two other women gave them less-than-welcoming stares. Before Karen could even sign in, Dr. Prasad herself came out and asked Karen if they could speak privately. Once in Dr. Prasad's office, Dr. Prasad said, "Karen, I'm really sorry to have to do this, but I don't think I can continue being your doctor."

Karen said, "What? You've been my doctor for almost my entire life. Are you serious?"

Dr. Prasad said, "Unfortunately, I am. I want you to know that I have nothing against you and I don't even mind what you're doing. Even if I did, I'd still be your doctor. I don't pass any kind of moral judgment on any of my patients."

Karen said, "Okay. Then why are you turning me away?"

Dr. Prasad said, "I'm sure you saw the crowd outside. They've been there for three days. I don't know how they knew I was your doctor, but they found out somehow, and now they're scaring my other patients—and everyone who works in this building, for that matter—and those people are starting to complain to me. I just can't put all of these people through this. I hope you understand that I don't want to be doing this, but I just can't, in good conscience, continue being your doctor."

Karen said, "Wow. What happened to the Hippocratic oath?"

Dr. Prasad said, "Come on. I don't want to argue about this. I've found another doctor for you. She's a great prenatal doctor and a pediatrician, just like me. I've known her since medical school, and she said she'd be happy to help you. No one knows we talked about it, so you should be able to remain anonymous with her. It will be easier for everyone involved, including you. I know you can't enjoy driving through that mob outside to come in here. Do you enjoy it?"

Karen said, "No. Of course not."

Dr. Prasad handed Karen a business card with the information for her new doctor and said, "Karen, I am truly sorry to have to do this. I've never turned a patient away before. But I think we both know this is best for us all."

As Karen walked out of her office Dr. Prasad said, "Good luck, Karen. I really mean that."

chapter
twenty-four

James had been on the road for a few days and had no more interactions with anyone he considered a possible angel. He was thankful that God had sent him two angels on his first day of the journey, and although he hoped the weeks ahead of him would bring him more, James was anxious not to seem selfish or ungrateful in this desire.

His drive through New Mexico was uneventful. The sand and rock formations in the landscape were filled with colors, many more than he had ever seen at home. James saw beauty and majesty in this and thanked God for making such a wonderful world.

As he drove into Arizona, James stopped to eat at a McDonald's. There, in the booth next to him, he saw a mother, father, son, and daughter eating together. It was a Sunday, and their clothing suggested that they had all just come from church. James knew it was rude to stare, but he found himself studying the family in detail. As he did, he found his gaze coming to rest on the mother more than the father or the children. She was pretty, and James briefly wondered what it must be like to make love to her. He felt ashamed immediately, but knew that his thought had come from a place of purity and not lust. He found her attractive, but there was something about her that was righteous and pious. She was dressed nicely but modestly. Her hair was pulled back in a tight bun, and she rarely looked up from her meal. He could tell that she was the woman God meant for that man, and that's what he really found attractive. It wasn't about her flesh. It was about her spirit.

Since leaving home, James hadn't given much thought to the possibility that he would never have a wife, never have a family. It was something he had forced himself to accept as a possible part of God's plan, but when he was faced with such an example of blissful Christian marriage, it was difficult not to want it for himself. He knew this was simply a test. It was merely God making sure that James was prepared for whatever he would be called to do, no matter what he might have to sacrifice. God had to know that nothing could distract him from his task, not even the promise of something that James had wanted since he was a child. James finished eating and left the McDonald's without giving the family who sat next to him another thought. He knew God was pleased with him.

As James made his way back toward the highway, he began to wonder what God's next sign would be. He still knew only that he was to make his way to California. He had personally selected Los Angeles as the exact destination, and since he'd seen no sign to contradict the choice, he continued on that path. Nonetheless, he hoped to see a sign very soon. He wasn't thinking about his next steps out of confusion or fear, but rather out of excitement. James found that he felt happiest and most alive when he could see God working in front of him, when he could feel God's hand guiding him to his divine purpose. It was when James was thinking about this that he received what was unmistakably God's next sign. On a telephone pole next to the freeway on-ramp James was about to take were two posters, one above the other. The top poster was for an event called the Arizona Praisefest. It read, "In Jesus's Name We Celebrate! Prayer Sessions! Bible Giveaways! Spiritual Music! All Weekend Long! Bring Your Family! Arizona Praisefest!" James noticed that this event had taken place the weekend prior but underneath that poster was another that read, "Flagstaff Gun Show This Weekend—Coconino County Fairgrounds." James was less than an hour from Flagstaff, and he knew there was no way God would have put that poster directly under the Arizona Praisefest poster if he wasn't meant to go to that gun show.

On the drive to the gun show, James thought very specifically about what God had told him on that third day in his apartment. He tried to recall the exact words God used, but found it difficult. He knew it didn't matter. God had revealed his plan, and James was certain that he was doing what was required of him, but ever since that day he had wondered how exactly he would be asked to carry out the plan. He knew that he had to get to California, and he knew that God would eventually demand more than just his presence—that he would be called to action and he would have to be prepared. James thought that certainly the gun show had something to do with this preparation. As he pulled his car into the parking lot at the Cococino County Fairgrounds, he assumed that God had brought him there to meet another angel. He thought it was a strange place for an angel to be, but he knew not to question God. There was a reason he was at the gun show. Some new directive or piece of information regarding his journey was at that gun show, and James would find it.

People in every kind of camouflage apparel James could imagine filled both the outdoor and indoor sectors of the gun show. The sight wasn't entirely foreign to James. Many people in Kansas were avid hunters, outdoorsmen, militia members, and recreational gun owners. It was a culture he was familiar with, and he didn't feel out of place at the Flagstaff show at all. As he meandered through the different booths he waited for some indication from God that he should approach a specific booth or person.

James passed booths that sold Nazi and Confederate memorabilia, night vision goggles, and self-published manuals with titles like *Surviving the Race War*. Then, as he started down a new aisle of booths, he saw what he knew he was meant to see, the reason he had been directed to this place. At the far end of the aisle, he saw a banner depicting Jesus reaching down through the clouds and handing a man a rifle. Under the image were the words *It's your God-given right*. The image reminded James a little of the paining that hung above Pastor Preston's desk. Beneath the banner was a booth operated by one man with various handguns in glass cases. James knew instinctively that this was the booth he needed to visit. This was the sign he had been waiting for.

As James approached the booth and started looking at some of the guns on display, the man behind the counter said, "Hey there, partner. I'm Corey. How can I hook you up today?"

There was only one God. He was very real and He was the father of Jesus Christ. Any and all other modes of belief in anything supernatural, including major religions or things like witchcraft and horoscopes, were punishable by an eternity in hell. God was loving, but he was also capable of raining down immense suffering and pain to his enemies, and he wanted his Christian followers to have the same capabilities, as they were made in his image. To this end, God invented the gun, and made it an indisputable right that any Christian American could own and carry one. Science was fine, as long as it was used to make things to destroy your enemies. It was a waste of time and resources to pursue scientific exploration of things like space and climate change. These were things over which only God could have any influence. Sex was something God ordered to only take place between a man and his wife—not a man and his husband, a man and his wife. It was meant to be an act that produced children, and trying to tamper with God's plan by using any form of contraception, or by denying a man his God-given right to procreate through disobedience as a wife, was a sin punishable by an eternity in hell. Children, especially male children, were precious. They were the vessels by which any man could pass on his legacy, including his faith in Jesus and his collection of firearms. These were things that Corey understood to be true.

James told Corey that he didn't really know what he was looking for, but he was compelled to come to the gun show. Corey said, "Okay. Have you ever owned a gun before?"

James told Corey that he had not, and he wasn't exactly sure he was supposed to get one.

Corey said, "Well, you came to a gun show, partner. What other reason would you have to be here?"

James cursed himself for not picking up the inherent logic in God's initial sign. Why would God have sent him to a gun show if he didn't intend for him to get a gun? The road could be a dangerous place, and although God could obviously protect James in a variety of ways, he clearly wanted James to be able to protect himself. This was a lesson that God was trying to teach him. James told Corey that he was certainly open to the idea of getting a gun, but he didn't know much about them.

Corey said, "Okay. No problem. What's your primary reason for getting one today? Self-defense? Recreation?"

James explained that he wasn't really sure about that. He just knew that it was time to get a gun.

Corey said, "Well, I can't argue with you there, friend. When the good Lord says it's time, then by God, it's time, right?"

Corey slapped James on the back, and James felt at ease with him. He wondered if Corey was possibly the third angel on his trip. His last statement, about obeying God when he says it's time, made James feel that Corey was very likely that angel.

Corey said, "Well, partner, I've got all kinds of stuff here today. You want a pistol? A revolver? A rifle? A shotgun? AR-15?"

James explained that he thought a pistol would be best suited for him personally. Corey said, "All right, I hear you. So what kind of price range are we talking here?"

James told Corey that he didn't have a lot of money, but the thing that drew him to that specific booth was the image of Jesus Christ providing for one of his children. At this Corey said, "Hallelujah, brother. Now you know I can't just give anything away, but I can damn sure help out a fellow Christian. I mean, that's what God put us on this earth to do, right? Help out other Christians and tell everyone else to go to hell." Corey laughed and slapped James on the back again. James laughed, too. He couldn't help but like Corey, and it was easy to imagine him as a kind of rambunctious, rough-around-the-edges angel, up in heaven making the other angels laugh just as he was doing here on Earth.

Corey took a gun out of the case and handed it to James. It was the first time James had ever held a gun. It was heavier than he expected. It felt solid. Corey said, "That there, my friend, is the Glock 17. Most popular gun in the great country of the United States of America. Police use it. Military use it. Families use it. Sportsmen use it. Unfortunately, criminals use it, too. It's got a decent weight, it's dependable, and it's really just an all-around solid weapon."

James asked Corey how much the gun cost. Corey said, "I usually let that one go for five, but you're a Christian, and I can tell you're not bullshitting me about that, so I'm not gonna bullshit you about this. I can let you have that weapon right now for four fifty, and that's a special Christian discount."

James explained that he was on a very tight budget and he wouldn't be able to afford anything that costly. He asked Corey if he possibly had any cheaper guns. Corey said, "I do, but I'm telling you, that's the weapon you want. That's the weapon Jesus wants you to have. The cheaper weapons are mostly used, and they're a little tricky sometimes. I just wouldn't feel right sending you off with one of them. You know, it's your first weapon. I want to know that I'm sending you off with a good weapon you can depend on, that doesn't take a lot of know-how to operate."

James agreed with Corey that he needed a gun that was simple to use, but maintained that he honestly couldn't afford to purchase a gun for four hundred and fifty dollars. Corey asked, "Well, what's your price range exactly?"

James knew he needed to save as much as possible for the rest of his trip, not knowing how long he'd be in Los Angeles or if he'd need to find a job once he got there. He also wanted to be honest with Corey. So he told Corey that he was comfortable spending around three hundred dollars. Corey said, "You're driving a hard bargain, and I know times are tough with money because of the current Muslim administration and the libtards ruining congress. So here's what I can do for you. I say four fifty, you say three hundred. What do you say we meet in the middle? Three seventy-five?"

This was a stretch for James, but Corey had treated him fairly in the negotiations, and James knew that this could be a test from God. Not accepting the offer might be a failure of the test, so James agreed. Corey said, "Great. Just great. I'm so happy to be able to give you your first weapon. I think you'll really enjoy it. Now, I just need your ID to get things started."

James handed him his driver's license and Corey said, "Oh, out of state. That's a tiny setback. I know this is probably a serious pain in the old backside, but we have certain gun laws that require a waiting period and a rudimentary background check to make sure you're not a felon. You're not, right?"

James indicated that he was not.

Corey said, "Okay, good. Usually at shows we can get around those things, but lately some of those libtards I was talking about earlier have really screwed things up for regular folks like me who sell firearms, especially where out-of-state weapon purchases are concerned. They've got their panties in a bunch over it, because some guy somewhere bought a gun in a different state from where he lived and then he shot up a 7-Eleven or something. I don't know. Some bullshit. Anyway, we're trying to watch our p's and q's for the time being, so we're doing the background checks on out-of-staters and blah, blah, blah. I have to tell you legally that it can take up to seven days, but honestly we get people processed in two, max. I know you're a good guy, but that ain't good enough for those pansies in Washington. And any dealer at this show will tell you the same. So I completely understand if you want to walk, but I'm telling you, you're not gonna get a better deal on a weapon like this at any other booth here, or at any gun shop in the country, and that's my hand to God."

James told Corey that he understood there were things that were beyond his control, and he appreciated the discount, so he'd be glad to wait a few days. With that, Corey handed him some paperwork to fill out and said, "Now, I just need a ten percent down payment to hold the weapon for you, and then you can either pick it up back here on the last day of the show, or I can have it waiting for you at my store, which is honestly a lot more convenient. Parking here, I'm sure you dealt with it, is a devil's dingle sometimes."

James finished his paperwork, handed Corey the down payment, and agreed to pick the gun up at Corey's store in a few days. He left the gun show comfortable in how he was progressing down God's path for him. He knew that God was providing him with a tool that would no doubt be very useful on his journey, a tool that God wanted him to have, and he was reminded of 2 Samuel 23:6–7: *But the godless are like thorns to be thrown away, for they tear the hand that touches them. One must use iron tools to chop them down; they will be totally consumed by fire.*

chapter
twenty-five

Karen walked down the cereal aisle. She had been craving Cinnamon Toast Crunch for the past week, and there was never enough in her parents' house. When her mother offered to get some more on her next grocery run, Karen knew that wouldn't be soon enough to satisfy her, so she decided to go herself. She loaded her cart with seven boxes of the cereal, leaving two for any other customers, and then checked the status of her donations on her phone. The site had collected just under twelve million dollars, and time was starting to slip away. She was relieved that her plan was working so well, but she was forcing herself to face the serious prospect that she'd have to undergo an abortion relatively soon. Even if she'd been able to avoid developing any significant emotional connection to the fetus growing inside her, she knew that just the sheer amount of time she'd been pregnant would make it harder to endure than if she had dealt with it when she originally wanted to.

She sometimes fantasized that Paul would go with her to the clinic, drive her back to their apartment when it was over, and spend a few days with her afterward, allowing them time to reconcile. She could imagine a future in which she published her paper or maybe even an entire book about the details of the ordeal, became a known public intellectual who would be asked to weigh in on a great variety of social issues, rekindled her relationship with Paul where it left off, and lived a life that was full of meaning for herself. She imagined this life more and more as the days ticked away. It became a kind of goal, even though it was more a fantasy than anything.

As Karen put her phone back in her pocket and headed to get some hummus and Cheese Nips, she brushed one of her breasts with the back of her hand and it came away slightly wet. She looked down to see that both of her breasts were leaking through her shirt. She had experienced many things during the pregnancy that she found to be disgusting. Vaginal discharge of varying viscosities, constant sweating, large and belabored bowel movements, stretch marks, skin so dry that it sometimes flaked off around her growing belly—and the fundamental fact that there was a living thing moving inside her—were just a few things that Karen found unsettling, but this new development almost made her vomit as she left the cereal aisle of the grocery store.

Turning the corner, she very nearly ran into another woman pushing a cart in the opposite direction. Karen said, "Sorry," to which the woman replied, "You *are* sorry. I know who you are, and I have to say that I think what you're doing is child abuse. It's just the worst thing a mother could ever do. I mean, do you even have a soul?"

God, the soul, and the spirit were all just names people gave to the same energy that flows through everything. Specific religions were all wrong, in that this energy that binds all living things wasn't sentient and didn't create anything. The energy was just always there. Space, and everything beyond our planet, might be interesting to scientists, but it would never have any real impact on the day-to-day life of the average person, so it was a waste of time to think about. Sex was fine, and it didn't have to happen only within the confines of a legal relationship, but people needed to be responsible about it, much more responsible than they were in contemporary society. Too many women had children because they weren't careful, and too many kids were neglected or parented improperly, and it was destroying the fabric of society. Having a child was something to be done only after a great deal of consideration, and raising a child was among the most important things a person could do. Raising a child meant bringing another person into the world and giving it the tools it would need to do the same someday. Having a child was the only purpose for which people existed. These were things that the woman in the grocery store understood to be true.

Karen said, "Well, luckily, I'm not a mother, so you should have no problem with it."

The woman in the grocery store said, "Yes, you are. You're carrying a human child right now. That makes you a mother."

Karen said, "Actually, it's delivering the child that makes you a mother legally. So I'm not a mother, and I very likely never will be."

The woman in the grocery store said, "You're disgusting," and then pushed her cart past Karen's, making sure to hit it as she pressed forward. Karen shook her head and wondered if anyone else in the grocery store would feel the need to chastise her while she was there. She made her way to the snack aisle, put a few boxes of Cheese Nips in her cart, and got some hummus. She checked out without another incident, but when she left the store, she was surprised to find that a group of a dozen or so paparazzi had gathered outside the exit. They all called her name while they snapped pictures of her, their flashing cameras disorienting her.

Karen was almost used to seeing groups of people gathered both in support and protest wherever she went. She didn't enjoy the experience, but she understood it. Her purpose was to engage people, to make them think, to make them debate the legitimacy of the pro-life forces in America, and they were having that debate in the context of supporting or attacking her. But being hounded by paparazzi was a different thing entirely. The flashes of the cameras and the urgent and aggressive tone of the paparazzi were all too much for Karen. She covered her face instinctually as she made her way to her car, got in the driver's seat, and started the engine. She wanted desperately to leave the situation, but the paparazzi swarmed in front of her car, still yelling at her and taking pictures. She honked the horn and moved the car forward a few inches, which got them to move enough for her to drive out of the parking lot.

She drove faster than she should have, and when she stopped at her first red light, she found that she was breathing heavy and sweating. She looked back over her shoulder to make sure she wasn't being followed, and in that moment, she began to understand that her life was no longer her own. This was something she had not anticipated. She started crying, aware that she had no real sense of what further impact this all might have on her life. She had no way of predicting what would happen next, how far she might actually be forced to remove herself from society.

Once she was back at her parents' house, she realized that she'd left the groceries she'd paid for in her cart just outside the grocery store. She cursed herself for being so fragile and allowing such a simple thing as a group of photographers to affect her that much. She walked into the kitchen where her mother was having coffee. Lynn could tell something was wrong with her daughter. She said, "Honey, are you all right?"

Karen said, "No. I'm not. A lady at the grocery store stopped me in the aisle and insulted me, which was weird, and then when I was leaving, there was a group of paparazzi taking pictures and shouting at me. I got so flustered that I left all my groceries in the parking lot. I just kind of lost my mind for a minute. It was really scary. Mom, this is just . . ."

Lynn said, "Too much to handle? If it is, you can still change your mind."

Karen said, "I don't know. No. I'm not changing my mind. But I think it might be better for me to kind of hang around here."

Lynn said, "Did any of them follow you here? You know your father and I don't want those photographers camped out in our front yard."

Karen said, "I don't know if they did or not, but if they could find me at a grocery store, I'm sure they can find me here, Mom."

Lynn said, "You may be right. Let's hope that doesn't happen. Do you want me to go get the groceries?"

Karen said, "No. I don't want you and Dad involved in this at all if it can be helped. I'll call Tanya or something."

An hour later, Tanya showed up at Karen's parents' house with several boxes of groceries. Karen said, "Thank you so much."

Tanya said, "No problem. So it was pretty bad today?"

Karen said, "Fucking terrible. I've never dealt with anything like that. They were like animals or something. Tanya, they stood in front of my fucking car yelling at me while I was trying to drive away. I didn't tell anyone I was going to that grocery store. They just showed up. That was an hour ago, and look at this shit." Karen held up her phone and showed Tanya a Christian watchdog website that had posted a very unflattering photo of Karen that afternoon as she was crying and trying to leave the grocery store. The caption read, "Devil Mom Tries for Sympathy with Fake Tears."

Tanya said, "Yeah, but that's one of those dipshit sites like Americans for Prosperity or World News Daily. Who cares?"

Karen said, "I care. Those sites might be the only ones running captions like that, but the photos are all over the Internet. I never wanted my face to be part of this thing. My identity is totally beside the point, and it's tainting what I'm doing. Beyond that, I don't know if I can leave my parents' house again. What kind of fucking existence is that?"

Tanya said, "It's the one you made for yourself."

Karen said, "My mom was saying it's not too late just end this. I know it's crazy, but that doesn't sound like such a bad idea anymore."

Tanya said, "You're a real piece of shit if you end this now."

Karen said, "What? I thought you'd be into that idea."

Tanya said, "Seriously? You're being a pussy. Would you want to quit if no one knew it was you? If you were still anonymous?"

Karen said, "No. Of course not. I'm saying that quitting is starting to sound better and better, because I'm no longer anonymous. That's the reason I would quit if I was going to."

Tanya said, "So you'd be fine to get everyone just as riled up and pissed off as they are right now, just as long as you're not the one they're blaming?"

Karen said, "That was always my plan. The idea was the only thing I wanted out there. I never wanted to be out there with it myself."

Tanya said, "But the idea *is* out there, and you are, too. You can't just stop because you're experiencing some personal blow-back. You know how I feel about this, but you have to stick it out now. You have to prove your point, and that means following it through to the end. If you don't, you'll still have gone through all the shit, but without getting the result you were looking for. You can't change the facts: you got kicked out of school, you lost your boyfriend, and now you're holed up at your parents' house, completely robbed of your privacy. All of that has already happened.

Things can't really get much worse. Or they could, I guess, but you get what I'm saying. Things are not good. Don't let everything you've gone through be for nothing. At least get to the end."

Karen hugged Tanya. "You're the best fucking friend of all time. Jesus."

Tanya said, "Every person has looked at the world and wanted to change it. But most of us just hope it will change on its own."

chapter
twenty-six

James walked into Corey's gun store, which was called Right to Bear. Corey said, "Hey there, partner. What'd I tell you? Two days. No more, no less. You're all set. I appreciate you taking the time to wait. I'll toss in a box of ammo and a cleaning kit because you were patient about it."

James thanked him, and said that he'd also like some instruction on how to use the gun.

Corey said, "You never even fired a weapon before?"

James explained that he hadn't.

Corey said, "Well, you're in luck today, friend. We got a range here, too. I'll be happy to take you back and show you everything you need to know."

James paid for his new gun, and then Corey gave him some eye protection and earplugs. Then Corey pointed up to the wall behind the register and said, "Who do you want to fire some rounds into this afternoon?"

Taped up to the wall were several paper targets. Some were nondescript black silhouettes, others were images of generic criminals pointing guns toward potential victims. Others were more Middle Eastern in aesthetic, featuring men in turbans with AK-47s or rocket launchers. And there were several targets featuring the images of various military and political figures. There was a paper target of Osama bin Laden with one of his eyes shot out, as well as a cartoon version of Bin Laden at the bottom of the sea. There were two different Vladimir Putin targets, one featuring him on a horse, the other in a business suit. There was an image of Hillary Clinton smoking a cigar. There were three different Barack Obama targets, including one that had the words *This Is for Benghazi* printed across his face in a graffiti style. James selected a standard, faceless black silhouette.

Corey said, "That's a good one. Standard, no frills. I like it." As Corey went to the bin where the targets were kept he said, "What do you think of that Karen Holloway?"

James explained that he didn't spend too much time thinking about her.

Corey said, "Good strategy. Doesn't deserve a second's worth of thought. I mean, can you believe that little piece of trash? Don't get me wrong, though. You know what I'm saying?"

James had never thought of Karen Holloway in a romantic or sexual way, because he knew she wasn't Christian, and for James that eliminated any possibility of finding her attractive. She was a person who was actively disobeying God and very clearly attempting to derail his glorious plan. She was in league with Lucifer, which meant that she was only an enemy to James, nothing more.

When James failed to respond to the innuendo, Corey said, "Well, whatever floats your boat, man, as long as it's women."

James assured Corey that he was only interested in women,

but that Karen Holloway was not the type of woman he'd ever be interested in. Corey said, "Fair enough, boss. I mean, I can imagine givin' it to her, but I can't imagine being in the same room with her, so I guess that'd make it pretty tough. Anyway, let's head on back and get you set up."

Corey instructed James to put on his protective eyewear and his earplugs, as well as a pair of soundproof ear muffs, which Corey called "cans." Corey then led James into a small room and closed the door behind them. Corey had to yell to James in order to be heard through the various ear protection they both were wearing. Corey said, "Now, when I open this other door, we'll be in the range, and it's kind of loud. We got a guy in there right now firing off a Desert Eagle, in fact, so it's gonna be real loud. Takes a second to get used to weapons going off around you, but you'll be fine. You ready?"

James nodded, and Corey opened the door to the range. James jumped a little at the first sound of a gun being fired and couldn't stop himself with each new shot that was fired. Corey said, "Told ya. Nothing to be afraid of, though. You'll be fine. We haven't even had a suicide in here for over six years."

Corey took James to an open lane. It happened to be lane number seven, and James took this to be a sign from God that purchasing this gun from this man was the right thing to do, the next step in God's plan. James had thought that Corey might have been an angel, but his comments about being sexually attracted to Karen Holloway made it seem far more likely that Corey was just another person, like James, whom God was using in his plan, and there was nothing wrong with that.

Corey clipped the paper target into two brackets that were connected to a long wire running the length of the room. He pushed a button and the brackets moved away, taking the target along. Corey said, "We'll put her at ten yards and see how you do," then opened the box of ammunition and took the gun out of its case. He said, "Okay, let's get down some basics. This is your new weapon." Corey slid the top part of the gun backward, and it clicked into place. James had seen a gun set this way before, with the slide locked back, in movies when characters ran out of ammunition. Corey said, "All right, this part here is the slide. You can lock it back like this with this lever. You always want to check your chamber, this little part here, to make sure you don't have a live round in it. So you lock it back like this, then you load your clip. I assume you haven't done that, either?"

When James nodded again, Corey pushed a button on the front part of the handle, and a clip slid out. He said, "This little button here is your clip release. You just push it and the clip comes out." Corey put the gun down and grabbed a few bullets from the box. He pushed one of the bullets down into the clip and then another. He said, "To load your clip, you just take a bullet, make sure the back, this flat part, is facing toward the back of the clip, push it down, and slide it back. Then you take another one and you do the same thing on top of the first one. So on and so forth until you get ten of them in there. Used to be that you could get a fifteen-round clip pretty easy, but times have changed. The libtards made it so we only get ten now. Anyway, here, give it a try."

James took the clip from Corey and pushed a bullet in. He looked at Corey for approval. Corey gave him the thumbs-up and said, "Keep going. Do the rest of the clip." James loaded a few more bullets into the clip before it began to get prohibitively difficult to push the bullet down far enough to be able to slide it all the way back.

Corey said, "It gets harder the closer you get to ten, because the spring in the clip gets pushed down more and it gets tighter, but if you ever forget how many you have in there already, just look at the back of the clip. There are little holes so you can see how many you got in there."

James saw that he only had eight rounds in the clip and forced another two in, hurting his fingers slightly in the process. James handed it back to Corey, who picked up the gun and said, "Okay, now comes the easy part. You just pop it in like so." Corey slid the clip in and James heard it click. Corey said, "Then you push that lever down." As Corey pushed the lever down, the gun's slide jolted forward. Corey said, "And you got a round chambered, and now you're ready to kill a pregnant demonic slut. Come on over here."

Corey led James over to the front of the lane and put the gun in his hand. James noticed that the bullets made it even heavier than before. Corey explained how to stand and how to hold the gun, then said, "But the most important part of shooting is learning to avoid anticipating the kickback. See, every time you fire, that slide blows back and your weapon will automatically eject the spent casing. Most people, the first time they shoot, have a great first shot. Then every shot after that is worse and worse, because they lean into the gun in anticipation of that kickback. You have to just get that out of your mind. You want to line up your sights so that the middle dot is between the other two, then just squeeze the trigger slowly. Don't pull it. And don't even think about the kickback. Just let it happen. Got it?"

James indicated that he thought he understood and Corey said, "All right, take your first shot, brother."

James went through the steps Corey had just taught him, raised his gun, targeted the silhouette's head, slowly squeezed the trigger, and nothing happened. He turned around and looked at Corey, who was standing behind him, supervising. Corey said, "Oh, and I forgot the most important thing. You have to click the safety off." Corey came over and pointed to the safety on the gun. He said, "That little dude right there. Just click it down. That engages the firing pin and you're ready to rock-and-rolla, Ayatollah."

James disengaged the safety, took aim once again, and slowly squeezed the trigger. This time the gun fired a single shot. James expected the kickback to be much more violent than it was, but he did close his eyes in reaction to the muzzle flash and the sound, so he was unable to see where his shot went. Corey noticed this and said, "That's all right, brother. You get used to the sound and the muzzle flash and everything. For a first shot, that ain't bad at all." Corey pointed downrange at the target and said, "You got him in the right boob."

James looked and saw that indeed there was a small hole in right side of the target's chest. He had missed the spot he was aiming for by maybe eight or ten inches. Corey said, "Keep on going, man. Empty that clip."

James took aim and fired nine more times. With each shot he felt he got a little bit better at understanding how to shoot. He reloaded his new gun and shot another ten rounds. With each shot his aim got progressively better until he was landing every shot within a few inches of where he was aiming. Corey was impressed. He said, "Damn, boy, you're a natural. I can't believe you've never shot before."

James felt that Corey was being honest, and he felt sure the only reason God would bless him with the gift of marksmanship was that he would need to use it at some point.

chapter
twenty-seven

After dinner, Karen's father, Robert, said, "Have you even been outside in the past week, or have you been cooped up in the house like an animal?"

Karen said, "I go out in the backyard and hang out."

Robert said, "That's not good. You need to be out doing things."

Karen said, "I don't think that's a good idea. I'd rather just lay low until whatever happens is going to happen."

Lynn said, "Lay low? You're past that point, I think."

Karen said, "You know what I mean. Just stick around here and not give them an opportunity to get any more photos of me. I did a fucking CNN interview. That should be the only public appearance I have to do."

Lynn said, "I don't think that's how it works, honey. When you put something in the world that gets people this fired up, they're going to want you to continue to be a part of it. What you do about that is obviously up to you, and we're happy to have you stay here as long as you want, but your dad just wants you to be happy, and I do, too. And you can't really be all that happy sitting around watching TV all day, can you?"

Karen said, "Much happier than getting attacked at a grocery store and then seeing pictures of it all over the Internet. And I don't just watch TV all day. I'm working on my dissertation."

Robert said, "Why? Are you going to try to get into some other school after this or something?"

Karen had considered this, but she hadn't yet committed to it in her own mind. She was continuing her work on the dissertation, in part, in order to stay focused on the purpose behind everything that was happening around her. Whether she used it to apply to a different philosophy program, or even tried to publish it herself, was irrelevant to her in that moment. It was just about continuing her work.

Robert said, "You've gotten into *something* here, that's for sure."

Karen said, "That is indeed for sure, Dad."

They finished eating dinner and Karen went to her bedroom. More and more, she found that lying on her bed in a specific position on her side was the only way to ease the pain in her back. She'd lie sometimes for hours at a time reading about herself on the Internet. Although the articles against her were far more violent in tone, she was surprised to find that there were just as many as the number supporting her. The supporters, though, usually defended her more on the basis of freedom of expression than because they supported her challenge to the Christian right. She did find a few prominent articles, however, that praised Karen's project as the event that the pro-choice movement was waiting for but had never had the guts or creativity to do for itself. These were the articles that gave Karen hope that what she was doing was making a difference, was changing people's minds, was forcing them to talk about this in a philosophical context rather than just the usual right-wing brainless screaming from a pulpit. One article equated what Karen was doing to the Emancipation Proclamation. It claimed that women were the most subjugated group of human beings on the planet and that this was a massive step toward ending that, toward forcing people to see the hypocrisy of patriarchal religious structures that claim to want the best for women even as they work to rob them of their reproductive rights.

She also read countless posts and articles that pleaded with her to give the child a chance to live, even if her financial goal wasn't met. Karen had to admit that the logic of this specific argument was sound. Most of these articles argued that Karen would be able to prove her point about the hypocritical nature of the religious right and take the high road at the same time if she didn't get the money but still had the child and gave it up for adoption or even decided to keep it. As she finished reading one such article, she noticed that she was unconsciously rubbing her stomach. She could feel the fetus moving inside her as she rubbed. The article's final line read, "If you do nothing else, just spend ten minutes thinking about what kind of person that child could become with you as a parent." She lifted her shirt and looked down at the strange thing her body had become. Two moles on the top of her stomach had begun to grow thick black hair. She had visible stretch marks that she found hideous. But she knew that when this was over they'd serve as lifelong reminders of what she'd done, and she knew that she'd come to love them. Most disgusting to her at this point was how her belly button had pushed itself out. Her new doctor told her that it would return to normal after the pregnancy, but for now it made her gag every time she saw it. In her mind, her protruding navel was worse than her leaking nipples.

The final line of that article struck Karen as a reasonable challenge, and she forced herself to take it. She felt that she shouldn't have to force herself to ignore her emotions, to close herself off from any thoughts or feelings she might be having. She put her palm flat on her stomach, where she felt the last movement, and thought about the tiny person growing inside her.

On the way home from her last doctor's appointment, Karen's mother had let slip the gender of the fetus, so Karen knew that it was a girl growing inside her. She imagined the girl to have blue eyes like Paul. She imagined them to be curious and smart and beautiful. She imagined this little girl growing up. She imagined herself going to a grade school PTA meeting and learning from the teachers that her daughter was the smartest student in the school, but that she also had a problem with authority. She imagined getting a call from a junior high principal because her daughter had punched a boy in the nose after the boy told her that he didn't think his future wife should have a job. She imagined her daughter telling her that even though everyone else was going to the prom, she wasn't, because she considered it an antiquated tradition that promoted discrimination more than anything else. She imagined her daughter getting into Harvard and being the first female student to do something so important that it forever altered the manner in which the school was run. She couldn't imagine what that would be, but she could imagine her daughter doing it. She imagined her daughter becoming a leader in whatever the feminist movement of her time would be. She imagined her writing books that incensed the public but nonetheless pushed things forward. She imagined her daughter growing old but keeping a photo of her mother with her all the time. She imagined her daughter loving her for a wide variety of things, but mostly for deciding to have her. She imagined her daughter reading through the mountains of words that would have been written about both her and Karen, and she imagined her daughter understanding why she had done it, and she imagined her daughter having respect and admiration for her mother and her project. And in all this she realized that this child was a part of Paul, too. It was a part of the person she had come to love most in the world. And this child might be the only way she could have some part of Paul in her life. It was something she'd never allowed herself to consider until that moment, and it made her extremely sad to think of this child in those terms, as the last piece of her relationship with Paul.

Karen felt a tear roll down her cheek and immediately told herself it was hormones. Then she imagined a different version of her daughter. She imagined her with the same blue eyes from her father, but then she imagined those eyes without the fire she saw in them in the other version of her daughter. She imagined this more likely child as a girl with little special curiosity about life or anything else. She imagined her daughter marrying an average man and having his average children, and never working, and never contributing to anything or thinking critically about the world around her. She imagined her daughter as a normal woman, trapped by her inability to see the dangers of traditional gender roles and relationships. She imagined her daughter as being happy, but that wasn't enough for Karen.

Karen knew that parents had some influence over the people their children became, but certainly that influence wasn't absolute, and statistically her daughter would be far more likely to be uninteresting than she would be likely to do anything of note or even to be likely to have an interesting conversation with her mother about any of this. For Karen, that would be more heartbreaking than anything else. And there was the dilemma for her. Even if she wanted to have the child and keep it without giving it up for adoption, she knew that the great likelihood was that her daughter would be completely and utterly normal.

She didn't consider herself to be normal by any means. She thought about how her parents had raised her, and how influential they had been in shaping the person she'd become. They had given her the room she needed to explore things for herself, and they never pressed religion on her or any publicly held views of what a woman should or could be. She knew she'd be the same way with any child she could ever have. But she had no real idea how much her upbringing had contributed to her adult personality, and how much it was the product of innate factors. She couldn't say how much of her would have been the same, no matter what her parents did. Things like intelligence and curiosity, Karen thought, were random. Despite any kind of parental impositions in a child's life, certain things were dictated at birth. And if her child had low intelligence, or no interest in intellectual pursuits, there was virtually nothing she could do to reverse that. This was her worst fear where a possible child was concerned, but it was a fear she'd never considered before that moment. It was a fear that betrayed in Karen a secret desire for a better life for her unborn child.

And beyond that, Karen could feel a bond forming with this child. She felt as though the child was on this journey with her, that some partnership in the overarching plot of this entire ordeal had been formed. That would be a difficult partnership to end. She'd already ended one relationship that meant more to her than anything, and she knew that losing another would be even more difficult.

She tried to put the question out of her mind and think instead about what the next few weeks would be like. She was quickly approaching the end of her second trimester, and although there had been a very significant uptake in donations as the end date approached, the account still had only twenty-seven million dollars. At this late date it was extremely unlikely that she would hit her goal, and abortion was a likely enough prospect that she had started looking into where she would have it done. She knew she would have to keep the location a secret, in order to avoid not only paparazzi but also the potential for harm to herself or anyone who worked there. When she called around, she found that every clinic was open to having Karen as a patient, and most of them even told her that they supported her and thought what she was doing was admirable.

She knew she would also have to make some kind of public acknowledgment of the results of her experiment. Every major news organization in the country had offered to cover a press conference live, if she chose to give one, but she wasn't yet certain that a live press conference was the way to go. She considered simply posting an update on her site and allowing that to be the only message she gave the public on the deadline. But as she thought more and more about the abortion itself, for the first time she realized that the apprehension she felt had little to do with the end of the experiment, or even the fear surrounding the procedure. She felt fear at the possibility that the life she was ending might just be one of the most amazing women she would ever meet.

chapter twenty-eight

Needing gasoline, James pulled into a gas station in Kingman, Arizona. When he went inside the pay for the gas, he realized that his remaining funds were quickly dwindling. As the man behind the register handed James his change, a dime slipped between his fingers, hit the floor, and rolled to a stop on another patron's discarded hot dog wrapper. On the wrapper was an advertisement for Terry Fator's puppetry show in Las Vegas. James quickly fixed on the sight as another potential sign from God. But this one was more intricate than some of the other signs he'd seen, more difficult to discern. But just as he knew that to hear God's voice he had to listen very carefully, James rationalized that to see some of God's signs a person might really have to look very closely at the things that were right in front of him.

The catalyst for the sign was a dime. James knew the number ten to be of great biblical significance. James had done exten-

sive study in the numbers of the Bible, and he knew the following things to be true. He knew there were four biblical numbers
that were indicative of perfection or completion: three, seven,
ten, and twelve. While all these numbers represented perfection,
each was linked to a different type.

Three was divine perfection. It appears 467 times in the
Bible. It is the first of the four spiritually perfect numbers. The
three righteous patriarchs before the flood were Abel, Enoch,
and Noah, and after the flood the righteous fathers were Abra-
ham, Isaac, and Jacob—both groups of three. There were
twenty-seven books in the New Testament, which is mathematically represented by the equation $3 \times 3 \times 3$. This is complete-
ness to the third power. Jesus prayed three times in the garden
of Gethsemane before his first arrest. He was crucified at the
third hour of the day at 9:00 A.M., which was three squared, and
died at the ninth hour, or 3:00 P.M. Three hours of darkness
covered the land while Jesus suffered on the cross. Three men
were crucified on that day. Christ was dead for three full days
and three full nights before resurrection. Only three people
saw Jesus's transfiguration on Mount Hermon: John, Peter, and
James. Only three people were allowed to ask God anything:
Solomon, Ahaz, and Jesus. God gave Israel three gifts: his law,
the land, and their calling. The Bible mentions only three angels by name: Michael, Gabriel, and Lucifer. Another angel is
charged to cry three woes to those on Earth, to warn them of
more trials to come. And the most important reference to three
was, of course, the Holy Trinity.

Seven was spiritual perfection. It appears 735 times in the
Bible and was the foundation of God's word. There were seven
days of the week, all created by God, who claimed the seventh
as the holy Sabbath. The Bible was originally divided into seven
major divisions: the Law, the Prophets, the Writings, the Gospels,
the General Epistles, the Epistles of Paul, and the Book of Revelation. The total number of originally inspired books was forty-nine,

represented mathematically by the equation 7 x 7. In the book of Hebrews, Paul uses seven titles to refer to Jesus: Heir of all things, Captain of our salvation, Apostle, Author of salvation, Forerunner, High Priest, and the Author and finisher of our faith. In Matthew 13, Jesus gives seven parables. In the Book of Revelations there are seven churches, seven angels, seven seals, seven trumpet blasts, seven thunders, and seven plagues. And, of course, Jesus performed seven miracles on God's holy Sabbath day.

Twelve was governmental perfection, symbolizing God's power and authority. It appears in the Bible 187 times. Jacob had twelve sons, each of whom represented a tribe, and from each tribe twelve thousand were to receive salvation during the end times. God demanded that twelve unleavened cakes be placed in the temple every week. New Jerusalem contains twelve gates. The walls of New Jerusalem are 144 cubits high, mathematically represented by the equation 12 x 12. Solomon appointed twelve officers over Israel. The first scriptural recording of Jesus's words occurred when he was twelve years old. And, of course, Christ chose twelve disciples with whom to surround himself.

Ten was the number of perfection of God's divine order. It appears 242 times in the Bible. It was the number of physical creation represented in the design of the human body by God himself, who gave us ten fingers and ten toes. In Genesis 1 the word *God* is used ten times. A tithe was dictated to be one tenth of a man's earnings, and it was said to be returned tenfold by God's grace. A Passover lamb was selected on the tenth day of the first month. Ten generations of man lived on Earth before the great flood. And, of course, God gave us the Ten Commandments, by which all things are to be governed. There was no need for an eleventh, nor would nine have sufficed. Ten was the number of laws man required to honor God's divine power in the way he saw fit. It was, to James, a perfect number.

All of this ran through his mind as he saw the dime lying on a piece of paper advertising Las Vegas. It was clear to him that whatever he was to do next would take place in Las Vegas, and a part of him knew that this is where God would help him gain enough money to complete his journey.

He picked up the dime and put it in his shirt pocket, knowing that it would be an instrumental tool in whatever was to happen next. He asked the man behind the counter how far away Las Vegas was, and the man told him it was only about an hour and forty minutes away. After a moment, James realized that that meant a hundred minutes, represented by the mathematical equation 10 x 10. It was perfection squared. He got in his car and headed to Las Vegas.

On the road, however, he started to worry that he was headed into the heart of sin. He knew Las Vegas was called Sin City, and he knew that it could tempt him in ways he had never thought imaginable. He took the dime out of his shirt pocket and held it tight in one of his hands. He was protected by God, and no matter how difficult his trip to Las Vegas would be, no matter how much Satan might try to pull him from his path, James knew that God would shield him.

As he got closer to the city, the traffic grew worse and worse. There were so many cars, and so many flashing lights, and the buildings were so big. He could almost feel the sin radiating from the city, pulling people in, destroying their lives and souls. He vowed that he would remain steadfast and uphold all his Christian principles for as long as God needed him to be in the city. He knew that if he could get through this, he could get through anything. He would be stronger for having lived through this, and as he parked his car in the parking lot of the Venetian, he thanked God for the opportunity to prove how devoted he was.

James walked from the parking lot into the hotel's casino floor and immediately felt he was in a place designed by the Devil. The noises and lights were so overwhelming that he was slightly disoriented. The smell of smoke was everywhere, and he knew it had to be a conscious effort by Satan to make himself feel more at home. He surveyed the area looking for an indication of what God might intend for him to do, and he saw an LED display next to a table of people. The LED board was simply a series of numbers. The top number was a flashing seven, and the two immediately under it were also sevens. Seven, seven, seven was the holiest number. James immediately went to the table and asked the person running the game what it was. She explained the basic premise and rules of roulette to him, and he took the dime out of his pocket. He placed it on the black ten before the same woman explained to him that there was a ten-dollar minimum on any bet at the table. James took this as a further sign that he was doing what God wanted him to.

He had a little more than fifty dollars. He put ten of it on the black ten and watched as the woman working at the table spun a tiny white ball around the rim of the roulette wheel. He watched as the ball's momentum slowed, and it finally fell into the spinning wheel where it was kicked around until coming to rest on black twenty. He watched as the woman swept everyone's chips and his ten-dollar bill away from the table, before allowing any more bets to be placed. He quickly tried to interpret what it could have meant. Twenty was twice the number he bet on, and twice the value of his bet. Ten times two was twenty, times two again was forty. This was roughly everything he had left. God sometimes demanded a great show of faith when he was testing his followers, and James knew of no greater show of faith than to trust God with everything in a place of sin. So James took the remaining forty dollars out of his pocket and placed it on the number ten. Once again he watched the woman spin the ball around the edge of the wheel, and once again he watched the ball fall and bounce. And this time the number it came to land on was the number ten. It wasn't surprising to James, and he openly thanked God at the roulette table for his victory. The woman running the table gave James several chips that totaled one thousand, four hundred dollars in value. He thought about cashing them in, but he started doing some math in his head.

Fourteen hundred divided in half was seven hundred, which was represented by the mathematical equation 7 x 10 x 10, or perfection times perfection times perfection, or perfection to the perfect power of three. This was clearly a sign to continue and place a bet on the number three. But then, just as James was about to put everything he had just won on the number three, he heard someone behind him yelling out the name *Timothy,* and he knew this to be a more certain sign from God. It couldn't be anything other than a reference to Timothy 6:10: *For the love of money is a root of all kinds of evils. It is through this craving that some have wandered away from the faith and pierced themselves with many pangs.* He realized that God's symbols in the numbers were a warning to stop, to leave this place with the gift God gave him before temptation swallowed his spirit whole.

James took his winnings to the cashier and left the casino with fourteen hundred dollars, which he knew would easily get him to Los Angeles and help him subsist while he awaited God's further instruction. He pulled out of the casino garage and made his way toward the freeway, where he saw a giant entrance sign reading, "Los Angeles – 270 miles." He looked at his GPS and saw that the final stretch of highway that would lead him into Los Angeles, where he would complete God's mandate, was the 10.

chapter
twenty-nine

Karen was tired. Not only was the fetus growing inside her getting big enough to keep her almost constantly exhausted and in physical discomfort, but she hadn't slept the night before. Her final deadline had arrived, and she was sitting in a car outside the same CNN building where she did her interview with Anderson Cooper. Having weighed all her options, she had concluded that announcing the results of her experiment on television would achieve the best effect and reach the most people. The night before, she had added a link to her site leading people to a live webcast of the press conference she was about to give.

Everyone already knew that her financial goal had not been met. The running tally on her website was at thirty-eight million dollars when the deadline arrived. There was no mystery about what had to happen next, but Karen would seize the moment to explain the outcome of her project and the decision she'd made about how she would handle the rest of the experiment.

She had driven to the studio with Tanya and her father. Her mother had decided to stay at home, explaining that she'd seen enough angry protestors at the doctor's office and she had no desire to go through the same thing again. As Karen drove slowly by the studio, she realized that her mother had made the right choice. Since she posted the announcement about her press conference on her website, huge groups of people, both protestors and supporters, had been sleeping outside the building in tents on the sidewalk. This time, however, there were many more police officers present than she'd seen at any point in the past. She wondered what each of them might think about her and about what she was doing. She wondered whether, in the event that she would require their real protection, they would be capable of providing it. It occurred to her that some of them might have no problem seeing her dead. She hoped that their sense of duty would spur them to protect her should it be necessary.

Her father said, "Jesus Christ, you really stirred up a hornet's nest."

Karen said, "Yeah. That was kind of the point."

Her father said, "Well, I know I haven't said this yet, but I want you to know I'm proud of you, and so is your mother. What you're doing and what you're about to do is on the fringe, for sure, but you really got the whole country's attention with your idea. That's pretty rare. So for what it's worth, we love you and we're proud. I just, you know, wanted you to know that."

She kissed her father on the cheek and said, "Thanks, Dad. That means a lot to me. Seriously."

Robert said, "Well, you mean a lot to us. Now, how in the hell am I supposed to get in the building with those shitbags blocking the entrance?"

Karen said, "The producers emailed to tell me to use a back

entrance around the corner. They have it blocked off from public access."

Robert drove the car around the back side of the building, where they found another entrance that was heavily guarded by police, and where there were no demonstrators in sight. The police escorted them into the building and back to the floor where she'd done her first TV interview. The main producer showed her the room where she'd be doing her press conference. A small table had been set up in front of a nondescript background drape, with thirty folding chairs for journalists. The producer told her that they couldn't vet them all in advance, but handed Karen a printed list of the most likely questions. Karen said, "Thank you. I can handle any question they throw at me, and they may not even know what they want to ask after I make my statement." At this the producer seemed confused, but she was too busy to engage any further. She showed Karen and Tanya and Robert to the greenroom and told them that they had about half an hour before the journalists would be allowed in. After they'd all taken their seats, Karen would be summoned to the pressroom.

In the greenroom, Tanya said, "I just can't get over how insane this is. Six months ago, you were complaining that you had no good ideas for your dissertation. Now you're not even in the PhD program, and there's a mob of people in the street who want you to die."

Karen said, "That's one way to look at it, I guess."

Tanya said, "You know what I mean."

Karen laughed and said, "Yes, I do."

Robert said, "At least the hard part's over."

Karen said, "That remains to be seen."

Robert said, "You're at the end of it. Once it's all said and done, which has to be in a few days, right? Legally?"

Karen said, "Yeah, legally."

Robert said, "Well, once it's done, it's done. Then there's nothing left for these people to care about. They might talk about it, but there won't be people with megaphones and signs. They'll move on to the next person or the next thing to be mad at."

Karen said, "Well, hopefully they'll still think about the question I'm raising here."

Robert said, "Honey, I know that's been your whole goal since the beginning, but you can't really get your hopes up about it. People don't change their minds that easily. They have too much pride. Eventually they have kids who see the world differently, and that's how real change happens. Old people die and the things they mistakenly thought were important die with them."

Karen said, "But you and Mom agree with what I'm doing, right?"

Robert said, "We support you."

Karen said, "I guess that's good enough."

They waited the rest of the half hour in silence.

At some point, Karen went to the window and looked down at the crowd below her. She was too high up for them to see her, but she could hear them on the street. She could hear some of them chanting, "Burn in hell! Burn in hell!" It was strange to Karen to have that much hatred directed at her. It didn't make her feel bad, exactly, or that what she was doing was wrong. It was just strange to know that complete strangers—many of whom considered themselves Christians—could be so full of hate and rage. This was part of the hypocrisy she wanted to expose and attack. In some ways, she thought that the discovery of her identity had aided her overall objective in this manner. In others, she felt it had been detrimental. Had she to do it all over again, she would have been much more careful. She would have posted the website from a public computer, maybe in an Apple store, so there would be no way to trace her identity without serious measures, such as a police review of security footage from the store, which she thought would have been unlikely because security footage was generally purged quickly unless a crime had been committed. She couldn't help but wonder whether the hundred-million-dollar goal would have been met if knowing her identity hadn't given people a target for their rage; whether remaining anonymous would have enabled people to focus on the philosophical question she was raising; whether people would have been more likely to think for themselves instead of giving into the easier, more primal emotional urges that come with assigning blame to an individual.

A producer came into the greenroom and told Karen it was time for the press conference. Karen followed her out and saw a room full of reporters waiting impatiently in their seats. Karen was escorted to her seat behind the table she saw earlier and was told that Anderson Cooper would be doing a small lead-in from New York, and then the cameras would cut to her, live in the studio. Karen sat down and waited.

Karen remained silent, looking out at the various reporters there. None of them returned her gaze. They were all busy looking at their phones or iPads or laptops or handwritten notes. Then a monitor showed the CNN feed. He said, "Hello, I'm Anderson Cooper. A few months ago I had the opportunity to sit down with Karen Holloway, who even then was among the most talked about people in the country, maybe in the world. She explained to us why she decided to solicit one hundred million dollars in donations as a trust fund for her unborn child—and, further, that if the donations failed to reach that goal, she would terminate that pregnancy. Today, CNN brings you an exclusive press conference with Karen, the day after her experiment came to a close without reaching that hundred-million-dollar goal. Now let's go to Los Angeles, and here is Karen Holloway."

Karen looked out to see a producer point and nod at her as her own image appeared on a monitor just behind the producer's head. Karen said, "Thank you to everyone who's watching this and who has been following this. Before I take any questions, I'd like to say a few things.

"As everyone knows by now, donations to the site I launched several weeks ago have fallen far short of the hundred-million-dollar goal. A total of about thirty million dollars in donations was registered on the site, all of which has now been electronically re-funded. This, in effect, proves my point. My original thesis was that the Christian right in this country has an agenda where women are concerned, and the pro-life movement was offered the perfect opportunity to disprove my point, but they failed. I hope that in the mind of the general public it's now abundantly clear that the Christian right does not actually care about the life of an unborn child. They were given the chance, with minimal effort, to save the life that's growing in me, and they failed to do so. They actively chose to let this child die. And that raises the question of why they would do that, after speaking out against abortion so vehemently and for so long. The only conclusion any rational person can draw is that they care far more about taking away a woman's choice than they do about protecting life, which they claim is their paramount goal.

"With this concrete proof of the hypocrisy in the pro-life movement, and more broadly in the whole of the Christian right, I hope we can collectively agree that this movement no longer warrants serious consideration as a political or social ideology. The failure of the Christian right to uphold what they claim as one of their primary objectives was something I expected. It was something, in honesty, that I was counting on to prove my point, and they delivered.

"That was about the only thing I expected in this whole ordeal that actually came to pass. Many more things happened that I didn't expect. My identity was discovered, which led to problems I could never have anticipated. I got kicked out of school. I lost the love of my life. My safety has been threatened. And, while all of that surprised me, the most unexpected result of this project should have been the one thing I was most prepared for. But I wasn't at all.

"The only thing that was guaranteed when I started this was that I would be pregnant for a while. I never really gave much thought to that until it became a fact of my life. I've done a lot of thinking over the past several months, and I've come to a conclusion that I would never have anticipated. Even though the monetary goal wasn't met, I've decided to have the baby and to raise her as my own child. The Christian right in this country may have abandoned this child to a death sentence, but I've found that I can't be as cruel. They have attempted to stifle my right to choose, but in the end, I don't think I could be making a better and more definite choice. And, as the final part of my pregnancy continues, I'd just ask the press and everyone else to give myself and my child privacy. Now I'll take any questions you may have."

The reporters gathered were slightly stunned. None of their prepared questions made sense now. Everyone in the room had assumed that Karen was going to have an abortion, and all their questions were based on that notion. After several seconds of silence, Karen said, "If there are no questions, I'll thank everyone for being here today and conclude this press conference."

One reporter raised his hand and asked Karen if this had been her plan all along, to use this entire scheme to shame the Christian right, to beat them at their own game of self-righteousness. Karen said, "No. I fully intended to have an abortion, just as I indicated on my website, but the best thing about letting women choose what to do with their own bodies is that we get to make a choice. And that's what I'm doing today. My mind has changed, and this choice reflects that. I think many people on the right would have you believe that pro-choice is synonymous with abortion, but it's simply not. I remain pro-choice, and I'm exercising my choice to do what I believe is right for me and for my child."

Karen waited for several more seconds, but there were no other questions from the reporters present. After a minute of silence, the feed cut back to Anderson Cooper, who said, "A shocking turn of events in the story of Karen Holloway. She has decided not only to have the child, despite missing her goal of one hundred million dollars, but she's going to raise it as well. I'm sure we'll be talking about this a lot in the coming days, but for right now, it seems that the reporters present were stunned, as are most people I would guess. Anderson Cooper for CNN."

chapter
thirty

James listened to every word of Karen's press conference on the radio as he drove toward Los Angeles. He couldn't believe she was going to keep the child. It seemed like a trick of some kind to James. Like Karen Holloway had played everyone for a fool. He couldn't fathom how evil she must be in her heart in order to do such a thing to people. Then he looked up and saw the words *Find Her* on a billboard. As he continued to drive he saw that the billboard had been slightly obscured and it actually read, "Find Her the Perfect Engagement Ring." Nonetheless, in that moment, it was very clearly a sign. God meant for him to find Karen Holloway. That's why he sent James to California, to Los Angeles.

He wondered why God would want him to find her or what he was supposed to do once he did. Maybe he was supposed to talk to her, to find out her true intentions or to just keep an eye on her for God, or maybe he was even meant to convert her. James had always been very self-conscious about testifying to strangers. He knew it was one of his duties as a Christian, but he also knew that it was his biggest weakness. He was shy around people he didn't know, and he'd always thought that if a person hadn't developed a relationship with God on their own, then he certainly wouldn't be able to introduce them. He knew that his ultimate purpose would be revealed in time, when God needed him to know it. All he knew for certain was that his goal was much clearer than it had been before, and this excited him. James realized that it was all part of the plan. Karen's trick couldn't fool God, and by extension it couldn't fool James. Even though she didn't get the money, she was still going to have the child. She had gone against her own rules in order to bring that child into the world. James knew of no better indicator of Satan's involvement in such affairs than trickery, which Karen openly employed. James began to think that it was possible, likely even, that God wanted him to convert Karen. The conversion of an open agent of Satan to Christianity would be a great blow to the Devil. He became slightly giddy at the prospect and then calmed himself. All he knew for sure was that Karen and her child were the reasons God sent James to Los Angeles, and that was more than he knew before coming to Los Angeles.

After the press conference ended, James turned his car radio to a Christian station on which two pastors and the host of the show were discussing the story and what they thought it meant. One pastor thought that Karen had done the right thing by keeping the baby. He said that although he had not donated to her site and he found what she did to be disgusting, he had always hoped that the child would live, and he was happy to see that it would. Whatever animosity any Christian may have felt toward her throughout this process, he warned, should be alleviated by her decision. He urged Christians to forgive her, just as Jesus would have done, because God had clearly taken a hand in her decision. James did not agree with this pastor's outlook and questioned whether or not this pastor was even a true Christian. Perhaps he, too, was an agent of Satan.

The other pastor chastised the first for abandoning one of the most fundamental tenets of their faith: oppose Satan at every turn, at all costs. This second pastor claimed that what Karen Holloway had done was a spiritual flip-flop. He maintained that forgiving her for what she did would be the spiritual equivalent of electing Osama bin Laden as president of the United States. He couldn't understand how she could be so vehemently in favor of aborting a child if she didn't get enough money, but then when the money didn't come in, she could just choose to abandon her initial threat. He claimed that her decision was a sign of weak moral and spiritual fiber, and possibly a trick of Satan himself to gain sympathy for this girl who was obviously working in his service quite possibly to give birth to the Antichrist. James agreed with this and thought that his own Pastor Preston must have felt the same.

Despite the first pastor's claims that all Christians should extend forgiveness to all sinners, as this was the most fundamental teaching of Jesus Christ, both the host of the program and the second pastor suggested that Karen Holloway be arrested and the child be turned over to the state after the delivery. They saw no reason to keep her in society after having committed such a heinous crime against God, which they likened to spiritual kidnapping. James turned the program off just as he drove into Los Angeles on the 10.

The traffic became more congested immediately, he noticed, but more than that, he was struck by the sheer scale of the city. He had assumed that Los Angeles would be similar to Las Vegas. They were both places of terrible sin, and it stood to reason in his mind that they would look nearly identical. Nothing could have been farther from the truth.

Las Vegas had been tiny compared to what he saw as he drove

down the 10. Los Angeles seemed to go on forever in all directions. Some of the buildings he saw from the freeway were old, but many were brand-new. There was no consistency in its look or feel, and this bothered James on a subconscious level. It was as if the city had just been thrown together haphazardly. It was frenetic and disjointed and chaotic, and it was endless. No matter where James looked, there was no reprieve from the city sprawl or from the brownish-yellow haze in the sky. There were so many people on the freeway that he couldn't even imagine what it must be like down in the city itself, where people lived. He felt pity for these lost souls condemned to roam this endless wasteland. This, he thought, was the real sin city. This was hell on Earth, and he would have to scour it in order to complete God's plan, in order to find Karen Holloway.

chapter
thirty-one

Karen pulled a pink jumper off the rack in a Babies "R" Us store and held it up. She said, "This one is cute."

Tanya, who was with her in the store, held up a different pink jumper and said, "I like this one. Jesus, I can't believe you're going to have a daughter. You know what I really can't believe, though?"

Karen said, "What?"

Tanya said, "You're having a kid before me. How the hell did that happen?"

Karen said, "Well, when a man loves a woman, he puts his penis in her vagina—"

Tanya said, "Screw you. You know what I mean."

Karen laughed and said, "I know. This is just so fucking weird."

Tanya said, "Shopping for baby clothes?"

Karen said, "Yeah, that's obviously pretty weird, but I meant actually being kind of excited for this. I really never ever thought in my entire fucking life that I'd have a kid, want to have a kid, be remotely excited about having a kid. I just feel like I'm not the person I always thought I was, I guess."

Tanya said, "That's the weird thing about life. You change."

Karen looked at her watch and said, "We have to get out of here. My appointment's in twenty minutes."

The two women put the baby clothes back on the racks and made their way into the parking lot. Once they were outside the store, two photographers followed them to Tanya's car, but they weren't screaming and they weren't trying to stop them from leaving. It had been a few weeks since the press conference, and while talk about her story hadn't really gone away, things were certainly changing. The media had shifted from debating whether Karen was the most evil person in the world to a milder celebrity-style fascination with the baby, and what magazine might get the first image of the baby after she was born, and even an occasional voice hailing Karen as a national hero. Her initial supporters rallied behind her even more passionately than before, and even many of her detractors felt compelled to take her side now that she was having the baby, which is what they'd been clamoring for since the beginning. Some of them cited what they believed to be the obvious influence of God in her decision, which slightly bothered Karen, but overall she was happy to be rid of the feeling that more than half of the country hated her.

The thing Karen disliked the most was how people had more or less stopped talking about the issue at the center of her story. It seemed like things were slipping back into the way they were, despite her best efforts to put a dent in the armor of the religious right. There was no significant exodus from the Christian denominations. Legislators in the Southern states were still passing laws making it harder for women to get abortions. It just seemed like it might all have been for nothing, and that was disheartening. Karen knew there was little she could do or say that she hadn't already done or said. She began to think that her parents were right: People tend to avoid making significant changes in their lives, no matter how beneficial that change might be.

This time, when Karen and Tanya pulled out of the parking lot, the photographers didn't even follow them to her pediatrician's office. Instead they merely took a few passing shots, and one of them even blew a kiss to Karen as they drove away.

Karen had been seeing Dr. Kang ever since Dr. Prasad recommended her. Although Karen had never wanted to switch doctors, she liked Dr. Kang and thought she was doing an excellent job. As she and Tanya walked into the doctor's building, they saw two more photographers outside. As they snapped a few pictures of Karen, one of them told her that he thought she was the hottest pregnant celebrity he'd ever seen, even hotter than Kim Kardashian.

In Dr. Kang's office, Karen went through the usual battery of questions and had a blood test to make sure everything was moving along as it was supposed to be. Dr. Kang said, "Everything looks good on my end. Is there anything that's worrying you?"

God was a waste of time as an idea, and humanity had only ever used that idea to subjugate people and cause misery. Studying the universe and the fabric of reality were the most important of all human endeavors, but so few people saw value in them that the sciences suffered from underfunding and understaffing. And, beyond that, the sciences had progressed to a level of such esoteric intricacy that it was near impossible for a lay person to understand even the basic ideas behind them, let alone the mathematical minutiae at their core. The best thing a nonscientific person could do was to help ease the suffering of as many people as possible in the course of a lifetime. Having children merely meant bringing one more person into existence who would have to endure that suffering and grapple with the same questions about reality and the nature of existence that everyone else did. These were things that Dr. Kang understood to be true.

Karen said, "I don't know. I've been having really weird and vivid dreams lately."

Dr. Kang said, "That's completely normal. We don't really know why that is. It might have something to do with hormones, but I tend to think it has more to do with your baby's brain development at this stage. She's really growing fast, and so is her brain. It's starting to develop certain functional processes that weren't there before. And, though your brains aren't connected, your bodies are, and I personally think that once her brain starts producing chemicals like serotonin and dopamine, you're very likely getting some fluctuations in your own levels because of her. Anyway, it's nothing to worry about. Anything else?"

Karen said, "Let's see. Back pain, leg pain, stomach itching, trouble sleeping, difficulty walking, weird hairs, weird moles . . . You know. The usual."

Dr. Kang said, "Well, the good news is you're almost done with all of that. The bad news is, you're going to have to have the baby to end it, which won't be very easy, of course. But I've already booked you a room at Cedars. Your delivery staff is the best I've ever worked with. I'll be there to make sure everything goes smoothly, and in a few weeks you'll be a mother."

Karen let that sink in. She knew that having a child meant she would be a mother, but that was the first time she'd heard the word used to describe her. It was strange, but it wasn't as terrible as she might have once imagined.

chapter
thirty-two

James had been in Los Angeles for almost a month, and he had been unable to decipher any of God's signs since his arrival. He knew it wasn't God's fault. He knew God was sending him signs. It was his fault that he'd been unable to see them. He was sure this was because of Satan's influence over the city. There was no other explanation. But that didn't change how even though he'd been living very sparsely and sleeping in his car since arriving in the city and trying unsuccessfully to find Karen Holloway with no outside help, James was running out of money. He had enough for maybe two or three more meals and a tank of gas, and that was all. So knowing that God always helps those who help themselves, James decided it was time to find work. It wouldn't have to be anything permanent, just something that would allow him to subsist in Los Angeles until God told him what to do next.

He checked the Internet to see if there were any Dillard's

stores in Los Angeles. There weren't, but he did find several malls, so he decided to start his job search there. He had plenty of experience on a cleaning crew and knew how to operate a floor buffer. He assumed it shouldn't be too difficult to find work in a city that big.

The first mall he visited was the Grove. It was an outdoor mall, so there would likely be little need for a floor buffer for the mall itself, but he reasoned that the stores themselves might be able to oblige him. After inquiring about employment at the general information booth, James was given an application. He filled it out and expected at least to be given an interview, but instead he was told that someone would look over his application, and if they had a position open, they'd call him back sometime in the next several weeks. This obviously wouldn't help James in the moment.

Next he visited the Westside Pavilion, an indoor mall that was much closer in nature to the mall he worked in back at home. He thought this would be an easier place to find employment, but after talking with another person at another general information booth, he was given another application, and was told again he would be contacted in a few weeks if they thought there was a position he could fill.

James visited three other malls and two Targets, all with nearly identical results. It wasn't until he visited the Beverly Center that he experienced something different.

When he approached the information desk there, he was met with an experience that at first seemed even worse than what he'd encountered before. The girl sitting at the desk told him that they had no openings at the mall, and it would be a waste of his time to even fill out an application because the mall used a private outside cleaning company to come in every night. Then, just as James turned around to leave, the girl said, "Hang on, though."

God was definitely real, and he definitely performed miracles, and he definitely wanted everyone to love each other and get along. War and murder and every bad thing on Earth were the result of mankind's bad choices. These things weren't punishments from God. They were just the logical conclusions of humanity misusing the free will God granted us. Science was incredible, but it was just one tool among many that God gave us so we could try to figure out things on our own. Sex wasn't necessarily only meant for marriage. There was no way that could even be possible, because sex had existed long before marriage. Having children wasn't an active goal most people should have, but if a girl was to get pregnant, she should obviously have the baby and raise it to the best of her ability. And if the father wants to be in the picture, even better, but it wasn't necessary. These were things that the girl at the Beverly Center information desk understood to be true.

When James turned back around, she said, "You know, my boyfriend actually works for a cleaning company that does, like, medical buildings and hospitals and stuff like that. I don't know if that's something you'd be interested in, but I could give you his email or something."

James thanked her and told her he'd love any help he could get. As she wrote down her boyfriend's email address, James noticed that she wore a golden cross around her neck. It seemed to glow a little bit as she was writing. James knew that this was his next sign from God. When it took her boyfriend only an hour to respond to James's email and set up an interview on the same day, James was excited to be back in the very obvious service of God. And when James was hired at the end of his interview to be part of a cleaning crew working on a few floors at Cedars-Sinai as well as some surrounding medical buildings, he knew that God's plan for him was moving much faster than it ever had before. And when he was given a nondisclosure agreement to sign, because some of the buildings he would be cleaning housed the offices of doctors who serviced celebrities like Angelina Jolie, Al Pacino, and even Karen Holloway, James knew that God was initiating the final phases of his plan.

chapter
thirty-three

In the weeks that followed Karen's press conference, she found herself inundated with phone calls and emails offering her public speaking engagements and requesting interviews for various publications, radio programs, and television shows, as well as publicists offering their services, and talent managers and agents promising that they could make her rich and even more famous than she already was. She even received an offer from a TV production company to shoot a talk show pilot, featuring Karen as the host. She declined the offers, but they still kept coming. Her morning routine, which used to involve checking her website to see how much money had been donated, now included emptying her inbox of the requests. At first she had written back to each request, citing her lack of interest in the public spotlight, but eventually she had resigned herself to moving all such email into the trash without even opening it.

Karen sat on the toilet with her phone in her hand, dealing with her latest and worst bout of constipation, and scrolled through her inbox. After deleting dozens of emails, she stopped on one that surprised her. It was from Paul. She hadn't talked to her ex-boyfriend at all since their last moment together in their old apartment. He'd kept his distance from both Karen and the public attention that came with her project, and she'd respected that by not contacting him, even though she'd wanted to several times.

Karen opened the email, which read, "Hey, I know we haven't talked in a while. I saw your press conference. I have to say I wasn't expecting you to do what you did. You're always full of surprises. Anyway, I don't know if you'd have any interest in this, but if you want to, I'd really like to see you. Maybe get coffee or lunch or something. Let me know, and I hope you're doing well. —Paul"

Karen reread the email twice, trying to decipher any hidden meaning, anything Paul might have been trying to imply through his word choice or context, but she could find none. She had wanted to hear from Paul so badly for so long that when she finally did, she found herself wanting more from the message. The email certainly wasn't negative in any way, but it wasn't as positive as she would have liked, either. Paul was the one man she had ever really loved, and this email gave her a glimmer of hope that she could save that relationship, but it wasn't affirmative enough to allay her fears altogether. Perhaps he just wanted to see her one last time before leaving town, she thought, or before moving in with a new girlfriend. So she replied with an email that read:

"It's really good to hear from you. This email is just as surprising to me as my decision might have been to you. I'd absolutely like to see you for lunch or something. Just let me know what your schedule is like over the next few days."

She pressed send and hoped to hear back from him soon. And she hoped his next email would contain some language that would give her an idea about what his intentions might be for this request to see her.

It took an hour, but when the response finally came it simply read, "I'm pretty open. I imagine your schedule is the busier of the two, so I leave it up to you. You can pick the place, too. I'll go anywhere."

So two days later as Karen sat in the lobby of the Cheesecake Factory in Woodland Hills, doing her best to avoid stares from a few patrons and agreeing to take one picture with a teenage girl who told Karen she was her hero, she still had no real idea why Paul wanted to see her. She was nervous about a great number of things. She hoped that Paul wanted to reconcile, just as she did. Beyond that, she was very visibly pregnant, and she wanted to look as good as she possibly could in a state that she considered to be uncomfortable at best. She noticed that she was starting to sweat and put one hand under her armpit to check just how intensely she was sweating. It was as she was pulling that hand out of her armpit that Paul walked in.

He smiled and said, "Hey, wow! You're really, really pregnant, aren't you?"

Karen smiled and said, "No shit."

They hugged awkwardly and then followed the hostess to their table. Once seated, Paul said, "So, thanks for meeting me and everything."

Karen said, "Of course. I was looking forward to it."

Paul said, "Me too."

Karen said, "Yeah, so why did you want to meet up? You didn't really give me any idea in the emails."

Paul said, "I just . . . I mean . . . I guess, first of all, I wanted to thank you for keeping me out of everything. I couldn't really stop myself from following the story while your site was up, and I know you got asked a lot about who the father was and what happened to our relationship and everything. I know it was tough, and I just wanted to say thanks."

Karen said, "Of course. You're welcome. You know, you could have said thanks pretty easily with an email or something."

Paul said, "I know. I also just wanted to see you, see how you were doing with my own eyes."

Karen said, "Okay. Really? That was it? You just wanted to thank me and see me in person?"

Paul said, "You always were such an asshole when I was nervous to talk about something."

Karen said, "I'm being an asshole right now?"

Paul laughed and said, "A little."

Karen said, "Well, I'm really fucking pregnant, so I get to be an asshole. That's how that works."

Paul took a deep breath, and he said, "Okay, look, here's the deal. Through this whole thing, I've always loved you. And there was something about not being a part of any of this decision that just made me worry that I wasn't that important to you anymore, like you just saw me as a sidekick in the relationship or something."

Karen said, "I'm sorry, Paul. You know—"

Paul said, "Just let me finish this."

Karen said, "Okay, sorry."

Paul said, "I think that was the reason I left you. I just felt like, if you could cut me out of a decision that big, then you could cut me out of anything in your life. I felt pretty disposable, I guess, and I didn't know how to deal with that. But over the course of this whole thing, I started to get why you did this, and I remembered how much I appreciate the dedication you have to your ideas, and the way you want to change the world. And those are all reasons why I fell in love with you in the first place. And when I really boiled it down, and honestly asked myself, if you had asked me about your plan before you went through with it, would I have been supportive or not? I know I would have been. I would have had to think about it, and I'm sure it would have freaked me the fuck out, but I would have been behind you all the way. You really did affect the world, Karen. That's just fucking amazing to me. So eventually I realized I had no reason to be mad or hurt by your decision. I only wanted to be with this amazing girl who I love and adore and who is doing things in the world that are fucking incredible. So, to answer your question, I asked you out for lunch because I wanted to tell you that I would love to give us another shot and be in your life and hopefully be in our daughter's life. And that's basically it."

Karen sat across from Paul silently for a few seconds, weighing what he just said to her.

Paul said, "So I guess I thought you might have a kind of immediate response to this, you know, one way or another."

Karen said, "You're the only person I'd ever want to be with. And, if you want the real truth, a huge part of the reason I decided to do what I'm doing is that this baby is a part of you, too. I love you, Paul."

Paul got up from his seat and crossed the table to kiss Karen. She started to cry and said, "I would not be crying normally, but this shit really screws with your hormones." They both laughed and kissed again. A handful of people nearby were staring and talking, and it occurred to Karen that they were probably speculating about the identity of Karen Holloway's mystery man.

Paul went back to his seat, sat down, took Karen's hand, and said, "Why'd you pick the Cheesecake Factory?"

Karen said, "I've been craving some dulce de leche cheescake like you wouldn't fucking believe."

They ate their meal and talked about the future. Karen told Paul that she'd be happy to have him move back into their apartment, and Paul told Karen that he would be there every step of the way for the rest of her pregnancy. For the first time in a long time, without giving a thought to public opinion or the possible repercussions for her now-completed project, Karen was simply happy.

chapter
thirty-four

As James vacuumed the carpet in the hallway of a doctor's office, he listened to a a podcast of Pastor Preston's sermon from the prior Sunday. Pastor Preston said, "Brothers and sisters, I know there's been a lot of talk about Karen Holloway, and some of you might still be on the fence about her and her decision. But I'm here to tell you today that the Lord has spoken to me, and he's told me that we have been given a glorious miracle right here and right now. Karen Holloway, whether she knows it or not, was moved by God's perfect grace to save the life of that child. She was an enemy to our Holy Father. She was an agent of Satan. We all saw that, and we all feared what she might do to that poor helpless soul, but Jesus Christ wouldn't let that happen. And it wasn't because of money, it was because of prayer. I know I prayed every day for that baby's soul, and I know you did, too, and now—"

James took his earphones out. He couldn't tolerate the hypocrisy of Pastor Preston's sermon. It was Pastor Preston who had condemned Karen Holloway as an agent of Satan and declared her unborn child to be the Antichrist, but now, as she was on the verge of delivering that child into the world, he seemed to have changed his position. James knew that Pastor Preston wasn't as devout as he once thought, certainly not as devout as himself. But he knew, even as he thought this, that he was wrong in judging Pastor Preston. James reasoned that a man who had spent his entire life in the service of Christ couldn't actually be at fault. The sermon and Pastor Preston's change in attitude must have been the work of Satan, who was clearly muddling the minds of as many people on Earth as he could to prepare them for the coming of his son, the Antichrist. If not even Pastor Preston was safe from the Devil's trickery and manipulation, then James knew he was in even greater danger. He rationalized that he might be the last agent of God left on the planet who hadn't been duped by the evil plan of the Devil, who might still have the ability to stop Satan from carrying out his own plan to usher in the Antichrist. He might be the last hope for the entire planet, and because God told him nothing to the contrary, James felt this must be true. He said a quick prayer asking God to grant him strength and to help him overcome every obstacle Satan might place in his path.

Although he was now absolutely certain his purpose in God's plan was not only to find Karen Holloway but also certainly to stop her from delivering her child into the world, James felt he was growing closer to knowing how he would be called to do that. He was convinced that it would be through testifying to Karen Holloway, showing her the true power of the Holy Spirit and ultimately converting her to Christianity. Once converted, she would see how she'd been manipulated by Satan and seek to have the child baptized, at which time the satanic spirit that dwelled within it would be destroyed. But he wasn't sure why he had not yet found his opportunity. He waited for signs from

God, and he knew they were right in front of him, but Satan was obscuring them. His task was difficult, but he would remain vigilant.

As he turned a corner with his vacuum cleaner into the first room off the hallway, he entered a room full of file cabinets. James saw that one of the drawers near the bottom of one of the file cabinets had been left ajar. As he bent down to slide it shut, he noticed that the drawer contained patient medical records. He knew this was no coincidence, and he checked the other drawers. They were all unlocked. This was another sacred boon from God. This was the result of God's own hand. He took a brief moment to wonder if God himself had been in that room only seconds ago, and then he wasted no more time searching through the cabinets for Karen Holloway's information. He wasn't sure that she was even a patient at this specific doctor's office, but he thought it was very likely that she was, or God wouldn't have sent him there, wouldn't have guided him into that room, wouldn't have left that one drawer open and the rest unlocked. He vowed to God that if he was able to find her records, he would take it as an undisputable sign that he was brought to Los Angeles to stop her from bringing about the end of the world by giving birth to the Antichrist.

James stood in front of the file cabinet containing the records for patients with last names ending in G, H, and I. He pulled a few files out and sorted through them, sure that he was about to uncover the home address of Karen Holloway. But before he could get through the files, his supervisor walked into the room and asked him what he was doing. James didn't want to lie—he knew it would require him to break one of God's commandments, one of God's perfect rules—but he saw no other option. He reasoned that God would forgive him this one sin if it was in the service of his greater purpose. He told his supervisor that when he came into the room there were some files on the ground and he was merely trying to put them back in the correct place. The supervisor explained that she'd been standing there for more than a few seconds and she witnessed James looking through the files. She knew he was lying, and it couldn't be tolerated. She terminated him without hesitation and told him that someone from the cleaning agency would contact him to let him know when he could collect his final paycheck. She then demanded that he turn over any keys or access cards he might have on his person as well as his employee identification badge. For a brief second James thought about withholding some of his access cards, but he immediately fought this dishonest impulse, silently cursing himself for lying in the first place.

James offered no defense for himself. He knew that what he had done was wrong. He knew that the open drawer and the unlocked file cabinets were all more tricks of Satan. He knew that he had lied to his supervisor only because Satan had tempted him. In the elevator, he cursed himself for being so stupid. Why would God ever want anyone to lie on his behalf? He should have known at the moment he felt the urge to lie that Satan was behind it. Who else but the Father of Lies? He hated himself for having come so far, having done everything right along the way, only to have his purpose invalidated by the very being he was fighting against.

He dropped to his knees in the elevator, clutched his hands together as tight as he could, and wept. James begged God for forgiveness. He apologized for succumbing to Satan's will without even knowing it. He admitted that he was nothing more than a weak-willed human being, fallible and prone to mistakes. He urged God to give him one more chance to carry out his final goal, which he was convinced involved stopping Karen Holloway's evil plan. He pleaded with God to take mercy on him and allow him to prove his obedience. He promised God that he would suffer anything in his glorious service as long as it meant that he was forgiven and considered righteous once again. He knew that even this faltering, even this giving in to satanic temptation, was somehow part of God's plan. It had to be. And that meant that God might still have James in mind to carry it out. So James asked him one final time, before the elevator got to the ground floor, to give him one last sign to guide him on the last leg of his journey. James promised God that if he could just be told what to do, he would carry it out.

James left the building and got in his car. He wiped his tears and started the engine. As the car started, the radio turned on, and James heard a morning DJ explaining that areas were being roped off near one of the exits from Cedars-Sinai hospital and paparazzi were already starting to camp outside the barriers. The rumor was that Karen Holloway was very close to her due date, and everyone was speculating that this is where she would emerge to give the world the first glimpse of her new baby.

James thanked God for this sign and promised him that no matter what the consequences were for him personally, he would carry out the plan.

chapter thirty-five

Karen was sitting on the couch as Paul unpacked some of his clothes and hung them back in their closet. Though her back and hips were still aching, she was happy. She was happy to be back in her old apartment, the place she had considered home for the past several years. She was happy that Paul was moving back in. She was happy to see what the rest of her life would be like with him and with their child. She had never thought she'd experience a moment like this, but she was glad for it and couldn't imagine it being any different.

Karen shifted on the couch a little to ease the ache in her lower back and heard a plainly audible pop. This was followed by the feeling of warm liquid filling her underwear, soaking her pants, and even through to the couch. She looked down to see that she was sitting in a huge puddle of liquid, and she knew her water had broken. Her heart started to beat faster and she began to sweat. She screamed, "Paul!" He ran into the room and she said, "We have to get to the hospital. This shit is happening."

Paul had been briefed by Karen's parents on the proper procedure for a smooth trip to the hospital and eventual delivery of the baby. Paul said, "Okay. Okay. Fuck. I'll get the bag of shit, and you—no, not you, I'll call your parents, too. You get . . . you get nothing. Just do what you need to do to get ready. Okay. Seriously. I'll get the shit, call the parents, and get the car running. Do you need help or anything? What's going on? Jesus fucking Christ."

Karen said, "Yeah. You get the bag, call the parents, and then wait for me. I'm going to change my pants because these are soaked. We might also need a new couch after this. And then maybe help me out to the car. Oh, shit, and call my doctor."

Paul said, "Okay," and proceeded to make the necessary phone calls as Karen went into the bathroom to clean up. As she walked, she could feel liquid leaking out of her vagina with every step. Even after taking her pants off, sitting in a tub for a few minutes, and putting on a new pair of pants, fluid was still trickling down her legs. After grabbing a bathroom towel, she had Paul help her out to the car, which he already had running and loaded with toiletries, clean clothes, baby outfits and other items they would need during the hospital stay. Then, once he was in the car, he laid the towel on the passenger's seat and Karen got in.

As Paul pulled out of the driveway, Karen looked at their apartment. She knew the next time they came to this place, to their home, they would not be alone. That phase of her life was over, and the realization scared her. She couldn't help wondering what her life would be like in that moment if none of this had happened, if she hadn't skipped a pill, if she had never gotten pregnant. She wondered what other dissertation she might have concocted. She'd still be in school working on it. She and Paul would have very likely never separated. She certainly wouldn't be on her way to the hospital to give birth to a child. And the world would have never known about her. For a moment she wondered whether that would have been preferable to the life she was about to lead. But then she let the matter drop. She didn't see the point in comparison.

Once they arrived at the hospital, Paul double-parked and helped Karen into the lobby. He stayed with her while she checked in and waited until a nurse brought out a wheelchair. Then Paul went out to deal with the car while the nurse helped Karen into the wheelchair and then started wheeling her back into the labor and delivery area of the hospital.

As she was sitting in the chair, Karen could still feel some fluid leaking out into her pants. She could also feel some of her first contractions. They weren't painful, but they were hardly comfortable. Karen could feel the muscles at the top of her stomach get very hard for a few seconds, then let up. It was almost like the onset of a muscle cramp, but not quite. She could understand how this would eventually become increasingly painful.

Once Karen was wheeled into her room, the nurse helped her into a hospital gown and told Karen that she could leave her socks on if she preferred to. Karen hadn't given it much thought, but decided to leave them on, thinking that there was no point in suffering cold feet along with all the other agony she was about to endure. This nurse helped Karen up into the hospital bed and told her that another nurse would be in shortly, as well as the doctor who would be overseeing the delivery of her baby. Karen said, "Did you call Dr. Kang, my doctor?" The nurse explained that Dr. Kang had been notified, but it was unlikely she'd be able to make it. The nurse assured Karen that this was all normal protocol, and the doctors who were on duty at the hospital had delivered thousands of babies and were more than qualified to deliver hers.

The nurse then inserted an IV into the back of Karen's hand. Karen was told that this IV would deliver necessary replenishing fluids, which she was certain to lose a lot of during the birth, as well as antibiotics for group B strep. Then the nurse said,

"Okay, now I'm going to have to do a little check to see how dilated you are."

Religion was important. It was the only thing that gave people a reason to live. It was the only thing that gave people an idea that something might exist after this life. And helping people in this life was the surest way to get a good spot in the next one. Science had its place in making the lives of people on Earth better, but beyond that there wasn't much point in it. Space exploration was a waste of time and money. Sex was something that people outside of marriage could engage in, but it was much better if it was between a husband and wife, because it meant more. Having a child was one of the most important things a person could do, if not the most important. Not only was it important on a concrete level to continue the species, but it was also deeply fulfilling on a personal level. Helping people to bring new lives into the world was almost as fulfilling. These were things that the nurse understood to be true.

The nurse put on a rubber glove and squirted some lubricant on her fingers, rubbing it over as much of her hand as she could. She said, "Okay, spread your legs a little, and let's see how close your— Do you know the sex?"

Karen said, "She's a girl."

The nurse said, "Okay, let's see how close your daughter is to coming out and saying hello."

Karen tried to remain still as the nurse inserted what felt like her entire hand into Karen's vagina. The pain was intense and sharp. The stretching of the skin was like nothing she'd ever experienced. It felt as though it might rip, but it didn't. The pain was made more intense as the nurse forced her hand deeper into Karen's vagina. She could feel pressure from the baby moving down toward her vagina, and pressure from the nurse's hand moving up into it. She tried to breathe and think of something else. The nurse removed her hand, giving Karen immediate relief, and said, "You're at a five, which is coming along pretty well.

We want to get you to about a ten, and then you start pushing, and with any luck, that'll be all we have to do."

Paul came in the room and said, "Hey, your parents are here. Do you want them to come in or wait in the waiting room?"

Karen said, "I guess they can come in if they want."

Paul said, "Okay," and went back out in the lobby to get them.

The nurse brought out several large pads and helped Karen position herself so that they could be placed under her lower back, buttocks, and vagina. Karen said, "What're the pads for?"

The nurse said, "Childbirth is pretty messy. We like to try to keep things as neat as possible. Makes it easier on everyone. I'll probably be changing these out a few times during the delivery, too."

A doctor came into the room. He said, "Hello, I'm Dr. Gibson. I'm going to be delivering your baby today. How are we doing?"

There was certainly no God. Humanity was the result of random particles coming together in exactly the right way to form life that evolved over millions and millions of years. There was no greater meaning or purpose to anything. Science was the best way to know everything about existence and our place in it. Medicine, specifically, was one of the best ways to know everything about humanity. The need for sex was a basic primal instinct, and one that still served our population very well, and it had nothing to do with love. That was a great misconception. Eventually there would be no need for sexual procreation, and our drive to seek out sexual interaction would evolve away. Until that time, babies needed to be brought into the world safely. These were things that Dr. Gibson understood to be true.

The nurse said, "She's at a five, and everything looks normal."

Dr. Gibson said, "Great. You feeling okay?"

Karen said, "A little nervous, but other than that, yeah. I'm okay."

Dr. Gibson said, "This your first?"

Karen said, "Yeah."

Dr. Gibson said, "You have nothing to worry about. We're going to take good care of you and your baby. Is anyone else coming into the delivery room for you, or . . . ?"

Karen said, "Oh, yeah. My parents and my, uh, boyfriend are coming in right now."

Dr. Gibson said, "Okay, okay, perfect. New boyfriend or old boyfriend—like, father-of-the-baby boyfriend? Sorry if I'm prying, I just followed your story pretty closely. I guess you could say I'm kind of a fan. Sorry."

Karen couldn't help smiling. She said, "No need to apologize. He's my old boyfriend, and we're back together. He is the father."

Dr. Gibson said, "Okay. Great. Great. Anyway, I'll be back in a little bit once things really start moving. But everything looks great so far." Then Dr. Gibson left.

The nurse said, "He really did follow your whole story. We all did, really. Anyway."

Paul, Robert, and Lynn came in the room together. Lynn said, "Oh my God. I can't believe this is actually happening. Oh, Jesus. Robert, can you believe this?"

Robert said, "It's something. That's for sure. Do you want us in here, honey?"

Karen said, "Of course. If you guys want to be in here, I totally want you in here."

Lynn moved over to Karen and hugged her. She said, "I know this has been insane, but I'm so happy this worked out like this and Paul is here. It's just perfect."

Karen said, "It's not really perfect. It's already starting to hurt pretty fucking bad, and I imagine it gets worse. So not perfect at all."

Lynn said, "Are you going to have an epidural?"

Karen said, "As soon as it's available. My back is fucking killing me."

The nurse said, "If you can move from side to side a little bit, that can sometimes help."

Karen started moving back and forth as she gripped her mother and Paul for stability. She said, "Not really helping much. I'm also dying of thirst and I'm hot. Sorry to be complaining so much."

The nurse laughed and said, "I think you're going to be complaining a lot more. I'll get you some water and some ice."

For the next few hours, Karen ate ice, drank water, and rocked back and forth while her parents and Paul tried to soothe her as best they could. The contractions were coming much closer together, and they were much more painful than they had been in the beginning. Karen's hair was matted to her forehead with sweat, and the pain was so bad that that she had begun gritting her teeth with each successive contraction. Seeing the obvious signs of labor, the nurse said, "I think it might be time to deliver this baby. Let me just do one more check."

She lubricated her hand and slid it back into Karen's vagina. The pain was much more intense than the first check, and Karen screamed. The nurse said, "I know. I know it hurts, but we need to see if you're ready. And it looks like you are." The nurse removed her hand from Karen's vagina and said, "Let me get Dr. Gibson."

A minute later Dr. Gibson entered the room and said, "Okay, you ready to do this?"

Karen said, "I want an epidural."

Dr. Gibson said, "Are you sure?"

Karen said, "Abso-fucking-lutely."

Dr. Gibson told the nurse to get the anesthesiologist. Karen could feel the baby's head descending, putting an almost unbearable amount of pressure on her vagina and anus. She started breathing through her gritted teeth, emitting an audible hiss as spit trickled out of the corners of her mouth. She said, "I need those fucking drugs right fucking now."

Another contraction made her entire body tense up as the anesthesiologist entered the room and told her that she'd have to sit up and relax her back so the needle could be correctly inserted into her spine. Paul and Lynn helped prop her up and Karen felt a cool liquid on her lower back where the anesthesiologist was sterilizing the injection point. Without warning, Karen felt a sharp stabbing pain in her spine as she was told not to move, and then it was over. She lay back down on the bed and Dr. Gibson said, "Okay, you should be pretty numb from the waist down within a minute or so, but hopefully you'll still be able to feel the contractions. On the next one, I want you to start pushing when you feel it coming on, all right? And if you can't feel them, that's fine. Nothing to worry about. It just means the epidural worked a little too well, and I'll have to tell you when to push."

Karen nodded in agreement, still holding on to Paul and Lynn with all her strength as Robert stood in a corner watching. He was in the room when Lynn gave birth to Karen, and he realized he had forgotten how gruesome a scene childbirth could be.

As the drugs started to take effect, Karen was both relieved and scared. Her legs felt paralyzed. She knew this effect was temporary, but losing the ability to move didn't exactly put her at ease. She could definitely feel her next contraction, but it was an ambiguous feeling—not necessarily painful, just kind of unpleasant. So she pushed, and as she did, she defecated all over herself and the table. The smell of feces was strong and immediate. She was embarrassed, and she felt like vomiting, but the trauma she was suffering during childbirth was more immediate to her than the need to feel any shame or even disgust.

She said, "Sorry, guys."

Dr. Gibson said, "No need to apologize. This is very common when you're trying to pass a baby through your body."

The nurse was already changing the pads under Karen and wiping her down. Even after the cleaning, the smell of feces remained throughout the rest of the event.

With the next contraction, Karen pushed even harder. She wanted this entire thing to be over with as soon as possible. The physical and psychological trauma was more profound than she had ever anticipated. She wondered how the human race survived after the invention of birth control. Had she known how painful the act of giving birth was, she never would have decided to keep the baby.

After two hours of pushing with every contraction, defecating all over herself one more time, urinating on herself, bleeding from her vagina, and sweating, the baby was still not born. Dr. Gibson said, "Okay, I think the epidural may have limited your ability to push with enough force to get her out. So we're going to give you a little help."

Another nurse came in with a small device that looked like a suction cup with a vacuum attached to it. Dr. Gibson said, "Every time you push, I'm going to use this to pull, all right?"

Karen nodded in agreement. For the next two contractions, they attempted this method of joint effort, but the baby still would not emerge. Dr. Gibson said, "Well she's certainly got a big brain, because her head just does not want to come out. So we're going to make the opening a little larger."

Karen said, "Sorry, what? How?"

Dr. Gibson said, "Just a tiny cut right at the back of the vagina. You won't feel it at all because of the epidural, and the baby should come right out. We're almost there. I promise."

Karen said, "Are you fucking serious? You're going to cut my vagina?"

Dr. Gibson said, "It's an episiotomy, yes. It's pretty standard procedure when we're at this point but the baby still isn't coming out. We don't have to do it, but I've delivered a few babies, and I can tell from our situation, here, that if we don't do it, your vagina is likely to rip anyway."

Karen wanted to vomit again. She was sitting on a table covered in her own urine, blood, and feces, in alternating states of agonizing pain and discomfort, and now she had to have her vagina surgically altered. She knew she had no choice, though, and she wanted the process to be over, so she nodded in agreement. She saw her father look away as Dr. Gibson cut her vagina, and she felt Paul's grip on one of her hands weaken as he looked down and saw blood rushing out of her vagina where the incision was made. He staggered and turned white. Dr. Gibson said, "If you need to sit down, there's a chair behind you."

Paul looked away from the blood-soaked pad under Karen and said, "I'm fine. I just didn't really expect it to be that much blood."

Karen said, "Can you not say shit like that right now, please?"

Paul said, "Sorry."

Dr. Gibson said, "Once we get the baby out, we'll stitch it back up and you'll be good as new. Okay, now, one more good push should do it. You ready?"

Karen nodded her head, and on the next contraction, she pushed as hard as she could, screaming through the entire process. Dr. Gibson used his suction assistance, and the baby was delivered. Karen was immediately relieved in a way she had never felt before. The pressure that had been building daily in her body for nine months was just gone. There was no scaling it down or slowly tapering it off. It went from being unbearable to nonexistent in a matter of seconds. And more than just a physical relief, Karen felt like the journey she had been on was over. It had come to a conclusion, and she felt good about that.

The nurse stitched the cut at the back of Karen's vagina. Dr. Gibson took Karen's daughter, cleaned her, sucked the mucus from her nose and mouth, and a few seconds later Karen, still covered in her own filth, heard her daughter crying. Dr. Gibson laid the baby on Karen's chest and said, "Congratulations. You have a brand-new healthy baby girl." Karen looked at her as Paul and her parents leaned in close. It was strange to see this tiny person on her chest, this person who would depend on her for the rest of its life, this person she would worry about for the rest of hers.

Paul said, "This is so weird. I never believed anyone when they said this moment changed the way they felt about kids, and that it was beautiful and all that, but here we are in a room that smells like your crap. You're covered in sweat and pee and whatever else. And it really is beautiful. She's beautiful."

Paul leaned in and kissed his daughter on the forehead as she cried and snuggled against her mother. Lynn said, "I'm so happy." She looked at her husband and said, "We're grandparents now."

Robert said, "I know. It's good. I feel really old, but it's good."

The nurse then moved up to Karen's stomach and told her that she needed to push a few more times to deliver the placenta. As Karen pushed, the nurse pulled on the umbilical cord that was hanging out of Karen's vagina and simultaneously massaged her stomach moving the mass of tissue out of her uterus and eventually through her vagina. This was not as traumatic as giving birth, but to Karen it was equally disgusting.

Dr. Gibson said, "We're going to take her now and put her in observation for a few hours just to make sure everything is all right, which it looks like it is, and we're going to get you to recovery. You all are welcome to be wherever our new mom feels comfortable having you."

The nurse took Karen's daughter away, and another nurse wheeled her into a recovery room. Paul, Lynn, and Robert went out into the waiting room. In the recovery room, the nurse explained to Karen that it was pretty important to try to urinate to get things moving again. So Karen sat on a toilet and forced herself to urinate to the best of her ability, the epidural still having some effect. When she looked in the toilet, there was some urine, but most of what was in the toilet was blood. The nurse assured her that this was normal and the bleeding would subside in a few days.

Karen remained in the hospital for the next twenty-four hours, per Dr. Gibson's recommendation, and her daughter spent most of those twenty-four hours nestled in her arms. Paul stayed by Karen's side the entire time.

The following morning, Tanya arrived with balloons and flowers and Karen's parents brought some breakfast. They all talked about what name should be given to this little girl who was the center of so much attention for the past months, but Karen had made no decision on the matter. Lynn said, "So you never even thought a little bit about what you might want to call her?"

Karen said, "I thought a lot about it, actually, but nothing ever seemed right." Then to Paul she asked, "Have you thought of any names?"

Paul said, "I've thought of a million names, but I'm with you. It's such a big thing, I don't know. We don't have to name her right now, do we?"

Robert said, "Well, you have to have something on the birth certificate."

Karen said, "But we have time. We don't have to do that right away. I kind of want to hang out with her. See what she's like. You know?"

Paul said, "I couldn't agree more."

Tanya said, "You're going to give the press a conniption if your baby doesn't have a name."

Karen said, "Who cares?"

Tanya grabbed the baby's finger and said, "I'm with you. I think it would be great to keep them guessing, but there are a whole bunch of photographers and press people outside. They have them roped off, kind of out of the way, but they're definitely going to be getting a bunch of pictures when you come out and they'll want to know what her name is."

Paul said, "Isn't there some back way we can take or something?"

Robert said, "Yeah, do we really have to deal with them?"

Karen said, "You know what? Let them get their pictures and then this is all over. Once they have a picture, it'll calm them down and hopefully things can get back to being a little more normal. So let's go out the front door and let them see what they want to see."

Paul said, "Are you sure?"

Karen said, "Absolutely."

James sat in his car, parked on the street near where the press had gathered outside of Cedars-Sinai. He'd been there as long as they had, for a little more than a day. On the radio, he had listened to coverage of Karen Holloway being admitted to the hospital and speculation on how much the baby would weigh, how long it would be, what color its eyes would be, if it would be born with hair and what color that hair might be, as well as what name the child might be given. This disgusted James. He didn't understand how the entire world could so quickly be swayed by her tricks, by Satan's tricks.

James prayed as much as he could in between listening to coverage of the event on the radio, asking God to give him one final sign, some instruction on what was certainly the most important part of the plan. He closed his eyes tight and tried to envision God as he asked him for help. Just then, James's head lurched forward when a news van pulled in too close behind him and ran into his car. The truck only tapped his bumper, it did no damage, but it was enough to jar James out of his silent meditation to God.

As a camera crew rushed out of the van toward the hospital, a woman with them asked James if he was all right and handed him a business card. She told him to call the news station if he had a claim to file, but she didn't really have time to stay and deal with it. She had to get to the hospital entrance.

James tossed the business card in the passenger's seat, and that's when he saw it: God's final sign. The news van hadn't hid his car hard at all, certainly not hard enough for the glove box to pop open, but that's exactly what happened. The glove box was open, and sitting there inside it was the gun James bought in Arizona. James knew what God was asking of him. Just as Pastor Preston had said, before he was corrupted by Satan: Christians were at war with the forces of Satan, and in war, blood must be shed.

James remembered when he heard God's voice back in his apartment. God told him that he would be called on to make a great sacrifice. James knew that if he did this, if he did what God was asking, he would be making the greatest sacrifice any person is capable of: sacrificing his own life.

He noticed the group of photographers and press people start to stir. They all looked at the hospital door near where they had been sectioned off. The door opened, and a family emerged, with Karen Holloway at the front, being pushed in a wheelchair holding a baby. The press went into a frenzy, with cameras whirring and reporters shouting things to Karen. The police officers on the scene were doing their best to keep the press at bay, but some of them made their way around the barricades to get microphones closer to Karen. James knew that God had created this confusion specifically for him, specifically to complete his divine purpose.

James opened his car door and casually walked across the street so as not to draw any undue attention to himself. He merged into the throng of reporters and photographers unnoticed, made his way around a barricade, slipped in behind a reporter who was interviewing Karen, removed the Glock 17 from inside his jacket, pointed it at Karen's baby, and fired seven shots in rapid succession, then dropped the gun, put his hands on his head, and kneeled on the ground.

Paul, Lynn, Robert, and Tanya screamed in horrified shock as the police apprehended James and wrestled him to the ground.